Elsie's Friends at
Woodburn

The Original Elsie Classics

Elsie Dinsmore
Elsie's Holidays at Roselands
Elsie's Girlhood
Elsie's Womanhood
Elsie's Motherhood
Elsie's Children
Elsie's Widowhood
Grandmother Elsie
Elsie's New Relations
Elsie at Nantucket
The Two Elsies
Elsie's Kith and Kin
Elsie's Friends at Woodburn
Christmas with Grandma Elsie
Elsie and the Raymonds
Elsie Yachting with the Raymonds
Elsie's Vacation
Elsie at Viamede
Elsie at Ion
Elsie at the World's Fair
Elsie's Journey on Inland Waters
Elsie at Home
Elsie on the Hudson
Elsie in the South
Elsie's Young Folks
Elsie's Winter Trip
Elsie and Her Loved Ones
Elsie and Her Namesakes

Elsie's Friends at Woodburn

Book Thirteen of
The Original Elsie Classics

Martha Finley

CUMBERLAND HOUSE
NASHVILLE, TENNESSEE

ELSIE'S FRIENDS AT WOODBURN BY MARTHA FINLEY
PUBLISHED BY CUMBERLAND HOUSE PUBLISHING, INC.
431 Harding Industrial Drive
Nashville, Tennessee 37211

Any unique characteristics of this edition:
Copyright © 2000 by Cumberland House Publishing, Inc.

Cover design by Gore Studio, Inc., Nashville, Tennessee
Photography by Dean Dixon Photography
Hair and Makeup by Calene Radar
Text design by Heather Armstrong

Printed in Canada
2 3 4 5 6 7 8 9 10 TR 08 07 06 05

CHAPTER FIRST

THE TWENTY-FOURTH had been cold and stormy—a keen, biting wind blowing continuously during the greater part of the day, bringing with it a heavy fall of sleet and snow.

The weather on Christmas Day was a slight improvement upon that—the wind being less boisterous and the snowfall only an occasional light flurry, but the sun scarcely showed his face. And as evening drew on, the moon shone but fitfully and through scurrying clouds. The ground was white with snow, but as it had drifted badly, the roads were not in condition for sleighing, so Max Raymond and Evelyn Leland made the journey from Woodburn to the Oaks in a closed carriage.

Captain Raymond handed Evelyn in. Max took a seat by her side and gallantly tucked the robes about her feet, remarking that it was the coldest night of the season so far.

"Yes," she said. "But I suppose we shall have still colder weather before the winter is over. This is nothing to some I have known in my old home in the north."

"Oh, no!" returned Max. "I remember it used to be very much colder where we lived when I was a little fellow."

Eva smiled, thinking he was not nearly grown up yet.

"Hardly a breath of wind reaches us in this closed carriage," she said. "I shouldn't care if the ride was to be twice as long."

"No, nor I," said Max. "But I dare say we'll have a fine time after we get to the Oaks."

"Yes, but I am so sorry your father thought best to decline the invitation for Lulu. I shall not enjoy myself half so well without her," sighed Evelyn.

"I'm sorry, too," Max said. "I know it was a great disappointment to her when papa told her she was not to go. I don't know why he refused to let her, but I do know that he always has a good reason when he denies any of us a pleasure."

Eva said, "Of course, I am quite sure he is the best and kindest of fathers." She then began talking of the approaching festivities at the Oaks, and those whom they expected to meet there.

"Do you know who has been invited besides ourselves?" asked Max.

"I believe I do," replied Evelyn. "There are to be two or three sets: little ones—Walter Travilla, and the eldest two of Aunt Rose Lacey's children—as mates for little Horace and his sister; Rosie Travilla, Lora Howard, and myself for Sydney and Maud; you, Ralph Conly, and Art and Walter Howard for their brother's companions; besides Bertram Shaw, a school friend of the Dinsmore boys, who, for their sakes, has been asked to the Oaks to spend the holidays."

"Eva," queried Max, "do you know exactly what relation Horace Chester Dinsmore and his brother and sisters are to the rest? They seem to call everybody cousin, even Grandpa Dinsmore."

"Yes, I was asking Aunt Elsie about them the other day," replied Eva. "She told me their father was first cousin to Grandpa Dinsmore—his father's brother's son. When he died, he left them to Grandpa Dinsmore's care. He made him their guardian, I mean, and as Uncle Horace and his wife were kindly willing to have them at the Oaks, they were invited to make it their home till they are grown up. It's a lovely place, and I know they are very kindly treated, but I can't help feeling sorry for them because both their parents are dead."

"Nor I," said Max. "For no matter how kind other folks may be to you, it isn't like having your own father or mother. I'm ever so fond of Mamma Vi, though," he added with emphasis. "I'm just as glad as I can be that papa married her."

"And that she married him," put in Eva, laughingly. "I think it was a grand match on both sides. She is so sweet and lovely, and he in every way worthy of her."

"My opinion exactly," laughed Max. "I am very proud of my father, Eva."

"I don't wonder. I am sure I should be in your place," she said. "Ah, see, we are just turning into the grounds! The ride has seemed very short to me. But it's quite a little journey yet to the house. I admire this winding drive very much. It gives one quite a number of beautiful views, and it's really obliging of the moon to come out just now from behind that cloud and show us how lovely every thing is looking. I think newly fallen snow gives such a charming variety to a landscape.

"There's witchery in the moonlight, too," she went on, glancing out through the windows, now on this side, now on that. "It is no wonder Grandma Elsie is so fond of this place where, as she says, she lived so happily with her father and

Grandma Rose when she was a little girl and up until she was married."

At that moment a turn in the road brought the front of the mansion into full view. Lights were gleaming from every window, seeming to promise a warm welcome and an abundance of good cheer—a promise whose fulfillment began presently as the carriage drew up before the door.

"You are the last, my dears, but none the less welcome," Mrs. Dinsmore said, as she kissed Evelyn and shook hands with Max.

"Thank you, ma'am. I hope you have not kept your tea waiting for us," returned Eva more than a little anxiously.

"Oh, no, my dear. We had been told not to expect you to tea, so we did not wait."

"And Rosie Travilla has only just come," said Maud, taking possession of Evelyn and hurrying her away to the room appropriated to their joint use during Eva's stay.

"These rooms that used to be Cousin Elsie's have been given up to our use for the present," she said. "This was her bedroom. There is another adjoining it on that side, and her dressing room on the other side has been turned into a bedroom for the time—so that we six girls are all close together. And we have her boudoir for our own private little parlor, where we can be quite to ourselves whenever we wish. Isn't it nice?"

"Yes, indeed!" returned Evelyn. "Oh, Rosie, so you got here before me!" she cried as Rosie came running in, followed by Sydney, each greeting the others with a hug and a kiss.

"Yes, a little. But where's Lu?"

"The captain thought it best for her to stay at home, and she preferred to do so, since Gracie is so unwell as to need her nursing."

"How nice and good of her!" cried Sydney. "But I'm ever so sorry not to have her with us, for I like her very much indeed."

"I love her dearly," said Evelyn. "I've never seen a more warm-hearted, generous girl, and it's beautiful to see how she and Gracie love one another."

"I really think the captain might have let Lu come, and I am sorry for her disappointment," said Rosie sincerely.

"She was disappointed at first," said Evelyn. "But after Gracie took sick she wouldn't have come if her father had given permission. She told me so, saying that she couldn't enjoy herself at all, knowing her darling sister was suffering without her there to comfort and amuse her."

"Vi would have done that quite as well, I am sure," remarked Rosie.

"And so we're only five instead of six," said Maud. "Well, we'll each one of us just have to try to be all the more entertaining to the rest. Your dress and hair are all right, Eva, so let us hurry out to the parlor where the others are. They'll be wanting us to take part in the games."

The door opened as she spoke, and an attractive little girl, about Evelyn's age, looked in. It was Lora Howard, the youngest of the Pine Grove family.

"Come, girls," she said. "We're waiting for you. Oh, Eva, how do you do?"

"What's the game to be?" asked Rosie. "I suppose it will be some sort of a romping one to please the little ones."

"Yes, let's play either 'Pussy Wants a Corner,' or 'Blindman's Buff,'" replied Lora, leading the way to the scene of festivity.

For some time mirth and jollity ruled the hour. The older people joined in the sports of the young with the double motive of watching over them and adding to their enjoyment, and then light refreshments were partaken of. After that the servants were called in, and the head of the family read aloud a short Psalm. He offered a brief prayer, giving thanks for the blessings of life and the pleasures of the past day and asking for the protecting care during the silent watches of the night of Him who neither slumbers nor sleeps.

Then the goodnights were spoken, and all quickly scattered to their rooms.

The little ones were carried off by Mrs. Dinsmore and their nurses. The five young girls retreated to the suite of rooms set apart to their use, and the lads—seven in number—trooped up the broad stairway leading to the second story.

"Max, we will all—you and I and Art and Walter Howard—share this room," said Frank Dinsmore. "You see we have to crowd a little—there being such a lot of us—but it'll be all the jollier, don't you think, boys?"

He had led the way, as he spoke, into a most inviting-looking room—large enough to seem far from crowded, even with the beds filling every available corner.

"Yes, indeed!" the others responded in chorus. Art added, "The more the merrier, and we'll have no end of good time, if I'm not mightily mistaken."

A door of communication with another room stood wide open, and through it they could see the three older lads, gathered closely about a blazing wood fire.

"Walk in, boys," called Chester, addressing Max and his companions, as he saw them sending curious glances in that direction.

"We're expected to go to bed, aren't we?" queried Max in reply, coming in last and speaking with some hesitation.

"We're not at boarding school, my lad," laughed Chester. "No one has given orders as to the exact hour of retiring, so far as I am aware."

"Of course not," said his brother. "Cousin Horace and Cousin Sue are not of the sort to be over-strict with a fellow, and they would never think of laying down the law to visitors, any way."

"And it's not late," added Walter, accepting the chair Chester had set for him.

"Come on, Max, we're a respectable crowd, and we won't damage your morals," said Ralph, lighting a cigar and beginning to smoke it.

"I should hope not," said Chester. "I presume if any such danger had been apprehended, he would hardly have been allowed to come to the Oaks."

"Are his morals supposed to be more easily damaged than those of the common run of fellows?" asked Bertram Shaw, regarding Max with a sneering, supercilious stare.

"I am inclined to think they are," said Ralph.

"Come, come now, I'm not going to have Max made uncomfortable," interposed Chester, good-naturedly. "He's my guest, you know. Here, sit down, laddie, it's early yet," pushing forward a chair as he spoke. "Have a cigar?"

"No, thank you," returned Max. "I tried one once and got enough of it. I was never so sick in my life."

"Oh, that's nothing unusual for a first trial. Likely it wouldn't have the same effect again, Max," said Bertram.

"Better take one. You'll seem twice the man if you smoke than you will if you don't."

The box of cigars had been passed around to all, and each of the other boys had taken one, but Max steadily refused.

"My father says it is injurious to boys and will stunt their growth," he gave as a reason. He then added, with a laugh, "It's my ambition to be as tall as he is and like him in every way."

"Very right," remarked Frank. "But do you mind the smoke?"

"Oh, not at all."

But the next minute he saw something that he did mind. A table was drawn into the middle of the room, and a pack of cards and a bottle of wine were produced from some hiding place and set upon it, while Chester invited them all to draw up their chairs and have a glass and a game.

The others accepted without hesitation, but Max rose and, with burning cheeks and fast-beating heart, uttered a protest.

"Oh, you can't be going to drink and gamble, surely! What would Uncle Horace say if he knew such things were going on in his house?"

"No, my son," said Chester, laughingly. "We're not going to do either. We'll not play for money, so it won't be gambling, and the wine isn't strong enough to make a fellow drunk—no, nor anywhere near it. So you needn't be afraid to join us."

"No, thank you," returned Max firmly. "I cannot think it right or safe to drink even wine, or to play cards, whether you put up a stake or not."

"No, 'twouldn't be safe for you, I presume," sneered Ralph. "He's awfully afraid of his governor, lads. So we'd best not try to persuade him."

"Do you mean my father?" demanded Max, more than a trifle hotly.

"Of course, my little man. Whom else should I mean, you silly boy?"

"Then I want you to understand that I never would be so disrespectful to my own father as to call him that!"

"It's not so bad," laughed Chester, while Bertram frowned and muttered something about a "Muff and a spooney," and Frank said, "Come, now, Max, sit down and have a game with us. Where's the harm in it?"

"Don't urge him," sneered Ralph. "He's afraid of a flogging. He knows he'd catch it, and the captain looks like a man that wouldn't mince matters if he undertook to administer it."

Max's face flushed more hotly than before, but he straightened himself and looked his tormentor full in the eye as he answered. "I don't deny that I should expect a flogging if I should weakly yield and do what my conscience tells me is wrong, even if my father had not forbidden it, as he has. But I'm not ashamed to own that I love my father so well that the pained look I should see in his face when he learned that his only son had taken to such wicked courses would be worse to me than a dozen floggings. Goodnight to you all," he said, as he turned and left the room.

"Coward!" muttered Ralph, as the door closed softly upon him.

"Any thing else than that, I should say," remarked Chester. "I think he has shown himself the bravest of us all. Moral courage, we all know, is courage of the highest kind."

"Yes, boys, I am sure he is right, and I, for one, shall follow his example," said Arthur, rising. And with a hasty goodnight, he too disappeared.

Walter and Frank exchanged glances.

"I think, myself, we might be at better business," remarked the one.

"That's so!" assented the other, and they, too, withdrew to the next room.

Max had taken a tiny volume from his pocket and was seated near the light, reading.

"What have you there, old fellow?" asked Frank, stepping to his side, laying a hand on his shoulder, and bending down to look. "A Testament, I do declare!"

The tone expressed astonishment, not unmixed with derision.

Max's cheek flushed again, but he replied without hesitation and in his usual pleasant tones, "Yes, I promised papa I would always read at least one verse before going to bed at night."

"And say your prayers, too, I suppose?"

Max felt very much as if he were called to march up to the cannon's mouth, as a glance showed him that not Frank only, but the other two boys also, were standing regarding him with mingled curiosity and amusement. His heart quailed for a moment, but the remembrance of what his father had once told him about having to pass through such ordeals in his youthful days gave him courage to emulate that father's example and stand to his colors in spite of the ridicule that seemed so hard to face.

"Not only that, but I know that God's eye is on me, His ear open to hear what I say," was his next thought. "I will not dishonor either my earthly or my heavenly father."

All this passed through his mind in a second of time, and he hardly seemed to pause before he answered in a firm, steady voice, "Yes. I did promise that, too. Even if I had not, I should do it. Don't you think, you fellows, it would be mean and ungrateful for a boy that is so well off as I am, and has been having such a splendid time all day long, to tumble into his bed without so much as saying thank you to the One he owes it all to?"

"Does look like it when you put it so," muttered Arthur quietly.

"And then," proceeded Max, "who is there to take care of us while we and everybody else are fast asleep? It may be we'll wake in the morning all right if we don't take the trouble to ask God to keep us alive and safe, for He's always a great deal better to us than we deserve, but don't you think it's wise to ask Him?"

"I reckon," said Frank, forcing a laugh, for Max's seriousness was rather infectious. "We'll not hinder you any way, old boy, and while you are in the way of asking for yourself, you can just include the rest of us, if you like."

"How old are you, Max?" queried Arthur.

"Thirteen."

"And I, though four years older, am not half the soldier you are."

Max shook his head. "I'm not brave at all. It was awfully hard to speak out against the cards and wine, and I did hope I'd have this room to myself till—till I'd got through with reading and the rest of it."

"Of course, but you went through the fight and stuck manfully to your colors for all your fright. I say, old fellow, you're worthy to be the son of a naval officer."

"Thank you," said Max, flushing with pleasure. "I wouldn't be worthy of my father if I couldn't brave more than I have tonight."

"Well, go ahead and finish up your devotions. We'll not disturb you," said Frank, turning away and beginning to undress for bed.

The Howards followed Frank's example, all three keeping very quiet while Max was on his knees.

They had all been brought up under religious influences, and while not controlled by them as Max was, they still felt constrained enough to respect his firm adherence to duty and the right.

CHAPTER SECOND

CAPTAIN RAYMOND HAD foreseen the distinct probability that his son would be subjected to such an ordeal and had tried—successfully as the event proved—to prepare him for it.

Max had been busy with his preparations for bed on the previous night, when his door opened and his father came in.

"Well, my boy," he said in his usual kind, fatherly tones, "I hope you have had a happy day and evening?"

"Yes, papa. Oh, yes, indeed! Never had a more splendid time in all my life!"

"In all your long life of thirteen years!" laughed the captain, seating himself and regarding his son with a proud, fond look.

"No, sir. And such splendid presents you and the rest have given me! Why, I'd be the most ungrateful fellow in the world if I wasn't as happy as a king!"

"Happy as a king?" echoed his father. "Ah, my boy, I should be sorry indeed to think that your life was to be less happy than that of most monarchs. 'Uneasy lies the head that wears a crown.'"

"I want to have a little chat with you," he resumed, after a moment's silence, his countenance and the tone of his voice much graver than they had been a moment since. "I heard today that

Ralph Conly, who exerted so bad an influence over my son some time ago, is to make one of the party at the Oaks."

"Is he, papa? Then I suppose you have come to tell me you can't let me go?" Max returned in a tone of keen disappointment.

"No," said his father kindly. "I do not withdraw the consent I have given. You may go, but I want you to be on your guard against temptation to do wrong. I am told Ralph professes to have reformed, but I fear it may prove to be only profession. I also fear that he and others may try to lead my son astray from the paths of rectitude."

Max looked very sober for a moment, then said with effort, "I'll give up going, papa, if you wish it—if you're afraid for me."

"Thank you, my boy," returned his father heartily, taking the lad's hand as he stood by his side and pressing it with affectionate warmth. "But I won't ask such self-denial. You must meet temptation some time, and if you go trusting in a strength not your own, I believe you will come off conqueror.

"Don't let persuasion, sneers, or ridicule induce you to do violence to your conscience, in either shirking a known duty or taking part in any wrong or doubtful amusement. Remember it would go nigh to break your father's heart to learn that you had been drinking, gambling, or taking God's holy name in vain."

"Oh, papa, I hope I shall never, never do such wicked things again!" Max said with emotion, calling to mind how he had fallen once under Ralph's influence.

"I know you don't intend to," his father said. "And I trust you will have strength given you to resist if the temptation comes. I know, too, that it is very difficult for a boy to stand out against the sneers, ridicule, and contempt of his mates. But how much better to have the smile and approval of God, your heavenly Father, than that of any number of human creatures! Do not be like those chief rulers among the Jews who would not confess Christ because they loved the praise of men more than the praise of God!"

"No, papa, I hope I shall not. Besides, I don't care half so much for the good opinion of all the boys in the land as for yours," he added, gazing into his father's face with eyes brimming over with ardent love and reverence. "I am proud to be your son, papa, and I do hope you'll never have cause to be ashamed of me."

"No, my boy, I trust you will be always, as now, your father's joy and pride," responded the captain, again pressing affectionately the hand he held. "Rest assured that nothing but wrong doing on your part can ever make you any thing else. Nor would even that rob you of his love."

"Then, papa, I think I shall never try to hide my faults from you," returned the lad with impulsive warmth. "I'm sure a fellow feels a great deal more comfortable when he isn't trying to make believe to his father that he is a better boy than he really is."

"Yes, when his effort is not merely to seem, but to be, all that he knows his best earthly friend would have him. You needn't stand in awe of me, Max, as of one who knows nothing by experience of sinning and repenting. I sometimes think you are a better boy than I was at your age, and I hope to see you grow up to be a better man than I am now."

"Why, papa, I never see you do wrong, and I don't believe you ever do," said Max.

"I do try to live right, Max," his father answered. "I try to keep the commands of God, honoring Him in all my ways and setting a good example to my children, but I am conscious of many shortcomings. And I could have no hope of heaven but for the atoning blood and imputed righteousness of Christ."

"And that's the only way any body can be saved?" Max said in a low tone between inquiry and assertion.

"Yes, my boy. All of human righteousnesses are as filthy rags in the sight of Him who is of purer eyes than to behold evil and cannot even look upon iniquity."

"Papa," Max said, after a moment's thoughtful silence, "I'm afraid you wouldn't think it from the way I act and talk, but I have really been trying to be a Christian ever since that time when I wrote you that I hoped I had given myself to God."

"My dear boy, I have noticed your efforts," was the kindly response. "I see that you try to control your temper, and you are always truthful, obedient, and respectful to me—kind and obliging to others."

"But you know, papa, it's only a few weeks since you came home, and you haven't found me out yet," replied Max naively. "I have often a hard fight with myself to go right, and sometimes I fail in spite of it. Then I grow discouraged, and so I'm ever so much obliged to you for telling me that it's a good deal the same way with you. It makes a fellow feel better, you see, to find out that even those he respects the most don't always find it easy to do and feel just as they want to."

"Yes, my dear boy, we have the same battle to fight—you and I—the same race to run. So we can sympathize with each other and must try to be fellow-helpers."

"You can help me, papa, but how can I help you?" asked Max with a look of surprise not unmixed with gratification.

"By being a good son to me and your mamma, and a good brother to your sisters. If you are all that, you cannot fail to be a very great help, blessing, and comfort to me. But best of all, Max, you can pray for me."

"Oh, papa, I do. I never forget you at night or in the morning, but—"

"Well?"

"I—I'm afraid my prayers are not worth much."

"Why not, my son? The Bible tells us God is no respecter of persons, but that He is ready to hear and answer all who come to him in the name of His dear Son, who is the one mediator between God and men. If you ask in His name—for His sake— you are as likely to receive as I or any one else.

"Now I must bid you goodnight, for it is high time you were asleep."

The next evening, about the time the goodnights were being said at the Oaks, Captain Raymond left Lulu, who had just passed a very happy half hour seated on his knee, in her own little sitting room and went down to the parlor where Violet was entertaining her guests.

There was quite a number of them, though it was only a family gathering. Mr. and Mrs. Dinsmore from Ion; Grandma Elsie, as Evelyn and the Raymond children called her; Lester Leland and his Elsie; Edward and Zoe; Herbert and Harold, who were at home from college for the Christmas holidays; the Laceys from the Laurels; several of the Howards of Pine Grove; and Calhoun and Arthur Conly from Roselands.

Violet looked up with a welcoming smile as her husband came in and made room for him on the sofa by her side.

"I was just telling Lester and Elsie," she said, "how beautifully Lulu is behaving, bearing so well the disappointment about her invitation to the Oaks and showing such devotion to Gracie in her sickness."

"Yes, she is a dear child and well-deserving of reward," he said feelingly. "It pained me to deny her the pleasure of sharing the festivities at the Oaks. Though, as matters have turned out, she would not have gone had I given permission, loving Gracie too dearly to leave her while she is not well. I have been thinking whether it may not be made up to her by allowing her to have a little party of her own next week, inviting her young friends who are now at the Oaks and perhaps some others, to come here on Monday and stay until Saturday. Does the idea meet your approval, my dear?"

"Yes, indeed!" cried Violet, looking really delighted. "How happy it would make her and Max. Gracie, too, I think, if we can only get her well enough to have a share in the sports.

"And, I believe," she added with a laugh, "I am child enough yet to enjoy it greatly myself."

"I hope so," her husband said, smiling fondly upon her. "You certainly are looking full young enough for mirth and jollity, and you must not allow yourself to grow old too fast in an endeavor to match your years with mine."

"No, captain, the better plan would be for you to match yours with hers by growing young," said Zoe, laughingly. "Can't you turn boy again for a few days?"

"I should not be adverse to so doing," laughed the captain. "I'll see what I can do, Sister Zoe. "May we look to you for some assistance in the work of contriving amusements?"

"Yes, indeed, if you give me an invitation to the party. I was not favored with one to the Oaks, you know, because of being a married woman. Though Ella Conly was, in spite of her superiority of years."

"Too bad!" returned the captain gallantly. "But we will not draw the line just where they did. Please, all the present company will please consider themselves invited for each evening's entertainment—mothers and all under twenty-five—for the whole time, from Monday morning to Saturday afternoon. I am taking for granted that my wife approves and joins me in the invitations," he added, turning smilingly to her.

"Oh, yes, indeed!" she said. "I hope you will all come." There was a chorus of both thanks and acceptances, some only partial or conditional.

"I promise you I'll be here when I can," Arthur said. "But you know a doctor can seldom or never be sure of having his time at his own disposal."

"You'll be heartily welcome whenever you do come," responded the captain. "Please take notice that you will be expected to be quite as much of a boy as your host."

"No objection to that condition," returned Arthur smiling. "If I don't outdo you in that, I'd be surprised."

"The next thing in order then, I suppose, will be to consider how our young guests are to be feasted and amused," remarked Violet.

"Yes," replied her husband. "But my wife is to be burdened with no care or responsibility in regard to either. Christine and I will see to the first — preparations for the feasting — and I imagine there will be no trouble about the other. The children themselves will probably have a great number of suggestions to make."

"Some of the older ones, too," said Zoe, eagerly, and she went on to mention quite a list of games.

"Besides, we can act charades and get up tableaux. Oh, let us try something I read about the other day in Miss Yonge's *The Three Brides.* It is a magic case with a Peri distributing gifts, oriental genii, turbaned figures, like princes in the *Arabian Nights,* along with singing and piano accompaniment. Oh, it would be fun and delight the children, I'm sure! I know we could manage it all among us very easily."

"It sounds charming," said Violet. "We must study it out and see what we can do. Shall we not, Levis?"

"I like the idea very much, so far as I understand it," he said. "Who will volunteer to take part?"

"Zoe and I may be counted on," said Edward with a smiling glance at his young wife.

"And Herbert and I," added Harold. "We've had some experience, and it's the sort of thing we both greatly enjoy."

"Yes, and we'll help with the charades and anything else, if we're wanted," said Herbert.

But it was growing late, so further arrangements were deferred to the next day. The company presently separated for the night — the Lelands and Edward and Zoe remained in the house, but the rest departed to their homes.

"Why, Gracie, here before me, though you're the sick one!" exclaimed Lulu, as early the next morning she entered the little sitting room they shared between them and found her sister lying on the sofa already dressed for the day.

"Yes," Gracie said. "I was so tired of bed, and Agnes said she would help me dress before mamma's bell should ring. So I let her, but I'm tired and have to lie down again a little bit."

"Yes, you're not nearly strong enough to sit up all day yet," returned Lulu, stooping over her to give her a kiss. "But you've been crying, haven't you? Your eyes look like it."

Gracie nodded, hastily brushing away a tear.

"Why, what ever is the matter?" asked Lulu in surprise. "I can't think of anything to make you cry, unless it's pain. Are you in pain, dear?"

Gracie shook her head. "No, Lu, but," sobbing, "I—I've been thinking 'bout that time I was so naughty, meddling with mamma's things, and—and—oh, you know the rest."

"Yes, but why does it trouble you now? It was all over such a long time ago."

"Yes, but papa doesn't know about it, and—oughtn't I to tell him?"

"I don't know," Lulu said reflectively. "But you needn't be afraid. He wouldn't punish you after this long while, especially as Mamma Vi knew all about it at the time and punished you herself."

"Such a little bit of a punishment for such a wicked, wicked thing," Gracie said. "Papa would have punished me a great deal harder, I'm most certain, Lulu."

"But he won't now; so you needn't be afraid to tell him."

"But he'd look so sorry, and I can't bear to see my dear papa look sorry for something I did."

"Then don't tell him. It isn't as if it had happened just the other day."

"But, Lulu, I oughtn't to let him think I'm a better girl than I am."

"Maybe he doesn't. You are a good girl—a great deal better than I am."

"No, I'm not. You would never, never do the wicked thing I did. But I'm afraid papa thinks I'm better, 'cause when—when he thought the baby was going to die, he was hugging me and kissing me. And he said, 'You never gave me a pang except by your feeble health,' and I said, 'I didn't ever want to.' But I forgot all about how bad I'd been that time, and that papa didn't know about it."

"What is it papa didn't know about, my darling?" asked a voice close beside the sofa. Both girls started in surprise, for their father had come in so quietly, his slippered feet making no noise on the carpet, that they had not been aware of his entrance.

He took Gracie in his arms as he spoke, sat down with her on his knee, drew Lulu to a seat by his side, kissed them both, saying in tender tones, "Good morning, my two dear children."

"Good morning, my dear papa," responded Lulu, leaning her cheek affectionately against his shoulder.

But Gracie only hid her face on his chest with a little, stifled sob.

"What is it, my precious one?" he asked, holding her close with loving caresses.

"Lu, you tell papa. Please do," she sobbed.

"Lulu may tell it, if you want papa to hear it," he said, softly smoothing her hair. "Otherwise, it need not be told at all. But if it is about some wrong doing that has been repented of and confessed to God and mamma, you need not dread to have your father know of it. For he, too, has been guilty of wrong doing many times in his life and needs to ask forgiveness of God every day and every hour."

"Papa," she exclaimed, lifting her head to give him a look of astonishment not unmingled with relief, "I don't know how to b'lieve that, if you didn't say it your own self. I never, never see you do anything wrong. But I want you to know 'bout this, so you won't think I'm a better girl than I am. Lu, please tell," and again her face was hidden on his chest.

"Papa, it was a long, long while ago," began Lulu, as if eager to vindicate her sister as far as possible. "It was only that she accidentally broke a bottle of Mamma Vi's. And then she was frightened—you know she's always so timid, and can't help it—and so, 'most before she knew what she was saying, she told Mamma Vi she never meddled with her things when she was not there to see her."

There was a moment of silence, broken only by Gracie's sobs, which were now quite violent.

Then her father said low and tenderly, "My dear daughter, I cannot comfort you by making light of your sin. Lying is a very great sin—one that the Bible speaks very strongly against in very many places. But I have no doubt that you long ago repented, confessed it to God, and received forgiveness. I trust you will prove the sincerity of your repentance by being perfectly truthful all the rest of your days.

"It was very honest and right of you to want me to know that you have not always been as good as I supposed. And so, my darling, I love you, if possible, better than ever," he added, caressing her again and again.

"Oh, I'm so glad to hear you say that, papa!" exclaimed Lulu, looking up into his face with bright and shining eyes.

"And you are no less dear than your sister," he said, drawing her closer to his side. "My child, I have felt very sorry over your disappointment in missing the festivities at the Oaks and have been trying to think of some way to make it up to you. How would you like to have something of the same sort here at home—a party of children and young people to come next Monday morning and stay through till Saturday?"

"Oh, papa!" cried Lulu, opening her eyes very wide in surprise and delight. "It 'most takes my breath away! Do you really mean it?"

"I do indeed," he said, smiling on her. "It will be your and Max's and Gracie's party, and we older folks will do all in our power to make the time pass pleasantly to you and your guests. We will have games and charades, tableaux, stories, and everything delightful that can be thought of."

"Oh, papa! How very nice! How splendid!" cried Lulu, springing to her feet, clapping her hands, and then jumping and dancing round the room. "Dear me! I've never once dreamed of such a thing! And it'll be ever so much nicer than going to the Oaks. I'm glad you didn't let me go because I couldn't be there now and get things ready for my own party, too. It's so much more splendid to be the one to have the party than one of the visitors. Isn't it?

Won't it be, Gracie? Oh, isn't papa just the best and kindest father in the world?"

"'Course he is," said Gracie, putting her arm round his neck and lifting her eyes to his with a very grateful, loving look.

"Does it give you pleasure, papa's darling?" he asked.

"Yes, sir," she answered with some hesitation. "If I won't be sick when they're here, and if I may sit on your knee sometimes."

"Indeed you may," he said. "Papa will try to take care that his feeble little girl has nothing to tire her."

"No, she needn't entertain," said Lulu. "I can do it for both of us. Oh, it is so nice, so nice, so perfectly splendid, to think we're going to have a real party of our own for several days together!" she cried, again clapping her hands, jumping, dancing, and pirouetting round the room.

Gracie laughed aloud at the sight of her sister, and so did their father.

"Why, Lulu, daughter," he said, "you seem to be going quite wild over the prospect! I am very glad indeed to have hit upon something that gives you such pleasure. But come here. I have something more to tell you about it."

"Oh, have you, papa?" she cried, running to him to put her arm round his neck and kiss him again and again. "What is it?"

"Ah," he returned, laughing, "I doubt if it is well to tell you. You are so nearly crazy already."

"Oh, yes, do tell me, please. I won't get any crazier. At least, I don't think I shall. I'll try not to."

So he told her of Zoe's suggestion, and that he intended it should be carried out.

A conservatory opened off of one of the parlors, and there, he said, they would have the magic cave.

"Oh, papa, how lovely, how lovely!" both little girls exclaimed, their eyes sparkling and their cheeks flushing with delighted anticipation.

"That entertainment will be for New Year's Eve," he said. "And the Peri must have a present for each one who visits her cave. That will necessitate a shopping expedition to the city today or tomorrow. Lulu, would you like to be one of the purchasers? Shall I take you to the stores with me?"

"Oh!" she cried breathlessly. "Wouldn't I like it? But," with a sudden sobering of demeanor and a tender look into the face of her little sister, "I—I can't leave Gracie, papa. She would miss me and be so lonesome without me."

"But I could stand it for one day, Lu. And I couldn't bear to have you miss such fun—such a good time—just for me," said Gracie with winning sweetness.

"And Mamma Vi will contrive that she shall not be lonely," the captain said, drawing them both closer into his arms.

"The mutual love of my little girls is a great joy to me," he added, hugging them in turn.

Just then a servant came into the sitting room, bringing Gracie's breakfast.

She ate it sitting on her father's knee, while Lulu, standing alongside, kept up a lively strain of talk on the all-absorbing theme of the hour. She had a good many questions to ask, too. And they were all answered by her father with his usual unfailing patience and kindness.

The proposed festivities were the principal topic of conversation at the family breakfast, also, for the ladies were deeply interested and the gentlemen not at all indifferent.

The storm had passed, the morning was fine, and the captain announced his intention to drive into the city, starting within an hour and winding up with the query, "Which of you ladies will volunteer to go along and assist in this important shopping?"

"Zoe would enjoy it, I am sure, and you could not have a more competent helper," Violet said, smiling kindly into the eager face of her young sister-in-law.

"I should not object, if I can be of service," said Zoe. "But don't you want to go yourself, Vi? I haven't a doubt that the captain would prefer your company to any other."

"I think I should abide by the tasks at hand," returned Violet in a lively tone. "Or rather by the little ones, baby and Gracie. Lulu must go with her papa—I would not have her miss it for a great deal—and I am eager to make the day a happy one to Gracie in spite of the absence of her devoted sister-nurse," she added with an affectionate glance and smile in Lulu's direction.

"Oh, Mamma Vi, thank you ever so much!" exclaimed the little girl. "I do think it will be just splendid to go with papa and help choose the things, but I can't bear to leave Gracie alone."

"You are a dear, good sister, Lulu," remarked Mrs. Elsie Leland. "It does one good to see how you and Gracie love one another."

"Thank you, Aunt Elsie," said Lulu, flushing with gratification. Then catching the look of proud, fond affection with which her father was regarding her, she colored still more deeply, while her heart bounded with joy. It was so sweet to know that he loved her so dearly and was not ashamed of her, faulty as she felt herself to be.

"Yes," he said, "their mutual affection is indeed a constant source of happiness to this father. I pity the parent whose children are not kind and affectionate to each other.

"Well, Mrs. Zoe," turning smilingly to her, "am I to have the pleasure of your company today and the benefit of your assistance and advice in the selection of the ornaments and gifts necessary or desirable for the successful carrying out of your proposed entertainment?"

"Thank you. I shall be delighted to go and give all the assistance in my power," she answered. "That is if Ned is willing to spare me," she added, turning to him with a merry, mischievous look and smile.

"I don't think I can," he said in a very sober and meditative tone. "But if the captain is sufficiently anxious to secure your valuable services to take me, too, my consent shall not be withheld."

"Then it's a bargain," laughed the captain, and Lulu's eyes sparkled. She was saying to herself, "Then I shall be sure to sit beside papa, because they always want to be together. So they'll take one seat in the carriage, and we'll have the other."

CHAPTER THIRD

X "Oh, Gracie, Gracie, I've had the nicest, the most splendid time that ever was!" cried Lulu, rushing into their own little sitting room where Gracie lay on a sofa, having that moment awakened from her afternoon nap.

"Oh, have you, Lu? I'm so glad!" she exclaimed as her sister paused for breath—for Lulu had rushed upstairs so fast in her joyful eagerness to tell everything to Gracie that she had not much breath left for talking.

"I've had a good time, too, looking at pictures, playing with baby, and hearing lovely stories that mamma and Aunt Elsie told me," continued Gracie. "But tell me 'bout yours."

"Oh, it would be a long story to tell you every little thing," said Lulu. "I enjoyed the drive ever so much, sitting close beside papa with his arm 'round me. He gave me such a loving look every once in a while and asked me if I were quite warm and comfortable. Then we went to so many stores and bought lots of things—some handsome and some not worth much—but just to make fun when we have the chance, you know. And papa was, oh, so kind! He let me buy every single thing I wanted to. He says I may label the presents this evening, and he will help me because it would be too much for me to do all alone—you know, to try and decide which present is to be given to which person."

"Oh, Lu, what fun!" cried Gracie.

"Yes, and you shall have some say in it, too, if you want to," returned Lulu, generously, throwing off her coat as she spoke and bending down to give Gracie a loving kiss.

"I'm to make out the list of folks to be invited, too," she ran on. "And write the notes with papa's help. He says this is to be all our own party—Max's and yours and mine—and he wants us to get every bit of pleasure out of it we can. Isn't he just the dearest, kindest father?"

"Yes, indeed."

"And, oh, Gracie, how nice it is to have him at home with us all the time and to live with him in this lovely home!"

"Yes, Lu, I think we ought to be ever such good children to him and Mamma Vi."

"So do I. Oh, here comes papa!" as a manly step drew near the door.

It opened, and the captain came in. Bending over Gracie, he kissed her several times, asking in tender tones how she was and if she had had a pleasant day.

"Yes, papa, oh, very! I've just had a nice nap and now I'd like to get up and sit on your knee a little while, if you're not too tired."

"I'm not tired at all, my dear, and I shall enjoy it perhaps as much as you will," he said, seating himself and complying with her request.

"Lulu, daughter, put your hat and coat in their proper places and make your hair neat."

"Yes, sir," Lulu returned in bright, cheerful tones, moving promptly to obey.

She was back again almost immediately. "Oh, Gracie," she said, "I didn't tell you about our dinner! Papa took us to Morse's, the best and most expensive place in the city. He let me choose just what I wanted from the bill of fare, and he paid for it."

"And my wise little girl, who thinks it so delightful to have her own way, chose several dishes that she found she could not eat at all," remarked the captain with a humorous look and smile directed at Lulu, who was now standing close at his side.

"Yes," she said, blushing vividly. "You told me I wouldn't like them, papa, and I found you knew best after all. But you and Aunt Zoe enjoyed them so that they weren't lost."

"Quite true," he responded.

"And then, papa let me choose again," Lulu went on, addressing Gracie. "And I took things I knew I liked."

"You did have a splendid time," remarked Gracie rather wistfully.

"I hope you will be able to go with us next year, my dear," her father said, hugging her tenderly.

"Oh, papa! Are we really to have another party like this next year?" queried Lulu in almost breathless excitement.

"That depends," he said. "If a certain little girl of mine should indulge in an outburst of passion while she is playing hostess to her young friends, I think the prospect of a party for her next year will not be a very brilliant one."

"Oh, I hope I won't papa. Please watch me all the time and do everything you can to help me keep from it," Lulu murmured, her arm round his neck and her cheek laid to his.

"I certainly shall, my dear child," he answered, putting his arm about her and drawing her into a close embrace. "And I am very hopeful in regard to it. You have been behaving so well of late. It gives me great pleasure to be able to say that."

She lifted dewy eyes to his. "Thank you, papa. Oh, I do mean to try as hard as I can!"

"Suppose we decide now who is to be invited," he said. "Gracie must have a say about that as well as the rest of us."

"I s'pose we'll have all the relations—least all that aren't too old—won't we, papa?" she asked.

"Yes, I think so—the same company they had at the Oaks for the whole time—and the grown people in the evenings, when we are to have tableaux or the magic cave or something else not too juvenile for them to enjoy."

"Papa," said Lulu, "I thought you said I was to have some choice."

"Yes, daughter, mention anyone else you may wish to invite."

"I don't care to invite anybody else, but—papa, please don't be angry with me, but I'd rather not have Rosie Travilla here." She hung her head and blushed, as she spoke in a low, hesitating way.

The captain looked a little surprised, but not angry. "Why not, my child?" he asked. "You ought to have very good excuse for leaving her out."

"Papa, it's because—because I'm afraid she'll get me into a passion."

"Ah," he said with an involuntary sigh, "I remember now that she was mixed up in some way with that unfortunate affair of a few weeks ago. But can you not forgive her for that?"

"Yes, papa, if I only could be sure she wouldn't say horrid things to me that—but, oh, I didn't mean to tell tales!"

"And I certainly don't want to hear any. Yet I should be far from willing to have your hard task of controlling your temper made harder for you."

"I don't want to be a tell-tale either," Gracie said timidly. "And I do like Rosie, but sometimes she isn't very good to Lu. Sometimes she teases her so that I think it's 'most more her fault than Lu's when Lu gets into a passion."

"Ah, this is news to me. Perhaps I have been too hard on my quick-tempered little daughter," he said in a remorseful tone, drawing Lulu into a closer embrace and pressing a tender kiss upon her forehead.

Lulu looked up with a flash of joy in her eyes, then dropping her head on his shoulder so that her face was half hidden there, she said, "I'll invite Rosie if you want me to, papa. If she teases me, I'll try to be patient."

"That's my own dear child," was his kindly response. "I should not like to have her left out, considering how very kind her mother and grandfather have been to my children and that she is your mamma's sister. I hardly think she will do or say unkind, trying things to you when she is your guest in your father's house. I feel quite sure she will not in my presence, and I shall arrange matters so that I can be with you almost all the time while your guests are here."

"Oh, papa, thank you!" cried Lulu, drawing a long breath of relief. "Then I'm quite willing to have Rosie here. I shouldn't like to hurt Grandma Elsie's feelings or Mamma Vi's or even Rosie's own by leaving her out."

"I am rejoiced to hear you say that. I trust there is little or no malice in your nature," he said, repeating his caresses.

"Papa, I think Lu's very good 'cept her temper," said Gracie, putting an arm affectionately round her sister's neck.

"No," said Lulu. "I'm willful, too. I've disobeyed papa more than once because I liked my own way best, and I'm bad other ways, sometimes. But I do love our dear father, and I am trying to be a better girl," she added, lifting her head to look affectionately into his face.

"Yes, daughter, I see that you are, and it makes me very happy," he said.

"Now, I have something else to tell you two that will please you, I think. We are all invited to spend tomorrow afternoon at the Oaks to see some tableaux they are getting up there, and I hope even my little Gracie will be able to go."

"Oh, how nice!" cried Lulu, while Gracie asked, "Will you go and take us, papa?"

"I hope to," he answered, smiling fondly down upon her. "Ah, there is the tea bell! Will you travel down to the table in papa's arms?"

"Yes, sir, if you would like to carry me, and it won't make you tired."

"It won't tire me at all, my dear child. I only wish you were heavy enough to be something of a burden," he said as he rose with her in his arms and moved toward the door, Lulu following.

"Oh, Lu, don't you wish you were in my place?" Gracie asked with a gleeful laugh, looking down at her sister over her father's shoulder.

"No, I'm so big and heavy that it must tire papa to carry me."

"Hardly," he said. "You remember it is not many weeks since I did carry you quite a distance?"

"But didn't it tire you, papa?"

"Very little; I was scarcely sensible of fatigue."

"Oh, it's nice as nice can be to have such a big, strong papa!" cried Gracie, giving him a hug.

It was quite a party, and a merry one, that gathered about the tea table, which had enlarged since breakfast by the addition of Violet's mother and her two college boys.

The talk, of course, ran principally on the holiday amusements going on at the Oaks and those in the course of preparation at Woodburn.

"They boast of being able to get up some very fine tableaux at the Oaks," remarked Harold. "And they expect to quite astonish us tomorrow."

"I hope you are going, captain, and will take Lulu and Gracie with you," Grandma Elsie asked, smiling kindly upon the two little girls as she spoke.

"Yes," he said, smiling also into the eager young faces. "I shall certainly take them both, unless something unforeseen happens to prevent it. My wife has already promised to go with us," he added with an affectionate glance at Violet.

"Yes, indeed! I shouldn't like to miss it," she said merrily. I believe Zoe and I are about as eager over these holiday doings as any of the children."

"I'm glad to hear it," he responded. "A man enjoys having a young wife even when he himself is not young."

"And the older he is, the younger he wants his wife to be," remarked Zoe in a lively tone. "At least so I have heard people say."

"But papa isn't old, Aunt Zoe!" exclaimed Lulu rather indignantly.

"My dear child," laughed her father, "it's no sin to be old, so you need not be so ready to take up the cudgels for me."

"Have you sent out your invitations, Lulu?" asked Zoe.

"No, ma'am, not yet."

"You will have a good opportunity to give them verbally tomorrow afternoon, if you'd like," remarked her father.

"But I—I don't think I want to, papa," she said. "I'd like to send nice little notes—only it's a good deal of trouble to write them."

"Oh!" said Zoe. "You can have plenty of help in it. I'll volunteer, for one."

"I, too, am at your service," said Grandma Elsie, and her offer was followed by several others.

"'Many hands make light work,'" said Zoe. "And we'll have the thing done in a few minutes after leaving the table. Then there'll be plenty of time for the selection of subjects for our tableaux, which I intend shall outshine those at the Oaks."

"You'd better not make any rash promises," said Edward, laughingly. "You have not seen those at the Oaks yet."

"Are we who abode in the house today to see your purchases now?" asked Mrs. Leland lightly, as they left the table.

"Why, no, of course not," cried Zoe with more than a little emphasis. "Half the fun will be in the surprises when the Peri hands out her gifts. Oh, captain," turning hastily to him, "is it to be decided beforehand who is to have what?"

"I think that would be the better plan," he answered. "I propose that you and Lulu share that privilege, if privilege you consider it."

"That I do," she returned quite delightedly. "And if you'd like, I'll help label them, so there need be no mistake in the distribution."

"Suppose you three attend to that business in the children's sitting room, while the rest of us repair to the library and write the invitations," suggested Violet. "Then you can join us and help in the selections for the tableaux."

"An excellent arrangement, my dear," replied her husband. "Shall we carry out our part of it, Madam Zoe?"

"With all my heart, Sir Captain," rejoined Zoe rather merrily.

"Then I will order our purchases carried up to the appointed place. Gracie, shall I take you up there to oversee us at our work?"

"Oh, papa, mayn't I help, too?" asked the little girl with a very wistful, coaxing look in her sweet blue eyes, as she lifted them to his face.

"Help, darling? What could such a feeble little one as you do?"

"I mean help say whose things are to be," she said.

"Ah, I did not understand! Yes, my dear, you may. The gifts are to be from you as much as from your brother and sister. So no one has a better right to a voice in the matter of distribution."

He was rewarded by a very bright look and a glad smile as she held up her arms to be taken.

He held her while giving his order to a servant whom he had summoned, then carried her upstairs, settled her comfortably in an easy chair, and wheeled it up beside a table whereon the day's purchases were presently piled.

Zoe and Lulu had followed. The captain politely placed a chair for each, then seated himself, and the work began—he writing the labels and they affixing them.

It was all done very harmoniously. There seemed to be but little difference of opinion, and Lulu behaved as well as could have been desired, gracefully yielding her wishes now and again to those of Zoe or her little sister.

That pleased her father very much, and she felt amply rewarded by his smile of approval.

"There, that job is finished, and done well!" announced Zoe at length.

"Why," exclaimed Gracie in a tone of mingled surprise and dismay, "there's nothing for papa! No, nor for you, Aunt Zoe, nor Lu either!"

"Oh, that is all right, little girlie!" laughed Zoe. "If we provided our own gifts we should miss the surprise, which is more than half the fun."

"Oh, yes!" she said. "I forgot that."

"You and I will contrive to find something for Aunt Zoe and Lu," her father said to her in a low aside, at which she clapped her hands and laughed very gleefully.

"Now we shall all go down to the library," he continued aloud. "Shall I carry you there?"

"I'm afraid it will make you too tired, papa, to carry me up and down so often," she answered. But her longing, wistful look plainly told of her desire to be with others.

So, with the assurance that she was a very light burden and that he enjoyed carrying her, he picked her up and bore her on after Zoe, while Lulu brought up the rear.

"We'll soon have to make this journey again," he said. "It will be your bedtime in about a half an hour, precious one."

"Oh, papa, can't I stay up a while longer tonight?" she pleaded.

"If you were well and strong, I should say yes without hesitation," he answered. "But I think you will find yourself weary enough to be glad to go to bed at the usual hour."

And he was right, for though much interested at first in the talk that was going on among the older people, her eyelids presently began to droop. Her head dropped on her father's shoulder, for she was sitting in her favorite place upon his knee.

"Ah, birdie, you are ready for your nest, I see," he said, passing his hand softly over her golden curls. "Papa will carry you up and put you in it."

"Yes," she murmured sleepily. "Lulu won't you come, too?"

Lulu hesitated and looked half inquiringly, half entreatingly at her father. She was very loath to leave the room while the interesting discussions in regard to arrangements for the anticipated amusements were going on—questions of drapery, scenery, costumes, and who should be given this part and who that, were being settled.

"You are free to go or stay, as you choose," the captain said in a very kind tone.

He only needed wait a moment for her decision. There was evidently a struggle in her mind for a brief space, but genuine love for her little feeble sister conquered.

"I will go, papa," she said. "I've been away from Gracie all day, and it would be too bad to refuse her."

"That is right and kind, daughter," he returned with an approving smile, as he rose with the little sleeper in his arms. Gracie was already too far on the way to the land of dreams to be aware of the sacrifice of inclination Lulu was making for her sake.

CHAPTER FOURTH

"GET ME GRACIE'S nightdress, and we'll put her to bed—you and I," the captain said pleasantly but softly to Lulu when they had reached Gracie's bedroom.

Lulu made haste to obey and stood by his side ready to give her assistance when needed.

"Poor darling," she said in a low tone, "how tired and sleepy she is, papa."

"Yes, she is not at all strong yet," he sighed, thinking to himself it was not likely that she would ever be anything but feeble and easily exhausted.

The child did not rouse to consciousness as they readied her for bed but was still fast asleep as her father laid her gently down upon her pillow.

He covered her up with tender care, then seating himself again, drew Lulu into his arms with a fond fatherly caress.

"Dear child," he said, "your unselfish love for your sister makes me very happy."

There was a flash of joy in Lulu's eyes as she lifted them to his. Then blushing and half hiding her face on his shoulder, she murmured, "But I don't deserve you to say that, papa, for I didn't want to come up with you and Gracie."

"No, but if you had had no desire to stay behind there would have been no self-denial in your yielding to her wish. You deserve all the credit I am giving you, Lulu. Now do you want to go back again?"

"If you would like me to, papa. Gracie is so sound asleep that she will not miss me."

"Yes, and if you are not too tired with all the shopping you have done today, you may stay up half an hour later than your usual bedtime," he said, taking her hand and leading her quietly from the room.

"Oh, thank you, papa!" she cried. "I don't think that I'm too tired, and I should like to so very, very much!"

"You are very greatly interested in what is going forward?" he remarked inquiringly, smiling down on her as they descended the stairs, her hand in his.

"Yes, indeed, papa! Oh, may I read the book that tells about the magic cave?"

"Some day, when you are a little older. At present you may read only what it says about that."

Once such a reply to such a question would have brought a frown to Lulu's brow, and she would have asked sullenly why she could not read the whole book now. But she was improving under her father's training and growing much less willful and more ready to yield to his better judgment, having become convinced that he was really wiser than herself and that he loved her too well to deny her any harmless indulgence.

So she responded in a perfectly pleasant tone, "Thank you, papa. I'll read only that part."

"I can trust you," he said. "I know you to be a truthful child, and I think, too, that you are learning to be an obedient one also."

Lulu was allowed to stay in the parlor as long as the older people did, as it so happened that they were ready to retire earlier than usual that evening. They separated and scattered to their respective rooms before ten o'clock.

Captain Raymond lingered behind to see that everything was made secure for the night. Passing into the library on his round, he was more than a trifle surprised to find Harold there.

"Ah, I thought you had gone upstairs with the rest!"

"So I did—part of the way at least—but the remembrance of something I heard this afternoon and which ought, I think, to give you pleasant dreams, brought me back to tell it. That boy of yours, captain, is a son to be proud of."

"So I have thought myself, at times, but feared it might be only a father's partiality," returned the captain, his face lighting up with pleased surprise. "What have you to tell me of him?"

"He had an experience over at the Oaks last night that might have easily proved too severe a test of moral courage to an older fellow than he, yet he came out of the trial with colors flying. I heard the whole story from Art Howard as we were driving together from the Oaks over to Roselands."

And so, Harold went on to give a detailed and perfectly correct account of what had taken place among the lads after retiring to their rooms for the night.

As it should be, he had an intensely interested and deeply gratified listener.

When he had finished, his hand was taken in a cordial grasp, while the captain said with emotion, "A thousand thanks, Harold! You can never know, until you are a father yourself, what joy you have brought to my heart. I have strong hope that my boy will grow up a brave, true Christian gentleman, neither afraid nor ashamed to stand up for the right against all odds."

"I believe it, sir. He's a fine fellow. I'm so proud of him myself that I regret the fact that there is no tie of blood between us."

The next morning Lulu was hurrying through the duties of getting ready for the day, saying to herself that she wanted a little talk with Gracie about the Peri's present to papa before he should come in to bid them good morning, as was his custom, when she heard his voice in their sitting room, which adjoined her bedroom.

Half glad, half sorry he was there already, Lulu made haste to finish her dressing, then softly opened the communicating door.

Her father was seated with Gracie on his knee, his back toward her, and before he was aware of her presence, she had stolen up behind him and put her arms round his neck and her lips to his cheek with a loving, "Good morning, my dearest papa!"

"Ah, good morning, my darling daughter," he responded, drawing her round in front of him into his arms and returning the kiss. "How happy it makes me to see you looking so bright and well. Beautiful, too," he added to himself, but that he did not say aloud.

"You've come in 'most too soon this morning, papa," she remarked, lifting laughing eyes to his.

"Ah! How is that?" he asked.

"Why, I was just coming in to consult with Gracie about the gift you are to get from the Peri, and now I can't, because it has to be a secret, you know."

"Papa," said Gracie, "please name over lots of things you would like to have, so we can choose one, and you needn't know which."

"Lots of things that I should like to have," he repeated. "I really cannot think of one. I have been deluged with beautiful and useful presents—the lovely bracket Lulu sawed out for me, the pincushion Gracie made with her own small fingers for my dressing table, Mamma Vi's beautiful painting that hangs over the mantel in my dressing room, the watch case from Max, besides the too-numerous-to-mention gifts from others not quite so near and dear as wife and children."

"But you've got to have something, you see, papa," laughed Lulu. "Whether you want it or not. Never mind, Gracie, we'll think up something. Perhaps Aunt Zoe can help us."

"Ah, that reminds me," the captain said. "We need to think of a gift for her. What shall it be, Lulu?"

"Suppose we say a ring, papa? When we were in that large jewelry store, I saw her looking at one with an emerald in it, and she admired it very much. Would it cost too much?"

"Perhaps not," he said. "I shall see about it."

"Did you like the things we gave you for Christmas, Papa?" asked Gracie, affectionately stroking his face with her little, white hand.

"Yes, indeed, particularly because they were all the work of your own hands! I could hardly have believed such tiny fingers as my Gracie's could do work so fine as that on the cushion she made for her papa. And Lulu's carving surprised and pleased me quite as much."

"Isn't it just lovely, papa?" cried Gracie with enthusiasm. "I can't do that kind of work at all."

"No, you are not strong enough."

"But I can't sew half so well as she can," added Lulu. "I'm not at all fond of plain sewing."

"I am sorry to hear that," remarked her father. "I think every woman should be skilled in that sort of work."

"I'd like sewing on a machine pretty well," said Lulu. "But it's slow, tedious work with a needle in your fingers."

"Then I fear I should not buy you a machine now, or you would never learn the skillful use of your needle. I want you to persevere with that, daughter, and I promise that as soon as your mamma tells me you have become an accomplished needle-woman, I will buy you the best machine that is to be had. And perhaps," he added with a humorous look, "it will not be necessary to forbid you to use it constantly."

"I don't believe it will, papa," returned Lulu laughingly. "I don't believe I should ever enjoy working it half so much as sawing and carving."

Just then the breakfast bell put an necessary end to their talk.

Shortly after the meal was over, Zoe drew Lulu aside and asked if she had decided upon the present from the Peri to the captain.

"No, not yet, Aunt Zoe. Have you thought of anything, yet?"

"Yes, one that is spoken of in the book we take the idea from—the idea of the magic cave, the Peri, and so on, I mean. It's a pen wiper with a donkey's head, and the words 'There are two of us.'"

"Why, Aunt Zoe! That would be just insulting papa! I shan't consent to it at all!" Lulu burst out rather indignantly.

"Oh, no, it would be only to make fun, and your father would understand it and be as much amused as anyone else."

"I don't like it. I couldn't bear to have such a thing as that given to him," returned Lulu. "I want to buy him a gold pen and holder that I saw in the city. I have money enough, and don't you suppose I can get somebody to go for it?"

"Oh, that will be easy enough," replied Zoe good-naturedly. "Edward is going in today, and I know he will do the errand willingly."

"Oh, that will be nice! Thank you," said Lulu in a tone of delight. "I must run and tell Gracie about it."

She was turning to go, but Zoe detained her. "Wait a moment," she said. "There are some pretty things to be made for adorning the magic cave. Do you want to help with the work?"

"Yes, Aunt Zoe, if you will show me what to do," Lulu answered a little doubtfully. "You know I'm not an expert needle-woman, but I think I should enjoy working with pretty things. It would be much more interesting than plain sewing."

"Yes, indeed, and you will take to it very readily if I am not greatly mistaken. I'll join you presently, bringing some of the materials, and show you what is wanted."

"Oh, if you please, Aunt Zoe! I'll be ever so much obliged. You'll find me in Gracie's and my sitting room," Lulu answered, hurrying away.

"Yes, that will be a nice thing to give papa," Gracie said in reply to Lulu's communication. "But what shall I give him? I want to give him something, too."

"Make him a pen wiper," suggested Lulu. "That would go nicely with a pen and pen holder, and you know he said he would rather have something we made for him ourselves."

"Oh, I'd like to so very much, Lulu, if only I knew how! Maybe mamma would give me some of the materials to make it of and show me how to do it, too."

"Yes, I'm sure she will," cried Lulu. "She's so kind."

At that moment Violet and Zoe came in together, bringing with them a quantity of material to be fashioned into dolls and fairies for ornamenting the magic cave, or to do duty as gifts to be dispensed by the Peri.

"If you girls are inclined to give us some assistance in this work, we shall be very glad indeed to have it," said Violet pleasantly.

"I should very much indeed, Mamma Vi, if you or Aunt Zoe will show me how," exclaimed Lulu eagerly.

"I, too, mamma," said Gracie. "Please, mayn't I make papa a present first? I was thinking of a pen wiper for him, if you'll please show me how to make a pretty one."

"Gladly, my dear. What would you think of a little book—its inside leaves of chamois, the cover of soft morocco, all fastened together with ribbon, and papa's name printed in gilt letters on the outside?"

"Oh, that would be ever so nice, mamma! But I haven't any chamois or morocco. Could anybody go and buy them for me in time?"

"I have some of each and will make you a present of as much as you need," Violet returned merrily, bending down to press a kiss upon the little, eager, upturned face.

"I have some liquid gilding, too," she went on. "So there will be no trouble about the lettering on the cover. I will do that part and perhaps your papa will not object because so much is your work."

"Oh, no, I'm sure he won't!" exclaimed Gracie. "And mamma, you're so very kind to help me so!"

Lulu was eagerly turning over the piles of pretty things, while Zoe gave her directions as to how to fashion them into the desired articles.

Violet went in search of what was needed for the pen wiper, and presently they were all four busily engaged, chatting and laughing right merrily as they worked. Violet and Zoe seemed to feel almost as young and free from care as the two little girls.

They were busily dressing paper dolls as fairies in wide-spreading tarlatan skirts highly ornamented with tinsel.

Lulu had dressed two, thought their appearance really beautiful and was highly delighted at her success. She was holding the second one up and calling attention of her companions to it, when Harold Travilla looked in to say that a quantity of things to be used in getting up the tableaux had come over from Ion. They had been taken by the captain's order to one of the unoccupied rooms, and mamma thought Vi, Zoe, and perhaps Lulu might like to look them over and select for the different characters.

"Of course we will," said Zoe, jumping up with alacrity, while Lulu hastily dropped her fairy into her workbasket, asking, "Oh, Mamma Vi, may I?"

"Certainly, dear. Gracie, too, if she wishes," Violet answered pleasantly. "You will have plenty of time to finish your gift for papa afterward, my dear little girlie."

Zoe had already hurried on ahead. Violet and Lulu followed more slowly, as Gracie was not yet strong enough to move quickly, and they would not leave her behind.

Reaching the room wither the packages had been conveyed, Gracie was comfortably seated in an armchair where she could overlook the proceedings without fatigue. The others gave themselves up to the fascinating business of examining the articles, discussing their merits, and the uses to which they should be put.

There were some very elegant silks, satins, velvets, brocades, and laces among them, and Lulu was quite lost in admiration. She thought it would be delightful to wear some of them, even for the little while a tableaux would last, and hoped it would be decided that she should take part in several.

At length, having seen everything and being seized with a desire to go on with the work in which she had become quite interested, she ran back to her own room without waiting for the others.

Reaching the open door of the sitting room, she paused upon the threshold, transfixed with astonishment and dismay. The baby, at the moment sole occupant of the apartment, was seated on the floor tearing up her fairies, while round her lay scattered in the wildest confusion, the contents of Lulu's work basket—skeins of silk and worsted tangled together; ribbons and bits of silk, satin, and velvet that Lulu had thought to fashion into various dainty little articles—all crumpled and wet, showing that Miss Baby had been putting them in her mouth and trying her pretty new teeth upon them.

Lulu's first impulse was to spring forward, snatch the fairy out of the baby's hand, and give the little mischief-maker an angry shake.

But she controlled herself with a great effort, and recalling the sad scenes and bitter repentance of a few weeks ago, refrained from rushing at the child. Instead she moved gently toward her, saying in soft and persuasive tones, "Oh, baby, dear, don't do so.

Let sister have that. There's a darling! Oh, you've made sad work! But you didn't know any better, did you, pretty dear?"

"Oh, Miss Lu! I'se awful sorry! I didn't neber t'ink ob my child doing sech ting!" exclaimed the baby's nurse, hurrying in from an adjoining room. "I was jes' lookin' at de Christmas tings scattered roun' an' hyar de chile gets hol' o' yo' workbasket 'fo' I sees what she 'bout."

"You ought to have watched her, Aunt Judy. It was your business to see that she didn't get into mischief," returned Lulu in a tone of sorrow. "All these pretty things are ruined, just ruined! And I'd taken so much pain and trouble to make those fairies for the magic cave," she went on, taking them up and turning them over in her hands with a despairing sigh.

"Never mind, daughter, there are plenty more pretty things where those came from," said her father's voice from the open doorway.

Lulu started and looked up in surprise. "Papa!" she exclaimed. "I did not know you were there. I did try to be patient with baby."

"And succeeded," he said, bending down to smooth her dark hair and giving her a tenderly affectionate look and smile.

Then he sat down and drew her into his arms, while Aunt Judy carried the baby away.

"Dear child, he said, "you have made me very happy by your patience and forbearance under this provocation. I begin to have strong hope that you will learn to rule your own spirit, which the Bible tells us is better than taking a city."

Lulu's face was full of gladness. "Now, I don't care if the fairies are spoiled!" she said with a happy sigh, putting her arm round his neck and laying her cheek to his. "I'm 'most obliged to baby for doing it."

Her father continued his hugs for a moment, then he said, "I am going for a walk. Would you like to go with me? I should be glad of your company and, I think you need the exercise."

"Oh, ever so much, papa!" she answered joyously. "There's nothing hardly that I like better than taking a walk with you!"

"Then you may go and put on your coat and hood, and we will set out at once."

It was a bright clear morning and the air was just cold enough to be bracing and exhilarating. Lulu felt it so and went skipping, jumping, and dancing along by her father's side, her hand in his and her tongue running very fast on the interesting subjects of children's parties, tableaux, and magic caves.

He listened with an indulgent smile. "I think my little girl is very happy this beautiful morning?" he said at length.

"Oh, yes, yes, indeed I am, papa!" she answered earnestly. "How could I help it with so much to make me so?"

"So, you are looking forward to a great deal of pleasure in entertaining your young friends this next week?"

"Yes, papa. It makes me glad. But that isn't all, you know." And she looked up into his face with an arch, loving smile.

"What else?" he asked, returning the smile with one full of fatherly affection.

"Oh, a great many things, papa, but most of all that you don't have to go away and leave us anymore. That makes this the very happiest winter of our lives so far—Maxie and Gracie and I all think it so."

"You may safely put my name on that list also," he said.

"You'd rather be with us than on your ship?"

"Much rather, daughter. I greatly enjoy these walks with you and the other pleasures belonging to life at home with wife and children."

"Papa, why did you forbid me to take walks by myself?" asked Lulu presently.

"Wait a moment," he said. Just then a turn in the road brought them face to face with a ragged, dirty man of aspect so forbidding that Lulu, though not usually a timid child, clung to her father's hand and shrank half behind him in terror.

The tramp noted it with a scowl, pushed rudely by them, and disappeared round the corner.

"Oh, papa," panted Lulu, "what a horrible looking man! He looked at me as if he'd like to kill me."

"How would you enjoy meeting him alone?" asked her father.

"Oh! Not at all, papa! I'd be frightened half to death, I think!"

"I, too, think you would, but what is more, I think he—and many another of the same class—would be a more dangerous creature for you to meet alone than any wild beast. Do you need any further reply to your question of a moment ago?"

"Oh, papa! No, indeed! And I shall never disobey you again by roaming about by myself. I see now that you were kind to punish me for it."

"I thought it far kinder than to let you run the risk that such disobedience would bring," he said. "And," he went on presently, "there are others who, though not so forbidding in appearance, are quite as dangerous. They coax and wheedle children and by that means get them into their power and carry them away from their parents and friends—only to lead miserable lives. I think it would break my heart to lose my dear little Lulu in that way. So, my darling, heed your father's warning and never, never listen to them."

"Indeed I'll not listen to them!" she exclaimed in her vehement way. "But I am sure nobody could ever persuade me to go away from you, my own dear, dear father!"

"Ah," he said with a sigh, "I think you forget how, a few weeks ago, you attempted to run away from me without permission from anyone."

"But that was because I thought you didn't love me anymore, papa," she answered humbly. "But now I know you do," she added, looking up into his face with eyes full of ardent affection.

"Never doubt it again, my precious child. Never for one moment doubt that you are very, very dear to your father's heart," he said with emotion, bending down to give her a tender kiss.

※ ※ ※ ※ ※ ※ ※ ※

CHAPTER FIFTH

THE CAPTAIN WAS carrying a basket. Lulu asked if she might know what was in it.

"Yes," he said, "it contains a few delicacies for a poor, sick woman whom we are going to see."

They had been pursuing a path running parallel with the highway, which had led them into a wood. Now the captain turned aside into another, leading to a hut standing some distance back from the road.

"Is it in that little cabin she lives?" asked Lulu.

"Yes, a poor place, isn't it? It hardly occupies as much space as one of our parlors. And there is quite a large family of children."

"I'm sorry for them. It must be dreadful to live so," said Lulu, her tones full of heartfelt sympathy. "But, papa, what makes them so poor?"

"I suppose they had no early advantages of an education—they are very ignorant at all events— but the principal trouble is idleness and drunkenness on the part of the husband and father. It makes it difficult to help them, too, as he takes everything he can lay his hands on and spends it for drink."

"Oh, I can never, never be thankful enough that my father is so different from that!" cried Lulu with another glad, loving look up into his face.

He only smiled in return and pressed the hand he held, for they had now reached the door of the cabin.

It was instantly opened by one of the children, who had seen their approach from the window.

One room, that to which they were admitted, served for kitchen, living room, and bedroom, and combined with a loft overhead and a shed behind, comprised the whole house.

The first object that met their eyes upon entering was the sick woman lying on a bed in one corner, and the first sound that saluted their ears was her hollow cough. She was very pale and so emaciated that she seemed to be nothing but skin and bones.

"How are you this morning, Mrs. Jones?" the captain asked in kindly sympathizing tones, as he drew near the bed and took the bony hand she feebly held out to him.

"P'raps a leetle better, cap'n," she answered pantingly. "I slep' so good and warm under these awful nice blankets you sent fur Christmas, an' the jelly an' cream an' t'other goodies — oh, but they was nice! I can't never pay you fur all yer good-ness — no, nor the half o' it. But the good Lord — He'll make it up to you somehow or other.

"An' ye've brung yer leetle gal to see me? That's kind. Mandy, set the cheer fur the gentleman — we ain't got but one, cap'n — an' find somethin' fur her to set on, Mandy."

"There, I cayn't talk no mo'; me breath's clean gone."

"No, you shouldn't try to talk," the captain said, taking the chair that Mandy had set for him after wiping the dust from it with a very greasy, dirty apron. "And don't trouble yourself, Amanda, to find a seat for my little girl. She is used to this one and likes it better than any other, I believe," he added with a tenderly affectionate smile into Lulu's eyes as he drew her to his knee.

"Yes, that I do," returned Lulu, emphatically, glancing proudly from her father to Amanda, who stood regarding them in open-mouthed astonishment.

"Well, I never!" she exclaimed the next moment. "Wouldn't I be s'rised out'n a year's growth ef pap should act that-a-way to me? And shouldn't like it nuther. The furder I kin git away from the likes o' him the better, I think, so I do."

The mother turned her face away with a groan.

"'Tain't no fault o' hern, cap'n," she said. "Ef Bijah wur like ye, sir, the childen'd be glad enough to git clost to him."

"Yes, love begets love," he said. Then taking up the basket, which he had set on the floor beside his chair, he said, "I have something here for you and should like to see you eat some of it now."

"What is it, cap'n?" she asked, as he handed her a large china cup filled with something white, creamy, and very tempting in appearance.

"They call it Spanish Cream," he answered. "I think you will find it good, and these ladyfingers, just fresh from the oven when I started, will go nicely with it," he added, setting a plate of them down on the bed beside her.

"Ladyfingers?" she repeated. "What's them? I never hearn of 'em afore."

"Sponge cakes," he said. "They are very light and neither rich nor tough, so I think you may eat freely of them without fear of harm."

"They're mighty nice, cap'n," she said when she had tasted them. "An' this here creamy stuff—I never tasted nothin' better. It wuz awful kind o' ye to fetch 'em, but I hain't got no appetite no more, an' so ye mustn't think hard o' me that I don't eat hearty of 'em."

"Oh, no, certainly not," he said.

"Shall I empty them things and wash 'em, ma?" asked Amanda, drawing near the bed and looking with longing eyes at the dainty food.

"Yes, but don't you uns eat 'em clean up from yer sick mother that cayn't eat yer bacon an' corn bread and taters."

"No, just a mite to see what ther like," returned the girl, dipping up a large spoonful of the cream and hastily transferring it to her widely opened mouth. A little crowd of younger children, who, from the farther side of the room, had been staring in silent curiosity at the captain and Lulu, burst out all together, "Gimme some, gimme some, Mandy. Ye shan't have it all, so ye shan't."

"No, ye cayn't none o' ye have none. It's all fer yer sick ma, and ye'd orter to be 'shamed to be axin' fer it," returned Amanda sharply.

"Let them have a taste all around," returned the captain kindly. "I'll have some more made and sent over by the time your mother wants it. But don't bother to wash the things. Just empty them and put them back in the basket."

"Yes, Mandy, ye might break 'em. Put 'em back jes so," panted the invalid from the bed.

When the children had quieted down, Captain Raymond, taking a Testament from his pocket, asked if he should read a few verses.

"Yes, sir. Oh, yes, ef yer ain't in too big a hurry. Please read about the blood — the blood that kin wash a sinner bad as me clean 'nuff to git to heaven. Them verses runs in my mind all the time. The Lord above knows I've need 'nuff o' that washin'."

"Yes, we all need it more than anything else, for in no other way can we be saved from the wrath to come! 'There is none other name under heaven given among men, whereby we must be saved!'"

Then turning over the leaves of his Testament, he read: "But now in Christ Jesus, ye who sometime were far off are made nigh by the blood of Christ.

"If the blood of bulls and of goats, and the ashes of a heifer sprinkling the unclean, sanctifieth to the purifying of the flesh, how much more shall the blood of Christ who through the eternal Spirit offered Himself without spot to God, purge your conscience from dead works to serve the living God?

"And these things write we unto you that your joy may be full. This then is the message that we have heard of Him, and declare unto you, that God is light and in Him is no darkness at all. If we say that we have fellowship with Him, and walk in darkness, we lie, and do not the truth; but if we walk in the light as he is in the light, we have fellowship one with another, and the blood of Jesus Christ his Son cleanseth us from all sin."

"Yes, yes, them's the blessed words!" she cried, clasping her hands and raising her eyes to heaven. "Oh, if I only knowed 'twas fer me—me that hasn't never tried to serve Him and now cayn't do nothin' but lie here and suffer!"

"If you bear your sufferings patiently it will be acceptable service to Him," the captain answered. "He pondereth the hearts. He sees all the motives and springs of action. And He will not let you have one pain or one moment of distress that is not for your good, making you fit for a home with Him in heaven, if you give yourself to Him in love and submission, and try earnestly to learn the lessons he would teach you.

"But never forget that salvation cannot be earned and deserved either by doing or enduring. It is God's free, unmerited gift, bought for His chosen ones by the blood and righteousness of Christ. He offers them to us, and if we accept the gift, God will treat us as if they were actually our own—as if we had been sinless like Jesus and had died the dreadful death that He died in our stead."

"I—I don't seem to see it quite plain, yet," she said. "Please, sir, ask Him to show me jest how to do it."

The captain willingly granted her request, kneeling by the bed—Lulu by his side.

His prayer was short, earnest, and to the point. His language was so simple that the poor sick woman, ignorant though she was, understood every word.

She thanked him in tremulous tones and with eyes full of tears.

"I hain't got long to stay," she whispered, faintly. "I hope I'm 'bout ready now, fer I've tried to give myself to Him. I wish I'd know'd you years back, cap'n, and that I'd begun to serve Him then."

Lulu seemed to have lost her merry spirits and walked along quite soberly by her father's side as they went on their homeward way.

"Papa," she asked with a slight tremble in her voice, "is that woman going to die?"

"I think she has not many days to live, daughter," he answered with a sigh, thinking how doubly forlorn her children would be without her.

"Then I'm very sorry for Mandy and the others. It's so hard for children to have their mother die!"

"And you know all about it by sad experience, my dear little daughter," he responded, bending a tenderly compassionate look upon her as she lifted her eyes to his.

"Yes, papa. So do Max and Gracie."

"Do you remember your mother?" he asked.

"Not just exactly how she looked, papa, but, oh, I've never forgotten how nice it was to have her to love, and for her to love us. Papa, I don't believe she had a temper like mine, had she?"

"No, daughter, she was very amiable and very sweet and lovely in disposition. As I have already told you several times, you inherit your temper from me."

"Papa, I'd never known you had a bit of a temper. Oh, do you think I can ever get to be like you in controlling mine?"

"Certainly, dear child. Can you think I would be so cruel as to punish you for its indulgence if I did not think you could control it?"

"No, papa, I know you'd never be cruel to me or to anybody."

Then going back to the former topic of discourse, she said, "It'll be a great deal worse for those children to lose their mother than it was for us to lose ours, even though it hurt so badly. For they won't have a good father left like we have. But, oh, papa, it did seem so very, very dreadful for all of us when you had to leave us and go off to sea so soon after mamma was buried."

"Yes," he replied in moved tones. "Dreadful to me as well as to my children!"

"But that's all over now, and we can have you with us all the time in a dear, sweet home of our own," she cried joyously.

"And a new mamma who is very sweet and kind to my once motherless children, I think."

"Yes, papa, she is, and it's very nice to have such a pretty gentle lady to—to do the honors of the house. That's what people call it, isn't it?"

"Yes," he returned, laughing in an amused way.

"And I s'pose you're a good deal happier than you would be without her?"

"Indeed, I am! Very much happier."

Lulu felt a burning desire to ask if he had loved her mother as dearly as did this second wife, but she did not dare venture quite so far. She asked another question instead.

"Papa, did you give those children shoes and stockings?"

"What put it into your head that I did?" he queried in turn.

"Oh, I saw they all had good ones on, and I don't believe their father ever bought them for them."

"No, and I fear they'll soon go for liquor."

"Papa, I have a woolen dress that's almost out at the elbows. Mamma Vi said I'd better not wear it anymore. May I get Christine or Agnes to patch it and give it to one of those Jones children? I think it would be about big enough for one of them."

"You may get Christine to show you how to mend it, and then you may give it to the little girl."

"But—I—I—don't like to sew, papa, and I'm sure Christine would be willing to do it."

"I presume she would, but, daughter, I want you to learn both how to do such work neatly, and what pleasure may be found in self-denying exertion for others. I am not laying a command on you. However, it would gratify me very much, if, of your own free will, you will do what I desire."

"Papa, I will," she said after a moment's struggle with herself. "I love to please you, and I know you know what is best for me."

"That's my own dear little girl," he said, smiling down at her.

CHAPTER SIXTH

"WHAT A NICE HOME ours is, papa!" exclaimed Lulu, as they turned at last into the grounds at Woodburn.

"Yes, I think so, and that we have a very great deal to be thankful for," he replied. "If God's will be so, I hope we may all see many happy years in it."

"The grounds are so lovely," pursued Lulu, "that I almost wish we could have warm weather a part of the time next week."

"I think we shall find plenty of amusement suitable for the house," her father said in a kindly tone. "Perhaps next summer, we will have an outdoor party for my children and their young friends."

"Oh, papa, may we? How delightful that will be!" cried Lulu with a joyous hop, skip, and jump. "Oh, it's just the nicest thing to have such a father and such a home!"

There seemed a pleasant bustle about the house as they came in. The conservatory was being prepared for the sport that was to be carried on in it, and sounds of silvery laughter and sweet-toned voices in lively, gleeful chat came floating down from above.

The captain and Lulu, following these sounds, presently entered Violet's boudoir, where they found the ladies busily engaged in making ready for the tableaux.

Gracie was among them and gave her father a joyous greeting—for the pen wiper was quite finished and laid safely in a place that he was not likely to look into.

He stooped to give her a kiss and ask how she felt. He then caught up the baby, who ran to meet him, crying in her sweet baby voice, "Papa, papa!" He tossed her up two or three times, as she crowed in delight, then seated himself with her on his knee.

"What is sweeter than a baby, especially when she is one's own?" he said hugging her close with many a fond caress.

"Papa, I do think she's the dearest, sweetest baby that ever was made," Lulu said, standing by his side and softly smoothing the baby's golden curls.

"In spite of her mischievous propensities, eh?" he returned laughingly, while little Elsie held up her face for a kiss, saying, "Lu, Lu!"

Lulu gave the kiss heartily. "Yes, papa," she answered. "I don't believe she's a bit more mischievous than other babies, and she doesn't know any better. I wonder if it's just because she's our own baby that she seems so beautiful and sweet?"

"Not altogether that, I am sure," he said. "Though no doubt it adds a good deal to the attraction. What do you think about it, mamma?" he asked, looking up fondly into Violet's eyes as she came to his other side.

"Oh, of course, I know she's the most darling baby that ever was born!" she returned merrily, bending down to kiss the little rosebud mouth. "Though, no doubt, you have thought the same of three others."

"Ah, how come you to be good at guessing?" he responded laughingly. "Yes, I remember that each one seemed to me a marvel of beauty and sweetness. I thought no other man had ever been blest with such darlings, and I'm afraid I must confess that I am of pretty much the same opinion yet," he concluded, gathering all three of his little girls into his arms and looking down lovingly upon them—for Gracie, too, had come to him and was standing beside her older sister.

"It can't be for goodness, as far as I'm concerned," sighed Lulu under her breath, but he heard her.

"No, nor for beauty, but just because you are my very own," he said, caressing them in turn, Violet looking on with shining eyes.

"Lulu, dear," she said, turning to her with a loving look. "I was sorry to learn that baby did such damage to your pretty things. I thank you for being so patient and forbearing with her—the little mischief!" She glanced smilingly into the blue eyes of the baby. "I shall make good your loss. I have plenty of bits of silk, satin, ribbon, velvet, and lace among my treasures to more than replace what she spoiled."

"Oh, thank you very much, Mamma Vi!" exclaimed Lulu delightedly.

"My dear," said the captain with a humorous look, "isn't the little mischief-doer as much mine as yours? Am I not, therefore, under quite as great an obligation as you to make good any loss the little one has occasioned?"

"Perhaps so," Violet returned. "But as man and wife are one, your easiest plan will be to let me do it, seeing you have no such supplies on hand."

With that, she pulled open a deep drawer in a bureau filled with such things as she had mentioned and bade Lulu and Gracie help themselves to all they wanted.

"Oh, Mamma Vi," they both cried in wide-eyed astonishment and delight. "How very good of you! But do you really mean it?"

"Yes, every word of it," laughed Violet. "Take all you want. I shall not feel impoverished if I find the drawer quite empty when you are done with it."

"No, you would still have your husband," remarked the captain with mock gravity.

"And baby," added Violet, taking the child from him.

The little girls were exclaiming over their treasures.

"What have you there?" asked Zoe as she came forward and peeped over their heads. "Oh, what quantities of lovely things! Some of them are just suited for dressing fairies, and several more are needed."

"Oh, may I dress one?" asked Lulu eagerly.

"Yes, indeed, if you like. Here, I'll help you select for it."

"Lulu," said her father, "you have forgotten to take off your hood and coat. Do so at once, daughter. You will be apt to catch cold wearing them in this warm room."

"I was just on the point of asking her if she wouldn't take off her things and stay a while," laughed Violet as Lulu hastened to obey.

Before the dinner bell rang, Lulu had again dressed two fairies that she thought quite an improvement upon the first two. She exhibited them to her father with pride and satisfaction, asking if he did not think them pretty.

"Yes," he answered with a smile. "I am hardly a competent judge of such things, but they are pleasing to my eye—all the more so, I suspect, because they are the handiwork of my own little girl."

Immediately after dinner the whole party set out for the Oaks, some riding, others driving. They arrived just as the exhibition was about to begin, and of course had no opportunity to speak to any of the young people—who were all engaged behind the scene—till it was over.

The spectators declared themselves much pleased with the whole performance—every tableau a decided success, and some of them really beautiful.

Lulu and Gracie, seated in front of their father and Violet, enjoyed thoroughly everything they saw, taking special interest in the tableaux in which Evelyn and Max took part.

In the last one Eva appeared as a Swiss peasant girl, and a very pretty one she made.

The instant the curtain dropped she hastened, without changing her dress, into the parlor where the spectator guests were waiting and made her way to Lulu's side.

"Oh, Eva!" cried the latter. "How pretty you are in that dress! And how perfectly lovely you looked in the picture!"

"Oh, hush, you mustn't flatter," returned Evelyn laughing, as she threw her arms round Lulu and kissed her with warmth and affection. "I'm so glad you came! You, too, Gracie," kissing her also. "I was afraid you might not be well enough."

"Oh, yes, I'm better," said Gracie. "Oh, I wouldn't have missed it for anything!"

"There was a great deal of laughing and talking going on, and Captain Raymond, exchanging remarks with some of the other grown people, had not noticed Evelyn till this moment. But now he turned toward her with a kind of fatherly smile and held out his hand, saying, "Ah, my dear, how do you do? Allow me to congratulate you on your successful performances and to hope you will repeat them at Woodburn next week."

"Oh, yes, Eva, you will won't you?" cried Lulu.

Eva smiled pleasantly. "I shall be glad to do anything I can to help with the sports, and I expect a very good time," she said. "It's ever so good of you and Aunt Vi to make another party for us young folks, captain."

"I shall feel fully repaid if it proves a happy time to you all," he replied.

"I must go now and change my dress," said Evelyn. "Captain, may I carry Lu off with me to the rooms we girls are occupying?"

"Yes, if you don't keep her too long. We will be starting home in about half an hour."

"Thank you, papa. I promise to be back by that time," said Lulu.

"And I'll see that she is," said Evelyn, and the two ran off together.

Lora Howard, the Dinsmore girls, and Rosie Travilla had already repaired to the rooms appropriated to their joint use. The moment Lulu appeared they all crowded around her with warm greetings, queries as to what she thought of their tableaux, and expressions of delight at the prospect of spending the greater part of the next week at Woodburn.

"I was quite vexed with the captain for not allowing you to accept our invitation, but I'll have to forgive him now," Maud remarked with a merry laugh. "I suppose he had some good and sufficient reason and is trying to make up for the loss to us now. Perhaps the right thing for us would be to retaliate by declining in our turn, but I must own I can't work myself up to such a pitch of self-denial."

"And I'm very sure I can't," said her sister.

"Lu," said Rosie a little shame-facedly, "I think it is very nice of you to invite me after all my teasing."

"I'm ashamed of having been so easily teased," responded Lulu with a blush. "And don't mean to be in the future, if I can help it. And I hope we shall be good friends. I am sure papa and Mamma Vi wish that we would."

"So nearly related—aunt and niece—you certainly ought to be the best of friends," lightly laughed Lora Howard.

"We're going to have tableaux, and act charades, and play various kinds of games. Papa is sure to see that we have a very good time—the best it is possible for him to contrive for us," said Lulu, quietly ignoring Lora's remark.

"My anticipations are raised to the highest pitch," said Sydney.

Evelyn had just finished changing. "Times up, Lu," she said, looking at her watch. "We must go back to your father."

The other girls had finished dressing, and the whole six at once adjourned to the parlor, where their elders were enjoying themselves together.

The lads were there also, and Max was standing beside his father, who held his hand in a warmly affectionate clasp. Bending down, he said in a tone that reached no other ears, "Max, my dear boy, I heard a report of you that has made me a very proud and happy father."

The captain's eyes were beaming, and at his words, Max's face flushed so joyously that Lulu, watching them from the farther side of the room, wondered what it could be all about. She hastened to them.

"Oh, Maxie!" she exclaimed, taking his other hand. "I'm so glad to see you! It seems as if we'd been a whole month apart."

Her father smiled down on the two at that—a fond and approving smile.

"Are you going home with us now, Maxie?" she went on.

"I don't know," Max answered with an inquiring glance at their father.

"Do just as you please about it, my son," replied the captain. "Your leave of absence extends to tomorrow afternoon, and if you are enjoying your visit, perhaps it would be as well to finish it out. Your going might interfere with some amusement that has been planned for the others as well as yourself."

Max said he was having a fine time and decided to stay.

"Can't Lulu stay too, captain?" asked Sydney, who happened to be near enough to catch the latter part of his sentence and Max's reply.

He deliberated a moment. "Do you want to stay, daughter?" he asked in a kindly tone, looking searchingly into Lulu's face. Her reply came promptly. "I think it would be very pleasant, papa, only I want to be at home to help get ready for my party—ours, I mean, because, Max, it's just as much yours and Gracie's as mine. Papa said so."

"And I think it's splendid that we are going to have it," said Max. "How good and kind you are to us, papa!"

CHAPTER SEVENTH

GRACIE WAS VERY tired when they reached home. Her father carried her immediately to her own room, saying she must be undressed, put to bed at once, and her supper brought up to her.

"May Lulu have hers up here with me, papa, if she's willing?" asked the little girl.

"I have no objection," he said. "Lulu may do exactly as she pleases about it."

"Then I will, Gracie," Lulu said, leaning over her sister and patting her cheek affectionately. "We'll have a nice time together, just as we have so often since you've been sick. I'm sure papa will send us a good supper. He never starves us or wants us to go to bed hungry as Mrs. Scrimp used to do, does he?"

"No," he said. "I should far rather go hungry myself, and it pains me to the heart to think that my darlings were ever treated so."

His tone and the expression of his countenance said even more than his words.

"Don't be troubled about it now, dear papa," said Lulu, putting an arm around his neck and laying her cheek to his—for he was seated with Gracie on his knee, while he busied himself in relieving her of her outdoor wrappings. "It's all over, you know, and we don't mind it. I do believe we enjoy this dear, sweet home all the more for having had such a hard time at first."

"My dear, loving little daughter," he responded, gazing tenderly upon her. Then he added with a sigh, "I wish I could think that hard experience had left no ill effects, but it is plain to me that you were injured morally, and poor Gracie will not soon recover from the damage to her health."

Violet came hurrying in just in time to catch his last words.

"What is it, dear?" she asked anxiously. "Was Gracie's little outing too much for her?"

"No, I trust not," he answered cheerfully. "I hope it will prove, in the end, to have been of benefit. But she is quite weary now, and Lulu and I are going to put her to bed. Bring her night dress, daughter."

Lulu hastened to obey, and Violet, drawing near, stooped over Gracie with a fond caress and a few endearing words.

"I am very sorry you are so tired, darling," she said. "I hope you will have a good night's sleep and wake in the morning feeling all the better for your little trip."

"Yes, mamma, I'm 'most sure I shall," said Gracie. "My bed is so soft and nice to sleep in."

"Shall I not take your place in helping to make her ready for it, Levis?" Violet asked in a sprightly tone.

"No, no," he said, "I'm much obliged, but consider myself quite competent to the task—besides, I think I hear baby calling you."

So, with a kind goodnight to Gracie, Violet left them alone again.

Lulu had brought the nightdress, and while helping her father, talked eagerly about the tableaux.

"I do think they were just lovely!" she exclaimed. "And Eva and Rosie looked so very, very pretty in those costumes. I want to take part in ours. You'll let me, papa, won't you?"

"Yes, daughter, but I hope you will not be selfish toward your guests in regard to the choice of characters, or in showing a desire to appear in too many. I want my little girl to be a polite and considerate hostess, and always modest and retiring—never trying to push herself into notice and never seeking her own gratification in preference to that of others.

"The Bible teaches us to please others in such things as are right, 'For even Christ pleased not Himself.' And He is to be our pattern."

"I'll try," she said with a thoughtful look. "Papa, I do believe you care more to have your children good than rich or beautiful or anything else."

"I do, indeed!" he returned. "It is my heart's desire to see them all followers of Christ and heirs of eternal life—for what is the short life in this world compared to the everlasting ages of the one we are to live in the next? And godliness hath the promise of the life that now is as well as of that which is to come. There is no real happiness, my child, but in being at peace with God."

Gracie was now ready for bed, and her father laid her in it, saying, "Lie there and rest, papa's dear child, till your supper is brought up. Then Lulu may get your warm dressing gown for you, and you may sit up to the table in your own little sitting room while you eat. Then you may go to bed again as soon as you are done your meal. And I think Lulu will be willing to stay with you till you fall fast asleep."

"Oh, yes. Yes, indeed!" cried Lulu. "I'll stay as long as she wants me."

"But, papa, you haven't kissed me goodnight," Gracie said, as he was turning away.

"No, darling," he answered. "I haven't forgotten it. I am going down now to order your supper sent up, and when I think you have had time to eat it, I shall come back to bid you goodnight."

Gracie was too tired to talk, but she made a good listener while Lulu's tongue ran fast enough for two all the time they were waiting for their supper and eating it after it came up—as tempting a meal as anyone could have reasonably desired.

Lulu's themes were of course the tableaux they had seen at the Oaks, those they expected to have the next week here in their own home, and such other amusements as had been planned for the entertainment of the invited guests.

"And aren't you glad, Gracie, that Maxie's coming home tomorrow afternoon?" she asked.

"Yes, indeed," returned Gracie. "Maxie's such a nice brother, and I'm tired of doing without him."

"So am I, but, oh, Gracie, how much worse it was to have to do without papa more than half the time, as we used to!"

"Worse than what?" asked the captain in a playful tone, stepping in at the open door leading into Gracie's bedroom.

The little girls were still at the table in their little sitting room.

"Worse than having Max away for a little while, papa," replied Lulu.

"But we think that's bad, too," said Gracie.

"It will soon be over. Maxie will be at home tomorrow," he said, sitting down beside her. "Are you enjoying your supper, my darlings?"

"Oh, yes, sir!" they both replied. Gracie added, "I'm done now, papa, and I'm ready to be put in bed again, when I've said my prayers."

The tea bell rang as he laid her down, so with a goodnight kiss, he left her to Lulu's care.

The Woodburn guests all went away early the next afternoon, most of them expecting to return on Monday. A little later Max came home, riding his pony that his father had sent for him.

Everybody gave him a warm welcome from his father down to the baby, who the moment she caught sight of him, held up her little arms crying, "Max, Max, take her."

"Why, of course I will, pretty child," he said, picking her up and hugging her in his arms. "How fast you're learning to talk, and are you glad to have your brother come home?"

The boy was more pleased than he cared to show.

She nodded her curly head in answer to his question, while Violet said, "We are all very glad, indeed, Max. We missed you in spite of having company every day while you were gone."

"And though I've had a fine time at the Oaks, I'm ever so glad to be back, Mamma Vi," responded Max. "I've found out the truth of the saying that 'there's no place like home.'"

"And I trust you will be always of that opinion," his father remarked with a pleased look.

"It is my ardent desire that to each one of my children their home in their father's house may seem the happiest place on earth."

"If it does not, it will be no fault of their father's," remarked Violet, giving him a look of proud, fond affection as she took the babe from Max. "We mustn't impose upon brother Max's good nature, little girlie," she said.

"Indeed, Mamma Vi, it's no imposition," he protested. "I like to hold her."

"Oh, Max," cried Lulu, "won't you tell us about the good times you've been having at the Oaks?"

"After a while," he said. "But now I want to go round and see how things look indoors and out."

"Oh, yes, you must see what papa's been doing in the conservatory, where the magic cave is to be. I'll go with you, shan't I?"

"Of course, if you like."

"We'll all go," said the captain, taking little Elsie from her mother. "Baby and all." He led the way, Violet following with Gracie clinging to her hand, Max and Lulu bringing up the rear, the latter talking very fast of all that was to be done for the entertainment of their expected guests.

Max was almost as much pleased and interested as even she could have wished.

"What lots of fun it will be!" he said when he had seen the alterations and heard all that was to be told about the new use to be made of the conservatory. "Papa, I think it's just splendid of you to give us youngsters such a party!"

"Splendid?" echoed his father with a humorous smile. "I presume that must mean that I am a shining example of paternal goodness?"

"I am sure you are," laughed Violet. "I never saw a brighter one."

"Thank you, my love," he returned. "And did you ever see a more grateful set of children?"

"No, never! I hope you feel that you have an appreciative wife, also?"

"She is far beyond my deserts," he answered softly, the words reaching no ear but hers—the children were again talking among themselves and paying no heed to what might be passing between their elders.

"No, sir," returned Vi with a saucy smile up into his eyes. "I utterly deny that that is so and stoutly maintain the contrary."

"My dear," he said laughingly, "have you so little respect for your husband's opinions?"

"Yes, sir, just so little," she answered merrily, "that is in regard to the matter under discussion."

"Ah, that last is the saving clause," he said with a look of amusement. "Shall we go back to the parlor? I see the children have forsaken us. Max seems half wild with delight at being home again — it is so new and pleasant a thing for him and his sisters to have a home of their own."

"With their father in it," added Violet. "I think they never forgot that that is the best part of it."

"As he does not that wife and children are the best part of it for him," responded the captain, quite feelingly.

"I think we are a very happy little family," Violet said with a joyous look and tone. "Really, Levis, it does seem extremely nice to be quite by ourselves occasionally."

Lulu made the same remark as they all gathered about the open grate in Violet's boudoir that evening after tea.

"Yes," said her father, bouncing the baby on his knee. "I think it does. Though we all enjoy visits from our other dear ones, yet sometimes we prefer to be alone together."

"Up, up!" said baby, stretching up her arms and looking coaxingly into her father's face.

"She wants you to toss her up, papa," said Lulu.

"So she does," said the captain. Then followed a game of romps in which everybody took part, much to Miss Baby's delight.

It did not last long, however, for her mammy soon appeared upon the scene with the announcement that baby's bedtime had come."

Everybody must have a goodnight kiss from the rosebud mouth, and then she was carried away, Violet following, while Gracie, as the next in age, claimed the vacated place upon her father's knee.

"That is right," he said. "And there is room for Lulu, too," drawing her to a seat upon the other. "Now, Maxie, what have you to tell us about the visit to the Oaks?"

Max had a good deal to tell and was flattered that his father should care to hear it. Drawing his chair up as close to his audience as consistent with comfort, he began talking with much liveliness and animation.

He said nothing about the unpleasant experience of the first night of his stay at the Oaks, or of certain sneering remarks to which he had afterward been occasionally subjected to by Bertram Shaw. But he told of the kindness with which he had been treated by his entertainers and of the sports and pleasures in which he had participated.

The captain noted with inward satisfaction that his boy's narrative was free from both censoriousness and egotism, and also that he seemed to have nothing to conceal from his father. He talked freely on as unreservedly as if is sisters had been the only listeners of his experience.

In fact, Max was becoming very thoroughly convinced that he could not have a wiser, truer, better friend, or safer confidant, than his father, and he was finding it a dear delight to open his heart to him without reserve.

Violet rejoined them presently, and Max found in her another attentive and interested listener.

But Max was not allowed to do all the talking. There were other topics of discourse beside that of his experience at the Oaks, and in these everyone took part.

They were all in a jovial mood, full of mirth and gladness, and time flew so fast that all were surprised when the clock, striking nine, told them the hour for evening worship had arrived.

As soon as the short service was over, the children bade goodnight and went to their rooms, and the captain, as usual since her sickness, carried Gracie to hers.

When he rejoined his wife, he found her sitting meditatively near the fire, but as he stepped to her side, she looked up with a bright smile of welcome.

"How nice to have you quite to myself for a little while," she remarked in a half-jesting tone, as he sat down with his arm round her waist and her hand in his.

"My dear," he said a trifle remorsefully, "I fear I may sometimes seem rather forgetful and neglectful of you. Do you not occasionally feel tempted to regret marrying a man with children?"

"Regret, indeed! Regret being the wife of the man who has never yet, in all the time I've known him, given me an unkind word or look?" she cried, almost indignantly. "No, no, never for one moment, my dear, dear husband!" she added, laying her head on his shoulder with a great sigh of content.

"My dear, sweet wife," he responded in accents of tenderest affection, pressing his lips again and again to hers and to her cheek and brow. "Words cannot tell how much I love you, or how precious your love is to me!"

"I know it," she said joyously. "I know you have given me the first place in your heart. Ah, I think mine would break if I saw any reason to doubt it. But please don't think ill of me as to suppose for a moment that I could be jealous of your love for your children, the poor motherless darlings, who have been half-fatherless, too, for the greater part of their lives!"

"Yes," he sighed. "When I think of all that I feel I cannot be too tenderly careful of them or too indulgent in all that I may with safety to their best interests."

"I am sure of it," she said. "I do enjoy seeing you and them together. Your mutual affection is a continual feast to my eyes. It often reminds me of the happy days when I had a father here," she added with a slight tremble in her sweet voice and tears in her beautiful eyes. "Oh, how we all loved him! Yet, not better, I am sure, than your children love you."

"Though, from all I have heard of him, I can hardly doubt that he was far more worthy of it," sighed the captain. "I fear I have sometimes spoken to my older two with unnecessary sternness. I think life in either army or navy has a tendency to abnormally develop that side of a man's character."

Violet looked up with a bright, roguish smile. "What a talent for concealing your faults you must have! I have known nothing of the sternness you deplore. But maybe you have been careful to seize your opportunity for its exercise when I was not present, darling."

"Probably I have, though not consciously with the motive your words would seem to imply," he replied, returning her smile and caressing her hair and cheek with his hand as he spoke. "Because reproofs have a better effect when given in private."

"Yes, that is very true," she said. "But I fear there are many parents who are not, like you, so thoughtful and considerate as always to wait till they have the child alone to administer a deserved reproof."

"Ah, how kindly determined is my little wife to see nothing but good in her husband!" he said with a pleased laugh.

She ignored that remark.

"Levis," she said, "I have been thinking, as I sat here alone just now, about the children's looks, and I was wondering at Gracie's being so entirely different from those of the other two. Max and Lulu resemble you so strongly that they would, I think, be recognized anywhere as your son and daughter — because they have your hair and eyes, indeed, all your features. Of course, I think them very handsome, noble-looking children—" she interpolated with another bright, winsome smile into his face. "But Gracie, though quite as lovely in every respect, possesses an altogether different type of beauty — of character also."

"Yes," he said in a meditative tone, "Gracie is like her mother."

"Her mother? Your first wife? You have never mentioned her to me before."

Her tone was inquiring, and he answered it.

"Because, my love, I feared — supposed at least — that you would hardly care to hear of her."

"But I do. I love the children, and but for her we should have had them. And she was so near and dear to them. If I knew about her, I should try to keep her memory in their hearts. Oh, if I were to die, I could not bear to think that my dear, little Elsie would forget all about me."

CHAPTER EIGHTH

"I CAN SCARCELY BEAR to even think of such a possibility," the captain said a trifle huskily, as he tightened his clasp of Violet's slender waist and went on. "It seems that one such loss should be enough for a lifetime. But it is just like my own sweet Violet to desire to have Gracie's children remember her with affection."

"Her name was Gracie?"

"Yes, our little Gracie wears her name as well as her looks. She also inherits from her the frail health, which causes us so much anxiety, her timidity, and her sweet gentleness of manner and disposition."

"She must have been sweet and beautiful," Violet said low and softly. "And you loved her very much Levis, dear?"

"Dearly, dearly, but no more than I love her sweet successor," accompanying the last words with a very tender caress. "I have often asked myself what I ever did to deserve the love of two such women."

"I should rather ask what they ever did to deserve yours," said Violet. "I think the hardest part of dying would be leaving you."

"Strange! Gracie told me it was so to her," he remarked in surprise.

"Poor thing! I cannot help pitying her," said Violet. "And I quite fill her place to you, Levis?" she asked with some hesitation and a wistful, longing look up into his face.

"Entirely, my dear love," he said, holding her close to his heart with oft-repeated and most loving caresses.

"Ah, then I do not feel jealous of the love you had for her, no matter how great it was. But please tell me more about her—of the life you led together and the time when—when she left you."

"Ah, that was a sad time," he said with great emotion. Then for some moments, he seemed lost in retrospective thought.

Violet waited in silence, her hand still in his and her loving eyes gazing tenderly into his grave, almost sorrowful face.

Presently he heaved a sigh, and in a low, absent tone, as if he were rather thinking aloud than talking to her, began the story she had asked for.

"It is just about fifteen years ago, now," he said, "when I first met Gracie Denby. She was then hardly more than eighteen—a fair, fragile-looking girl with delicate features, large, liquid blue eyes, and a wealth of golden hair.

"A gentle, timid, clinging creature—almost alone in the world, having neither parent, brother, nor sister—she was just the sort to win the enthusiastic devotion of a great, strong fellow like myself. I felt a protecting love for her from the first hour of our mutual acquaintance."

Violet was listening with deep interest, and as the captain paused in his narrative, she asked in her low, soft tones, "Where did you meet her?"

"At the house of my friend, Lieutenant Henry Acton. We were fellow officers on the same vessel, intimate friends, and getting a leave of absence together when our ship came into port one summer day, nothing would content Harry but for me to go home with him and see the pretty young wife he was so proud of.

"She and Gracie had been school girls together and were fast friends.

"Gracie, as I learned at length, was comparatively poor and not treated in a way to make her happy in the family of an uncle with whom she made her home, not of choice, but necessity. So she had gladly accepted the invitation of Mrs. Acton to spend some weeks with her.

"Well, to make a long story short, Harry and his wife were naturally very much taken up with each other, and Gracie and I were constantly thrown together, often left without other society. So, soon we did not, I think, care for any other. Before the first week was out I was deeply in love, and the second had not elapsed ere we were engaged.

"It was the evening before my leave expired, and the next day's parting was both sweet and sorrowful."

"You did not marry at once?" Violet inquired, as again the captain paused with a slight sigh and an absent air.

"No, I should have been glad to do so—was, indeed, very urgent for the right at once to claim her as my own and provide for all her wants, but—" He turned to Violet with a slight smile, "Ladies are, I am inclined to think, almost always desirous to defer the final plunge, even when they would be by no means willing to resign all prospect of matrimony."

"Yes, the step is irretrievable and so important—involving so much of happiness or misery—that it is no wonder we pause and shrink back on the brink of the precipice," she returned with an arch glance up into his face. "But go on, please. I am deeply interested. How long were you forced to wait, poor fellow?" she asked, stroking his cheek caressingly with her pretty, white hand. "I was only a little girl then, so you have no need to feel as though you should have waited for me."

"No, you were waiting and growing up to be ready for me," he answered with tender look and smile.

"Yes, so it seems, and it was just as well that you were enjoying Gracie in the meantime and that she was happy with you, as I am quite sure she must have been."

"I think she was," he said. "She often told me so, though our frequent partings wrung both our hearts.

"I had another leave of absence within the year, and then we were married. We went to Niagara for a week, then came back and began our housekeeping.

"It was only in a small way. Harry and I had taken a double house—that our wives might be close together when their husbands were off at sea, yet each have her own domicile—a plan which worked very nicely.

"On my next homecoming I found a new treasure. Gracie met me with Max in her arms, and perhaps you can imagine the joy and pride with which I took him into mine after the mutual tender embrace between his parents. I had been gone for over a year, and he was a fine, big fellow, old enough to be afraid of his father at first, but not many days had passed before he would come to me even from his mother, and strangely enough, it seemed to please her mightily."

"Ah, I can understand that," remarked Violet.

"I had a long leave that time," the captain went on. "And a very happy time it was. Of course, it was succeeded by a sorrowful parting, for I was ordered off to the coast of China. Again more than a year elapsed before I saw wife and children—Lulu had been added to my treasures in the meanwhile, you will understand, and having been apprised of the fact, I was very eager to see her as well as her mother and our son.

"That, too, was a joyful time, but my after-visits to my little family were saddened by my wife's ill health. Little Gracie came, too, and her mother was never well after her birth. Instead, she grew more and more feeble year by year till the end came."

A heavy sigh followed the concluding words, and for some moments he sat silent, his eyes fixed thoughtfully upon the floor.

"Were you with her at the last?" asked Violet in low, feeling tones.

"Yes, I have always been thankful for that. She was a Christian, and for her death had no terrors. She was glad to go except when she thought of the parting from her dear ones.

"'My dear little children! My poor soon-to-be-motherless darlings!' she moaned one day, as I sat by her side with her hand in mine. 'What is to become of them?'

"I assured her I would do my best for them, earnestly endeavoring to be father and mother both in one.

"'But, oh, you cannot, because you will be forced to leave them for months or years together,' she sobbed. 'Ah, the only bitterness of death to me is leaving them and you, my dear husband.'

"I could only remind her of God's gracious promise to the seed of the righteous and His tender care for all helpless ones and entreat her to trust them implicitly to Him. At length she seemed able to do so.

"She died in my arms with her dear eyes gazing into mine with a look of intense affection, which I can never forget."

He was silent only for a moment, then resumed his narrative.

"My leave of absence was so nearly expired that I had scarcely more than time to see her dear body laid in the grave and place my children in the care of Mrs. Scrimp—a sad mistake, as I have since thought, but seemingly the best thing that could be done then—when I was forced to bid my poor, motherless darlings good-bye and leave them.

"Ah, how they clung to me, crying as if their hearts would break and begging most piteously that I would stay with them or take them away with me. But, as you know, neither alternative was possible. Though it broke my heart as well as theirs, I was compelled to tear myself away, leaving them in their bitter sorrow and loneliness.

"Oh, I cannot think of it yet without sore pain!" he added in moved tones.

Then, after a moment's pause, "How thankful I am that now I can give them a good home and constant oversight! I find it sweet work to teach and train them and watch the unfolding of their minds. And how sweet to be able to hug and caress them whenever I will and to receive such loving caresses from them as I do every day! My dear and precious little darlings!"

"They are dear, lovable children," Violet replied. "What a good father you are, Levis."

"I don't know," he said doubtfully. "I certainly have a very strong desire to be such, but I fear I sometimes make mistakes. I have used greater severity toward Lulu than I ever did with either of the others, or ever expect to. It pains me to think of it, and yet I felt it my duty at the time. It was done from a strong sense of duty and seems to have had an excellent effect."

"It certainly does, and therefore you should not, I think, feel badly about it."

"The child is very, very dear to me," he said. "I sometimes think all the dearer because she is a constant care and anxiety. I dare not forget her for an hour but must be always on the watch to help her guard against a sudden outburst of her passionate temper. I strongly sympathize with her in the hard struggle necessary to conquer it.

"Her mother's invalidism was a most unfortunate thing for Lulu. Poor Gracie felt that she had no strength to contend against the child's determined will, so humored her and let her have her own way far more than was at all good for her. She was seldom or never called to account and punished for her fits of rage.

"Mrs. Scrimp's treatment following upon that was, I think, even more hurtful to Lulu, subjecting her to constant irritation as well as the absence of proper control.

"I am more and more convinced as I watch my children and notice the diversity of character that they exhibit, that it is very necessary to vary my system of training accordingly. The strictness and occasional severity absolutely needful in dealing with Lulu would be quite crushing to the tender timid nature of my little Gracie. A gentle reproof is all-sufficient for her in her worst moods, and she is never willfully disobedient."

"Nor is Max, so far as I am aware," remarked Violet with a look and smile that spoke of a fond appreciation of the lad.

"No, when Max disobeys or is guilty of any misdemeanor, it is pretty certain to be from mere thoughtlessness, which is bad enough to be sure, but far less reprehensible than Lulu's willful defiance of authority. That last is something which, in my opinion, no parent has a right to let go unpunished—much less overlook or ignore, as of little or no consequence."

CHAPTER NINTH

It was Sunday afternoon, and the house seemed quiet, Lulu thought, as she laid aside the book she had been reading and glanced at Gracie, who lay on the sofa near by. Her eyes were closed and her regular breathing telling that she slept.

Lulu stood for a moment gazing tenderly at her sister, then stole on tiptoe from the room, down the stairway into the hall below, and to the library door.

"I hope papa is there and alone," she was saying to herself. "I know Mama Vi's lying down with the baby, and Max is in his own room."

The door was ajar. She pushed it a little wider open and peeped in.

A hasty glance about the room told her that she had her wish. Her father sat in an easy chair by the open grate with his face turned toward her, and he did not seem to be doing anything—he had neither book nor paper in his hand. But his eyes were fixed thoughtfully upon the fire.

"Papa?" she said softly.

He looked up and greeting her with an affectionate smile, holding out his hand.

"Am I disturbing you?" she asked as she accepted the mute invitation, hastening with quick, eager steps to his side.

"No, not in the least. I was just thinking about you and wanting you here on my knee," drawing her to it as he spoke.

"Oh, how nice of you, papa," she sighed, putting her arm round his neck and gazing with shining eyes into his face. "I came because I was just hungry for loving and hugging!"

"Were you?" he asked, hugging her close and kissing her several times. "Well, you came to the right place for it. I have no greater pleasure than in loving and hugging my children. But how came you to be so hungry for that kind of fare? You have not been very long without it."

"No, sir, I was on your knee awhile last night, and I had a kiss this morning. But that kind of hunger comes back very soon, papa. And it's only your love and hugging that can satisfy it. I hardly care to have anybody else hug me. Oh, I'm so glad you're not like Annie Ray's father!"

"Who is Annie Ray, and what was her father like?" he asked with an amused smile.

"She's a girl that went to the same school I did when I lived with Aunt Beulah. One day when we were taking a walk together I was telling her about my father being far away on the sea, and how I longed for you to come home, because it was so nice to have you take me on your knee and hug me and kiss me.

"Then she sighed, the tears came to her eyes, and she said, 'Oh, how I'd like it if my father would ever do so to me! I'd give 'most anything if he would, but he never does. Even when I've been away on a visit for two or three weeks he only shakes hands when we meet again.

"'He isn't a cross father. He always gives me plenty to eat, good clothes to wear, and sometimes a little pocket money, but I'd rather do without some of those things if he'd hug and kiss me instead.'

"So I asked her, 'Why don't you go and kiss him? That's the way I do my father, and he always looks pleased and kisses me back.'

"'Oh, I wish I dared!' she said. 'But I don't for I am afraid he wouldn't like it.'"

"I should be more grieved than I can tell if I ever had reason to think one of my children felt so toward me," the captain said, stroking Lulu's hair caressingly, while his eyes looked fondly into hers.

"You need never be at all afraid, daughter, to come to your father to offer or ask for a caress."

"Unless I've been naughty?" she said, both inquiringly and in assertion.

"No, not even then, if you're ready to say you're sorry and don't intend to offend in the same way again.

"I noticed that you were unusually quiet on the way home from church. Would you like to tell me what you were thinking about?"

"First, about what the minister had been saying, papa. You know he reminded us that this was the last Sunday of the old year, and he said we should think how we had spent it, repent of all the wrong things, and resolve that with God's help we would live better next year.

"So I tried to do it. I mean, to think how I'd been behaving all the year. And I found it had been a very, very bad year for me," she went on, blushing and hanging her head. "All that badness at Viamede was after New Year's Day was past, and then I did such a terrible thing at Ion.

"Oh, papa, I most wonder you can be fond of me, even though I am your very own child!" she exclaimed, her head sinking still lower, while her cheeks were dyed with blushes.

"My darling, I, too, am a sinner," he said with emotion, holding her close to his heart. "I, too, have been taking a retrospective view of the past year, and I am not too proud to acknowledge to my own daughter that I fear that I have sinned even against her."

She suddenly lifted her head to look into his face in wide-eyed astonishment.

"Yes," he sighed. "I have been recalling the rebuke I administered to you the first time we met after the baby's sad fall, and it seems to me now that my words were unnecessarily severe, possibly even cruel.

"I had just come from my apparently dying babe and her heartbroken mother, and dearly as I have always loved my eldest daughter, my anger was stirred against her at that moment, as the guilty cause of all that suffering and distress.

"But I ought to have seen that she was already bowed down with grief and remorse and to have been more merciful. My dear child, will you forgive your father his extreme severity?"

"No, papa, I—I can't," she murmured, her head drooping so low again that he could not see the expression of her countenance.

"You cannot?" He sighed in surprise and grave disappointment. "Well, my dear child, I can hardly blame you, and I certainly would not have you say what you do not feel. But I had hoped your love for me was sufficient to prompt a different reply."

"Papa, you don't understand," she cried, lifting her head again, throwing her arms round his neck, and laying her cheek to his. "It's because I've nothing to forgive. I deserved it all—every word of it. You had a right to say those words, too, and they did me good, for it has helped me many a time to conquer my temper—thinking how dreadful to be anything but a blessing to you, my dearest father!"

"Thank you, my darling," he responded in moved tones. "Now when death has parted us there will, I trust, be no sting for the survivor in the memory of those words, as I felt that there surely would be if they were left unretracted."

"Papa, don't talk of death parting us," she said in tremulous tones. "I can't bear to think of it."

"I hope that we may be long spared to each other," he returned with grave tenderness.

"Do you mean you're sorry for having punished me, too, papa?" she asked presently.

"No," he said. "Because that was in obedience to orders, therefore undoubtedly my duty and for your good."

"Yes, sir. I know it was, and I know you didn't want to do it. But you had to because we must do what the Bible says."

"Yes, because it is God's word—the only infallible rule of faith and practice."

"What does that mean, papa?"

"Infallible means not liable to err. Faith is what we believe. Practice is what we do, and we must study the Bible to know both what to do and what to believe.

"It is an inestimable blessing to have such an unerring guide that in following its directions we may at last reach the mansions Jesus has gone to prepare for His redeemed ones. Oh, that I could know that my Lulu's feet were treading that path—the straight and narrow way—that leads to eternal life!"

"Papa, I do mean to be a Christian some day."

"How long are you going to live?" he asked with grave seriousness.

She looked up in stark surprise. "Why, papa, I do not know."

"No, nor do I. God only knows when He will call for you, or me, or any other of His creatures home. And if we are taken away from earth without having accepted His offered salvation through the death and merits of His son Jesus Christ, our opportunity to do so will be gone forever. The door of heaven will be shut upon us never to open again. Knowing this, how can I be other than very anxious and troubled about my dear child, while she continues to neglect this great salvation?"

"I wish I was as good as you are, papa," she said, nestling closer in his arms.

"My dear child, 'There is none that doeth good, no, not one.' 'All our righteousnesses are as filthy rags' in the sight of God, and it is only when covered by the spotless robe of Christ's righteousness that we can stand in His sight.

"It is offered to all, but only those who accept it can be saved. And no one can tell when, for him or her, the offer will be withdrawn."

"By death coming, do you mean, papa?"

"Yes, or by God saying of that one, 'Ephraim is joined to his idols. Let him alone.' It is a fearful thing to be let alone by God. Jesus said, 'No man can come to Me, except the Father which has sent Me draw him.'"

"Papa, how can we know if He draws us?"

"When we feel any desire to come to Jesus, when something—a still, small voice within our hearts—urges us to attend at once to our salvation, we may be sure that God the Father is drawing us and that the Holy Spirit is calling us to come and be saved.

"And none need fear to be rejected, for Jesus says, 'Him that cometh to me I will in no wise cast out.'"

"Papa, do you think I'm old enough?"

"Old enough to begin to love and serve God? Are you old enough to love and obey me and to trust me to take care of you?"

"Oh, yes, indeed, papa! It seems to me I've always been old enough for that."

"Then your question needs no further answer. If you can love, trust, and obey your earthly father, so can you your heavenly Father also."

"But I just can't help loving you, papa," she said, giving him another hug and kiss, which he returned. But then he asked, "Why do you love me, my daughter?"

"Oh, because you are my own father, take good care of me, and give me everything I have. You love me, too, and because you're so good and wise and kind."

"And have you not all those reasons for loving your heavenly Father? He created you, therefore you are more His than mine. He has only lent you to me for a time. His kindness and His love to you far exceed mine, and my wisdom is not ever to be compared to His."

"But, papa—"

"Well, daughter?" he said inquiringly, as she paused, leaving her sentence unfinished.

"I don't think I can be a Christian with such a dreadful temper as I have. I shouldn't think the Lord Jesus would want me for one of His children."

"My dear child, the more sinful we are the more we need Him to save us. Don't you remember that the angel said to Joseph, 'Thou shalt call His name Jesus: for He shall save His people from their sins'?

"And He himself said, 'I came not to call the righteous, but sinners to repentance.'"

"But, papa, oughtn't I to conquer my temper first? I—I'd be a disgraceful kind of Christian with such a bad, bad temper."

"No, daughter. If you tarry till you're better, you will never come at all. God's time is always now. Come at once to Jesus, and He will help you in the hard struggle with your temper."

Violet's entrance at that moment put an abrupt end to their conversation.

"Ah, Lulu," she said pleasantly, "you have been having a very nice time with papa all to yourself, I suppose?"

"Yes, indeed, Mamma Vi," returned the little girl, as the captain gently put her off his knee that he might rise and hand his wife a chair. "Papa, shall I go now and see if Gracie is awake and wanting me?"

"Yes," he said glancing at his watch. "It is nearly tea time."

"How fond the child is of her father," remarked Violet, smiling up into her husband's face as Lulu left the room.

"And her father of her," he responded. "I should count myself a rich man with one such child, but with four and a peerless wife beside, I am richer than all the gold of California could make me without them."

"It is nice to be so highly appreciated," she said with a bright, winsome smile. "I'm not the only one who is, for I'm perfectly sure that I drew the highest prize in the matrimonial lottery."

"I am to understand from that that I, too, am appreciated? Yes, I have no doubt that I am, at my full value," he responded.

"Little wife, I hope you find your new home not less enjoyable than the old, which I know was an exceedingly happy one to you."

"I have always had a happy home, but never a happier one than this that my husband's love and care have provided—it so sweet and restful!

"Oh, Levis, what a joy this newly expired year has brought me! I had not dared to look forward to a home with you for many years to come! I had thought of it as a great blessing that might come to me in middle life—not in my young days."

"Ah, God has been very, very good to us!" he exclaimed feelingly. "I trust we have many years to live and love together on earth, and after that a blessed eternity in the better land."

"Yes," she responded. "How that blessed hope—making even death only a temporary separation—adds to the joy of mutual love! It is dear mamma's great comfort in her widowhood."

"Yes," he said. "What an evident reality it must be to her that her husband is not dead but only gone before, and that they will be reunited one day, never to part again. Dearly as she no doubt loved him and sorely as she must miss him at times, her life seems to me both serene and happy."

"It is," said Violet. "Her strong faith in the wisdom and love of her heavenly Father makes her days to be full of peace and content."

Presently the summons to tea brought the family all together—except baby, who was still too young to know how to conduct herself at the table.

But she, too, was with the others when they gathered in the library, upon leaving the table at the conclusion of the meal.

She was the center of attraction, amusing parents, brother, and sisters with her pretty baby ways, till carried away to her bed.

Then Gracie was drawn lovingly to her father's knee, while Max drew his chair up close on one side, Lulu hers on the other.

"Now we will have our verses," the captain said, touching his lips to Gracie's cheek. "What is yours, Max, my son?"

One of the captain's requirements was that each of these three children should commit to memory a verse of Scripture every day, which verses were recited to him at morning family worship. On Sunday evening each had a new one, and all they learned through the week were recited again. Then their father talked familiarly with them about the truth taught in the passages they had recited—for all were upon one and the same subject, selected by him beforehand. But the verses were left to the choice of the children themselves.

God's love to His people and to the world was the subject at this time.

"The new one first, papa?" asked Max.

"Yes, and we will take the others afterward."

Then Max repeated, "God so loved the world that He gave His only begotten Son, that whosoever believeth in Him should not perish, but have everlasting life."

Then Lulu, "Herein is love, not that we loved God, but that He loved us, and sent His Son to be the propitiation for our sins."

Now it was Gracie's turn. "We love Him because He first loved us."

Her face was full of gladness as she repeated the words in clear, sweet tones. "I do love Him, papa," she added. "Oh, how could I help it when He loves me so?"

"Yes, strange that such wondrous love does not constrain everyone who has heard of it to love Him in return," responded the captain, and then he repeated a verse. "Yea, I have loved thee with an everlasting love; therefore with loving kindness have I drawn thee."

"Papa," said Lulu, "that verse reminds me of something the minister said in his sermon this morning about God never leaving or forsaking anybody that trusts in Him. But then afterward he told about a poor, dying woman that he went to see once—so very, very poor that she had hardly any furniture in her room, nothing to eat, and nothing but rags to wear or to lie on for a bed. And yet she was a Christian woman, and she said it was like heaven there in her poor, wretched room. She was just as glad as she could be because she was going to die and go to heaven. Papa, I don't understand. It does seem as if she was forsaken when she was so very poor that she hadn't anything at all even to eat."

"Forsaken, daughter, when she was so full of joy in the consciousness of Christ's love and presence and the certainty that she would soon be with Him in the glorious home He had gone to prepare for His own redeemed ones?"

"Oh, I didn't think of it in that way!" said Lulu. "Jesus was with her, and so she was not forsaken."

"I don't think it made much difference about her being poor," remarked Max, "when she knew she was going to heaven. What good do riches do when people are dying? They know they have to leave them behind. I've read that when Queen Elizabeth was dying she was so unwilling to go that she cried out, 'Millions of money for an inch of time!' She was dying in a palace with everything, I suppose, that riches and power could give her, but who wouldn't rather have been in that poor Christian woman's place than in hers?"

"Who, indeed?" echoed the captain. "In the dying hour the one question of importance will be, 'Do I belong to Christ?' For 'there is none other name under heaven given among men, whereby we must be saved.'"

The children finished the recitations of their verses, said their catechism also to their father, and then for an hour or more their voices united in the singing of hymns, Violet accompanying them upon a parlor organ.

Family worship closed the day for the children—their bedtime had come.

"Papa, it has been a nice, nice Sunday—this last one of the year!" Gracie said, as he was carrying her up to her room. "I hope all the Sundays in the new one will be 'most 'zactly like it."

"And so do I," chimed in Lulu, who was close behind them. "It has been a very nice Sunday. I'm glad it's 'most over, though, because I'm in ever such a great hurry for tomorrow to come. Papa, I really can't help thinking about the fun we're going to have."

"You can help talking about it, though, and try to turn your thoughts upon something more suitable for Sunday, my daughter."

CHAPTER TENTH

A FEW MOMENTS BEFORE the breakfast hour on Monday morning, Captain Raymond, as usual, went into the apartments of his little girls to see how they were.

He found them in the sitting room. Gracie with a Bible in her hands and Lulu—greatly to his surprise—busily plying a needle.

"Good morning, my darlings," he said, bending down to bestow a fatherly caress upon each. Then with a smiling glance at Lulu, "I am glad to see you so industrious, daughter."

"Yes, papa, see it's the dress for that little Jones girl. Christine basted the patches on for me Saturday and showed me how to sew them. I'm nearly finished now. Please look to see if I am doing it well."

"Very nicely, I think," he replied, examining the work. "Your stitches are small and neat. Would you like to take it to the little girl yourself, this beautiful morning, Lulu?"

"If there's time, papa."

"There will be. Your young friends are not expected much before the dinner hour. So if the weather is pleasant, you and Gracie shall have a little drive with me shortly after breakfast, and we will call at the Jones's house and leave the dress."

Both little girls exclaimed, "How nice, papa!" Lulu added, "I shall enjoy giving it to her myself. And I'll have time to go, for I got up quite early and have pretty nearly put my rooms in order already."

"I like to see you industrious, daughter," her father said kindly. "But I do not want you to overdo the thing by being up too long and taking too much exercise before eating—because that might injure your health."

"Yes, sir, but I had a glass of milk when Gracie had hers, and now I'm just nicely hungry for my breakfast."

"Well, I am glad to hear it," he said. "The bell will probably ring in about five minutes."

Gracie had laid her Bible aside and taken possession of her father's knee.

"I'd like to get up early and work, too, if I could," she said, laying her hand on his shoulder.

"Yes, I know you would, my dear," he responded, passing his hand caressingly over her soft curls. "But you are not strong enough yet."

"But she's useful, papa," remarked Lulu. "She has been helping me to learn my verse while I sewed by reading it over and over to me, and we've learned hers, too, in the same way."

"That was a very good plan," he said.

"They are such nice verses, papa," said Gracie. "This is mine—'He that loveth not, knoweth not God; for God is love.'"

"And this is mine," said Lulu. "'Hereby perceive we the love of God, because He laid down His life for us; and we ought to lay down our lives for the brethren.' What does the last clause mean, papa?"

"That the love between the disciples of Christ must be great enough to make them willing to lay down their lives—die for each other if necessary."

"It wouldn't be many folks I could love so hard as that," remarked Lulu, emphatically.

"Doesn't the Bible say we must love everybody, papa?" asked Gracie.

"Yes, 'Thou shalt love thy neighbor as thyself.' 'But I say unto you, love your enemies.'"

"There, I'm done!" exclaimed Lulu, breaking off her thread, throwing the mended dress over the back of a chair, and putting away her needle. "Papa," coming close to his side and leaning up affectionately against him, "it's just as easy as anything to love you and Gracie, and Max and Mamma Vi, and Grandma Elsie—and other people that are good and kind and pleasant, but I just can't love everybody. At least, not a bit as much as I love you," she said, giving him a hug and kiss.

"No, dear child, that is not required. It is right that parents and children, brothers and sisters, husbands and wives, should have a deeper, stronger love for each other than they can possibly feel for mere acquaintances or those whom they do not know personally. But we are to love everybody with a love of benevolence, wishing them well and being willing to help them when in poverty or in distress if in our power to do so.

"Also, we must be patient and forbearing under provocation. The love of benevolence, if we have it, will help us to be so and make us willing to yield honors and pleasures to others, even though it seem to us that we ourselves have the best right to them."

"Papa," said Lulu, "I know you mean that for me, and I do intend to try hard to be unselfish toward all my little friends while they are here. I asked God to help me when I said my prayers this morning," she added in a lower key.

"I am glad to hear it," he said, pressing his lips to her cheek. "It is only by His help that we can overcome in the fight with the evil of our natures.

"We will go down to breakfast now, for there is the bell."

The weather proved mild, the sun shone brightly in a cloudless sky, and the little girls greatly enjoyed the short drive with their father.

They called at the house where the Jones family lived, but did not intend to stay many minutes. Gracie did not get out of the carriage at all. The captain and Lulu alighted and went into the cabin but declined to sit down. Lulu handed the dress, done up in a neat bundle, to the girl for whom she had intended it, and she greatly enjoyed the girls's look of astonishment as she received it, her eagerly impatient tug at the string that held it together, and her scream of delight when success crowned her efforts and the dress—a far better and prettier than she had ever owned before—met her astonished gaze.

"'Tain't for me?" she cried. "Say, miss, you didn't never intend to gimme it, did ye?"

"Yes," said Lulu. "I brought it on purpose for you. Papa told me I might."

"Well, now! I never was so s'prised in all my born days!" was the child's half-breathless exclamation. "It's mighty good o' ye and yer pap, too."

"No, it wasn't a bit generous in me," said Lulu. "I was quite done wearing it, and besides, papa gives me new ones very often."

The captain had brought a fresh supply of delicacies for the invalid and had employed the moments while the children were talking in saying a few comforting words to her. He now bade her good-bye, and taking Lulu's hand, led her back to the carriage. The young Joneses, grouped in the doorway, sent after them glances of mingled curiosity, admiration, and envy.

"Papa," said Gracie, who was watching the slatternly, frowzy little crowd with a mingled curiosity and interest equal to theirs, "I think those children want a ride ever so much."

"Quite likely," he returned. "And if they were clean and neat, they should have it. But as they are, their occupation of this carriage even for a short time would render it unfit for your mamma, or indeed any of us, to enter again." He had lifted Lulu in and taken a seat by her side while he spoke, and now they were driving on their homeward way.

"I wish they could have a ride," said Lulu. "Papa, couldn't some kind of vehicle be hired for them?"

"Perhaps so, but who is to pay for it?" he asked.

"I will, papa, if the money I have left will be enough," answered Gracie.

"I'll help," said Lulu. "We haven't spent all you gave us for Christmas, papa, and we have this week's allowance besides."

"Well, I will see what can be done," he said. "I am glad my little daughters care for the happiness of others as well as their own."

"We'd be dreadfully selfish if we weren't willing to help other folks to a little bit of good times when we are going to have so much ourselves," said Lulu. "Oh, Gracie, aren't you glad the day for our party to begin has come at last?"

"Yes," answered Gracie. "I b'lieve I'm beginning to be 'most as glad as you are Lu, but I wouldn't be if papa hadn't said I may sit on his knee whenever I want to. And that he'll take care of me and not let me get too tired."

"I think my little feeble girl is feeling rather better and stronger today," the captain remarked, bending down to hug and kiss her.

"Yes, papa, I do b'lieve I'm 'most well," was the cheerful reply. "I feel just as happy!"

"I, too," chimed in Lulu. "And I'm all ready for the girls. My pretty rooms are in perfect order. Papa, may I have Evelyn sleep in my room?"

"Certainly, daughter, if it pleases her to do so. I think you could not have a safer friend than Evelyn.

"I am very glad to see my dear, little girls so happy," he went on. "But, my darlings, you must not expect to be entirely free from vexation and annoyance while entertaining your friends. There will be clashing of interests and differences of opinion, even occasions when some will have to yield their wishes and preferences to those of others. I shall be highly gratified if my three children show a readiness to do that and do it both cheerfully and pleasantly."

"We'll try, papa," they both replied.

And now they seemed to forget everything but the pleasure close at hand. Both girls were nearly wild over the prospect of the new delight of entertaining—

quite new to them—for hitherto that privilege had never been accorded to them.

Their father showed himself to be in full sympathy with them and allowed them to chatter and laugh to their hearts' content.

Lulu's good resolutions were, however, put to the test even before the coming of her guests.

Almost immediately upon their arrival at home, Christine, the housekeeper, sought an interview with the captain. After a few minutes' chat with her, he repaired to the apartments of his daughters.

"Lulu," he said, "we find that it will be necessary for you to accommodate more than one of your young friends here at night."

"Oh, papa, please don't say that," she returned coaxingly. "I thought it would be so nice to have just Eva, and nobody else, in here with me nights and mornings. Can't it be managed somehow?"

"I am afraid not," he said. "There will not be room for all unless we give you two companions."

"But I have only one bed, papa, and it will crowd us very much to sleep three in a bed."

"Yes, one will have to take the couch here, which will make a very comfortable bed. And that one, I think, should be my own little daughter, Lulu."

"Papa, you said I might have Evelyn to sleep with me, and there wouldn't be room for more than one on the couch."

He sat down and drew her to him.

"Yes, I did make that promise—or rather give that permission. And I do not withdraw it. If you insist upon it, you and Evelyn may occupy the bed, and some one of your guests will have to content herself with the couch. But would it not be more polite and kind on your part if you resign your bed to her and Eva and take the couch yourself?"

"Yes, sir, and I will if you say I must. I'll have to, of course."

"I don't say you must. I only say that I shall be far better pleased with you if you do and that it would be the right and kind thing for you to do. But perhaps you do not care to please me?" he added, noticing the unwilling expression of her countenance.

"Oh yes, papa, I do! I'd do anything to please you," she cried, smiling up into his face, putting her arm round his neck, and laying her cheek lovingly to his.

"Thank you, dear child," he said, holding her close to his heart. "And now you may choose which of your little friends you will have to share these rooms with you and Eva."

"Lora Howard," she said. "I'm better acquainted with her than with any of the others, except Rosie."

"Rosie will share her mother's room," said the captain. "An excellent plan, I think."

"And Rosie Lacy is to sleep with me," remarked Gracie. "Mamma told me so, and I'm glad, for I like Rosie ever so much. Lu, maybe you'll find it's good fun for so many of us to be close together."

"I dare say she will," said her father. "And she may invite Evelyn almost any time to come and stay for days and weeks and share her room."

"Papa," cried Lulu delightedly, "you are just the very kindest of fathers."

"I am well pleased that you think so," he said contentedly, repeating his caresses. "While for my part, I verily believe no dearer or more lovable children than mine are anywhere to be found."

Gracie had come to his side, and he passed an arm round her as he spoke, bestowing upon her hugs and kisses as loving and tender as those Lulu had just received.

"Yes, my dears," he went on, "I think you will find it quite enjoyable to have your little friends sharing your rooms for a while. But don't allow yourselves to be so taken up with sport as to neglect your morning and evening devotions. Never begin a new day or lie down to sleep at night, without thanking your heavenly Father for His goodness and mercy to you and yours and asking to be kept from danger and from sin. Never be ashamed or afraid though the whole world should know that you do this. Jesus said, 'Whosoever therefore shall confess me before men, him will I also confess before my Father which is in heaven. But whosoever shall deny me before men, him will I also deny before my Father which is in Heaven.'"

"Papa," said Lulu, "I don't think I'd hesitate to say my prayers before others, even if I expected they'd laugh at me. I mean if I could not go by myself to do it. But when we can find a private place where no one but God can see or hear us, oughtn't we to choose it for the purpose?"

"Yes, Jesus said, 'When thou prayest, enter into thy closet, and when thou hast shut thy door, pray to thy Father which is in secret, and thy Father which seeth in secret shall reward thee openly.' You have a private place in that little tower room opening into Lulu's bedroom, and there you and your guests can go by turns to pray in secret."

Then he told them how Max had shown his moral courage while visiting at the Oaks.

"I'm proud of my brother!" exclaimed Lulu when the tale was told, and her eyes shone as she spoke.

"I, too," said Gracie. "I'm afraid I might not have been so brave. But Eva and Lora say prayers, too, so we won't have such a trial as Maxie had."

At that moment there was a sound of wheels on the drive, and Lulu, running to the window, exclaimed in joyous tones, "It's the Fairview carriage with Aunt Elsie Leland, little Ned, and Eva in it. Oh, I'm so glad they've come the very first!"

"We will go down and welcome them," the captain said, taking Gracie's hand. "Do you feel able to walk, daughter? Or shall I carry you?"

"I'm a little tired, papa," Gracie answered, and he picked her up and carried her.

Meanwhile hasty, impetuous Lulu had flown to meet her friend, and as the captain appeared on the scene, Lulu was embracing her with as much ardor and effusion as if they had been separated for months instead of only a day or two.

"Oh, Eva," she cried, "I do think we are going to have the most splendid time that ever was! You are to share my rooms, and we'll go right up there if you like."

"I do like, or shall as soon as I have spoken to your father and your Mamma Vi," returned Evelyn merrily, putting her small hand into the large one the captain held out to her.

"I am very glad to see you, my dear," he said in a fatherly manner that made the quick tears spring to her eyes.

A sudden sense of her irreparable loss almost overwhelmed her for the moment, and she could not utter a word of reply.

He saw her emotion, drew her nearer, and bending down, kissed her as tenderly as if she had been his own.

"Lulu's father may have the privilege, may he not, daughter?" he asked in affectionate accents.

A grateful look was Lulu's only answer.

But now other carriages were driving up and guests, old and young, poured in so fast that there was a delightful confusion of affectionate embraces and merry greetings.

Lulu was in her element, playing hostess to her young girl friends, showing them to their rooms, and seeing that everything necessary for their comfort was provided. Meanwhile, Max did likewise by the boys with perhaps an equal sense of enjoyment, and Gracie entertained her little mates in her own quiet fashion in the lower rooms of the mansion.

Rosie Travilla, coming down a little in advance of the others, met the captain in the lower hall.

"I'm expecting to have a lovely time, captain," she remarked. "Zoe has been telling me about the magic cave."

"Has she? And would you like to step into the conservatory and see the alterations we have made there, Rosie?"

"Yes, indeed!" she answered. He led the way.

They were quite alone, and after she had seen and made her comments upon what had been done, he asked, "Would my little sister like to do her big, biggest brother, a favor?"

"Do you one, do you mean, captain? Certainly, if it's in my power?"

"Thank you," he said. He then added with gravity, "I regret that you apparently consider me so fond of my title. Would it be difficult or disagreeable to you to say Brother Levis instead of captain?"

"Not very," she returned, laughing. "But the title is more convenient, and it's for that reason I use it, and not because I ever have imagined you to be proud or fond of it."

"Well," he said, "if I were in your place I think I'd use the other—especially if ever the tables should be turned so that I wanted to ask a favor of my biggest and oldest brother."

"If you really care to have me do so, I might try," she replied with a merry look up into his face. "But is that the only favor you have to ask?"

"No, there is another that I am still more desirous to have you grant."

He paused for a moment, then went on, "I have a very fiery-tempered little daughter whom I love so dearly that it gives me great pain to punish her for her outbursts of passion."

Rosie's cheeks grew suddenly very hot, and her eyes were downcast.

"I am certain she is fighting hard against her besetting sin," the captain continued. "I am trying by every means in my power to help her, and the favor I ask is that you will join me in this by kindly refraining from provoking her even in sport.

"Please, understand, my dear little sister, that I am not saying you ever have intentionally provoked her. I know and acknowledge that it is no difficult matter to rouse her temper."

It cost Rosie a desperate effort to make the acknowledgement, but she forced herself to answer. "But if I did say it, 'twould be nothing but the truth, for I have teased her purposely more than once. But if you'll forgive me this time, cap—

brother Levis, I'll try not to do it again. I never thought of it as an unkindness to you."

"My children are very near and dear to me, Rosie," he said. "They are so near and so dear that any injury to them is much more trying than a personal one.

"But I am fond of my little sister, too—both for my wife's sake and her own," he added in a kindly tone and with an affectionate pressure of her hand that he had taken in his. "Of course, I forgive the past, while thanking you heartily for your promise in regard to the future."

"Does Lulu hate me?" she asked, tearfully and blushing vividly.

"I trust not, indeed!" he said. "I have no reason to think so. It would distress me greatly if I thought she did, and you must not imagine that she has been telling tales. With all her faults, she is above that, I think."

"Yes, I do believe she is," acknowledged Rosie.

Just then the door opened, and Lulu's voice was heard saying, "Oh, here she is! Rosie, we were look-ing for you. We're going to look at some of the things for the tableaux, and we thought you'd like to see them, too."

"Oh, yes, thank you!" cried Rosie. "Those things are always interesting. You're coming, too, aren't you, captain—er, I mean, brother Levis?" glancing back over her shoulder at him as she hurried toward the little group in the doorway.

He was about to say no, but an entreating look from Lulu caused him to change his mind and go with them.

He made his presence welcome to them all by the interest he showed in what interested them and the zest with which he entered into all their pleasures. Not at this time alone, but every day while the guests were there—always so far as concerned the children God had given him for his own.

❦❦❦❦❦❦

CHAPTER ELEVENTH

THE AFTERNOON WAS spent in rehearsing tableaux and the evening in playing games and acting charades.

For a while Gracie seemed to enjoy the fun, but an hour before the others were ready to give it up, her father perceived that she was growing weary. So he carried her off to bed.

"Shall I go with you, Gracie?" Lulu asked, glancing up from the game she was playing.

"No, Lu, you're having such a nice time, and papa and Agnes will 'tend to me," Gracie answered, giving her sister a sweet, affectionate smile.

So Lulu went on with her game. It was finished presently, and then she stole quietly from the room and upstairs to Gracie's bedroom.

"So you did come!" said Gracie, who had just laid her head on her pillow. "I like to have you, but oughtn't you stay with your company?"

"I just want to speak to papa, and then I'll go back to them," answered Lulu, going to his side.

He had seated himself by the bed, meaning to have a little loving chat with Gracie before leaving her for the night.

"Well, daughter, what is it?" he asked, putting his arm about Lulu and stroking her hair caressingly with the other hand.

"I was thinking, papa, that I won't have a chance for the least little bit of a goodnight talk with you, because there'll be company downstairs to see and hear everything. And you won't want to come into my room to say goodnight as you 'most always do when we're alone, because of Lora and Eva being with me there."

"But you are going to occupy the couch in your sitting room, and when you hear me coming you can shut the door between that and your bedroom. So what is to hinder us from having a bit of a private chat as usual?"

"Oh, yes, that will do nicely!" she exclaimed, her face lighting up with pleasure. "You will come, papa?"

"Yes," he said, giving her a kiss. "Now run back to your mates and enjoy yourself as much as you can till your bedtime comes."

The three little girls came up to their rooms in the merriest spirits, saying to each other that they had been having a lovely time. But they were careful to move and talk quietly for fear of disturbing Gracie and Rosie Lacey, who was now fast asleep by her side.

"It's quite too bad for us to turn you out of your bed, Lu," said Evelyn. "Let me take the couch."

"Or me," said Lora. "You two are such great friends that I know you'd like to be together."

"Thank you both," returned Lulu. "But you must have the bed, and you needn't pity me for having to sleep on the couch, for it is every bit as comfortable. Besides papa is coming up presently to bid me goodnight—and I know you won't care to see him. So, I'll shut the door between the rooms and have him all to myself."

"How nice of him!" exclaimed Lora. "My father never does that. I don't believe it ever so much as entered his head that he might, but mother does."

"Yes, I know it's nice," said Evelyn. "I remember how sweet it was to have papa come to me in that way. I'm glad for you, Lu, that you have such a father. I know if he were mine I should love him as dearly as you do."

"There, I hear his step!" cried Lulu. "So, goodnight, girls. Pleasant dreams," and she hurried into the next room, closing the door after her.

Her father entered by the other at the same moment. "Are you quite ready for me?" he asked.

"Yes, papa, I'm all ready for bed. I've put this warm dressing gown on over my nightdress and the warm slippers you bought for me on my feet, so I'll not take cold. Mayn't I sit on your knee a few minutes?"

"It is exactly what I want you to do," he said, taking an easy chair beside the grate and drawing her into his arms. He held her close for a moment then lifted her to the desired seat, saying, "There, hold out your feet to the fire and get them well warmed while we talk. Have you anything in particular to say to me?"

"Yes, papa. I wanted to ask you if I mayn't be the Peri tomorrow evening?"

He did not answer immediately. Putting her arm around his neck and looking coaxingly into his face, she repeated, "Mayn't I?"

He stroked her hair and kissed her before he spoke.

"I think," he said at last, "that here is a good opportunity for my little girl to put into practice her good resolution to deny herself for the sake of others."

"I don't like to," she said in a half-jesting tone and with an arch look and smile. "I wasn't born good, and I'd rather please myself."

"Yes, daughter, that is the way with us all. None of us were born good, and we all love self-indulgence."

"Papa," she exclaimed in her vehement way, "I don't believe you do! Not one bit! You're always doing kindnesses to other, and I think you're just as unselfish as possible!"

He was musing again and seemed scarcely to notice what she said.

"Do you suppose my oldest daughter might be safely trusted to keep a secret?" he asked presently.

"I hope so, papa. Will you try me?"

"Yes, it is merely a suspicion of mine that I don't want to trust to any ears but yours. I think—indeed, feel certain—that your Aunt Zoe desires as strongly as you do to be the Peri."

"Then, there isn't any chance at all for me!" pouted Lulu, an ugly frown on her downcast face.

"I hoped my little daughter would be generous enough to prefer another's pleasure to her own," the captain remarked with a slight sigh.

"Don't sigh, papa. Don't feel badly about it," she entreated, hugging him tight. "I will try to be good about it. I won't say a word to let anybody know I'd care to be the Peri, and I'll do my best to be cheerful, pleasant, and to make them all enjoy themselves."

"That is my own dear child," he said, caressing her. "It is all I could ask of you."

"And now that I think about it, I'm sure Aunt Zoe has the best right, because 'twas she who suggested having a magic cave and a Peri," Lulu said in her ordinarily pleasant tone. "Besides, she has always been kind to Max and Gracie, and 'most always to me, too."

"Perhaps always when you were deserving of it."

"Yes, papa, I suppose so."

"Well, daughter, it is high time you were in bed, so unless you have something more to ask or say, I will kiss you goodnight and leave you to your rest."

"That's all now, thank you, papa. Only — do you think I've been a pretty good girl today?" she asked with a wistful, longing look into his eyes.

"I do," he said. "You gave up very nicely about the sleeping arrangement. I have no fault at all to find with your conduct today, and I am very glad to be able to say so."

Her face lit up with joy. "Papa," she said, her arm still round his neck and her cheek laid to his, "I'm just the happiest girl in the world when you're pleased with me."

"And it gives me great happiness to be able to commend you," he returned. "Now, my darling, good night. Go to bed and to sleep as soon as you can."

The magic cave was to be a surprise to most of the young guests, and those who were in on the secret guarded it carefully. The doors of the parlor opening into the conservatory were found locked the next morning, while amusements of various kinds, suited to the differing ages and tastes, were provided in other parts of the mansion.

Before breakfast, the captain called Lulu into his dressing room and told her it had been settled the previous evening that Zoe was to be the Peri, Edward Travilla and Lester Leland the Genii. The turbaned figures at the entrance to the conservatory would be Herbert and Harold, the unseen musicians Aunt Elsie and Mamma Vi.

"I'm satisfied, papa," she said. "I think it's very good of them to be willing to help."

"Yes," he returned. "I think, too, that they will enjoy the sport. And I hope, daughter, that you also will get a great deal of enjoyment out of it."

"Oh, I haven't a doubt that I shall, papa!" she responded. "I think it will be splendid fun, and I've given up wanting to be the Peri."

"I am glad to hear it!" he returned. "I really think you will find it more amusing to be one of the outside throng. You will see and hear more of what is done and said than you could from the inside.

"Besides, as hostess you should be where you can give attention to your guests, seeing that each one has as large a share of the fun as you can secure for her, and that no one's comfort is neglected."

"That's work I shall like, papa," Lulu said, her eyes sparkling with pleasure. "And I suppose it'll be my business to find amusement for them all while Mamma Vi, Aunt Zoe, and the others are decorating the conservatory and the magic cave?"

"Yes, and I expect to give you some help in that."

"Will you, papa? Oh, I'm glad! All the girls say that you helped us to have a great deal nicer time yesterday than we could have had without you."

"I feel quite complimented," he said laughingly, stroking her hair and giving her a hug, for she stood by his side with his arm about her waist.

There was a light tap on the door, and Max's voice asked, "May I come in?"

"Yes," said his father, and he entered with a cheery, "Good morning, papa. Good morning, Lu. I want to talk a little about the fun for tonight. I've been thinking somebody should resist being blindfolded and led into the cave, like that Mrs. Cecil did—in the story, you know. I've been reading that chapter, and I think it would make more fun."

"Oh, yes," said Lulu. "Of course, it would! But who shall do it?"

"You, perhaps," returned Max in a sportive tone. "You have about as much talent in that line as anybody of my acquaintance. There aren't many folks who'd dare resist papa's authority for instance, as—"

"Max, Max! Don't tease your sister," interrupted their father gravely, for Lulu's eyes were downcast and her cheeks hot with blushes. "She has been very good and obedient of late, and I am sure has no intention of resisting lawful authority in the future."

"I beg your pardon, Lu," Max said with hearty goodwill. "I really don't think you have more or worse faults than I have myself."

"Yes, I have, Maxie. You're a thousand times better than I am," sighed Lulu, nestling closer in her father's embrace. "I get dreadfully discouraged with myself sometimes, and I do believe I'd give up trying to be good if I didn't know that papa loves me in spite of my badness."

"Papa does indeed, dear child!" the captain said in tender tones. "And he knows by experience how hard a fight it takes to rule a fiery temper."

"And perhaps there are other folks beside that care a little bit for you, Lu," said Max with an arch look and smile. "But say now, shall you or I play Madam Cecil's part?"

"You can if you want to," she added laughingly, quite restored to her good humor and cheerfulness,

"I do believe you can be stubborn, too, if you choose to be."

"I hope so," said their father. "A strong will is a very good thing if used aright. It would grieve me to think my boy lacked firmness and decision of character, for they will often be needed to keep him from yielding to temptation to step aside from the paths of rectitude."

A great variety of grand amusements had been provided, and all seemed to find the day pass quickly and pleasantly.

On leaving the tea table everyone repaired, by invitation, to the large parlor adjoining the conservatory, and many were the exclamations of delight as they caught a glimpse of the interior of the latter.

Rare and beautiful plants and shrubs were massed on each side of the central alley. Their branches hung with a myriad of tiny colored lamps and other glittering objects, including the fairies made by the ladies and Lulu. At the farther end could be seen the magic cave, also hung with fairy lamps and jewels. In the midst the Peri was arrayed in a rich oriental costume with her attendant genii, one on each side. Meanwhile two turbaned figures stood guard in front of the glass doors opening from the parlor, and soft strains of sweet music issuing from some unseen quarter lent an added charm to the witchery of the scene.

"Can we go in? Oh, can we go in now?" asked a chorus of eager young voices.

"Yes, one or two at a time," answered the captain, opening the door and motioning to Maud Dinsmore, who happened to stand nearest, to pass in.

She did so and was caught by the hand by one of the turbaned figures, who bowed low and waved her on toward the cave, while a voice sang to the accompaniment of the unseen musical instrument:

Hush! The Peri's cave is near:
No one enters scathless here;
Lightly tread and lowly bend,
Win the Peri for your friend.

At the same time a muslin bandage was thrown over her eyes from behind, her other hand taken, and she felt herself led onward toward the cave. As she and her conductors paused at its entrance, a whistle sounded long and loud at her back.

She turned hastily round, but it rang out again behind her—again and again, always behind her, turn which way she would. Meanwhile the singer slowly repeated:

Bend, bend, lowly bend,
Win the Peri for your friend.

She obeyed with ready grace. A voice said:

Homage done, you may be
of this merry company.

And with another blast of the whistle the bandage was taken from her eyes, and a string which seemed to have been made fast to her sash put into her hand, to which she gave a jerk, expecting to find the whistle attached to it. But instead there was a golden scarf-pin of delicate workmanship.

"Oh, how very pretty!" she exclaimed. "Am I to keep it?"

But only the song answered:

Away, away,
In the cave no longer stay,
Others come to share our play.

And one of the attendant genii drew her aside to make room for the next blindfolded victim, who was already being introduced in like manner as she had been.

All, both old and young alike, took part in the sport, going through the same ceremonies, and they had a very merry time. Indeed, the older people seemed to feel almost as young as the children for the time being.

Max carried out his plan of pretended reluctance, and in its way that added a good deal to the fun. The gifts, too, were a source of much mirth and jocularity. Most of them were pretty and valuable, but some were of little worth except for the sport occasioned by the incongruity of their bestowal.

Mr. Dinsmore received a baby's rattle, his son a lady's headdress, while whistles and tops and other articles equally inappropriate to the age and sex of the receiver were given to their wives and the other ladies.

Zoe received the ring she had admired and bestowed the uncomplimentary pen-wiper she had made upon one of her young brothers-in-law.

Beautiful watch charms from their father fell to the lot of Lulu and Gracie. They were much pleased, and the captain equally so with their present to him.

A few tableaux closed the entertainment for the enchanted evening.

The curtain rose first on a wedding scene — Lester Leland and his Elsie in bridal attire in the foreground, Calhoun Conly, dressed as a minister, and an attendant group of little boys and girls gathered about them, making altogether a very pretty picture, indeed.

In the second tableaux there were but two lone figures—Edward Travilla with his Zoe on his arm looking very lovely and bridelike in white satin, veil, and orange blossoms.

She had always regretted that the circumstances of their marriage had precluded the possibility of thus arraying herself for her bridal.

"What a lovely bride she makes!" and other similar remarks, reaching her ear, sent a rich color into her cheek and an unusual sparkle into her always bright eyes. But she did not move a muscle, and the curtain fell amid loud and prolonged applause.

It rose again in a very few minutes on another and even more handsome pair—Captain Raymond and Violet, also in wedding dress.

It was a surprise to his children, who were all now among the spectators. They gazed eagerly and with intense interest, Lulu almost holding her breath in her excitement.

"How sweet mamma looks!" murmured Gracie, close at her side.

"And how handsome papa is!" said Max, who stood near enough to hear the remark.

"He always is the very handsomest man in the world!" said Lulu.

"It's 'most like being at their wedding," remarked Gracie. "I wonder if mamma wore that very dress."

"Yes," answered Rosie, "that is her wedding dress, not altered at all. And the one sister Elsie wore was hers."

"It's nice that they've kept them so nicely," said Sydney Dinsmore. "I may live and die an old maid, but if ever I do get married, I mean to keep my wedding dress for my children and grandchildren to see."

They all had their eyes fixed upon the tableau while they talked.

But now the curtain fell, shutting out the sight.

"Oh, why didn't they let it last a little longer?" murmured several young voices. "It was such a lovely picture!"

"I'd have liked to look longer," said Gracie. "But I s'pose mamma would have been tired standing so still. Besides, I guess it's bedtime. I feel as if it must be," she murmured, pulling out the dainty little watch that was papa's gift.

"Yes, it is past my bedtime. But I'm not much tired, and I hope papa will let me stay up a little while longer."

"Oh, see!" cried Lora, as a door opened. "Here they all come, the three brides still in their wedding dresses. They're going to wear them for the rest of the evening, I suppose. How wonderful!"

But nobody listened to what she was saying. They had all risen to their feet and were crowding around the brides and bridegrooms with merry congratulations and good wishes.

Lulu and Gracie presently made their way to their father's side. He was laughing and talking with some of the other grown people, but when he felt the small hands clasping his, he glanced smilingly down at his darlings, then stooped and kissed them both.

"I fear my feeble little Gracie is very much fatigued by this time," he said. "Do you want papa to carry you up to bed now, dear?"

"I'm not so very tired, papa, and if you're willing, I'd like ever so much to stay up a wee bit longer," she returned coaxingly. "It's so nice to be at your wedding, you know. It seems as if it's your and mamma's wedding."

"Does it?" he laughed. "I wish I could have had my children at the real one. Yes, you may stay up a little longer and have some ice cream. We are going out to the dining room now for refreshments."

CHAPTER TWELFTH

WHEN EDWARD AND ZOE had retired to their own apartment on the breaking up of the company that evening, he led her up to a pier glass asking, "What do you think of the picture you see there, my dear?"

She gazed an instant, then, looking up at him with an arch smile and a charming blush, said, "I think the gentleman is extremely handsome," she said.

"I was asking of the lady," he laughed, drawing her closer to his side and bending to kiss the ruby lips. "You make a bonny bride, my darling, even bonnier that you did when first you gave me the right to call you mine. Look again, and tell me if you are not entirely satisfied with your own appearance in bridal array?"

She obeyed, again gazing intently for a moment, smiling, and blushing with gratification, for it was a very lovely face and figure she saw reflected in the mirror.

"Wouldn't you have liked to have me dressed just so when we were married, dear Ned?" she asked with another glance up into his face.

"Yes, sweet one, if it might have been. And yet it could hardly have made us happier at the present time than we are now, could it?"

"No, and yet I should have preferred a happier bridal than we had. I can never think of it without remembering the bitter sorrow that came to me at the same time. You were my only helper and comforter then, dear, dear Ned! And, oh, how kind you were! But you know you were almost a stranger, and I couldn't love and trust you as I have learned to do in these years that we have lived together. I was grateful to you then—though not half so grateful as I should have been—but half afraid of you, too. But I don't fear you now. No, not a bit," she concluded with a light and happy laugh.

"I hope not, indeed," he said. "'Perfect love casteth out fear.' How have you enjoyed yourself tonight?"

"Very much indeed. I think we gave mamma a pleasant surprise with our tableaux. She hasn't a particle of prying curiosity about her, and we were quite successful in keeping our intentions in regard to them a secret from her."

"Yes, I know. She told me it was a great treat for her to see her three daughters in bridal attire— that in her eyes they all looked very lovely and very bridelike."

"It's so nice of her to include me with the others. She is and always has been a real mother to me ever since the day you brought me to Ion. Well, I suppose I must doff my finery, for it is growing late."

"Yes, for tonight, but you must don it again some time for my benefit, if for no one else's."

There were new sports for the next day and the next—in most of which Harold and Herbert, the captain and Violet, Edward and Zoe, and sometimes even Grandma Elsie, took part in a way to make it extremely satisfactory to the children. They entered heartily into the fun and frolic, enjoying it, apparently, if not really, as much as the youngest of the company.

Almost entire harmony had prevailed until the last evening but one. Then there was a slight unpleasantness.

Lulu and the five girls who were her special guests were seated about a table engaged in playing "Letters."

The player who could make the largest number of words would win the game. Each drew a letter in turn from a heap in the center of the table, thrown randomly together, and was bound to select haphazard, not seeing what the letter might be till it was chosen and could not be exchanged for another more to the player's liking.

"Dear me!" cried Sydney Dinsmore, when the game had been going on for some time. "Rosie is going to win for certain. Just see! She has more words than anybody else. But I'd like to know how it is that she always hits upon a vowel, while I get nothing but consonants and of course can't make out my words."

"That's a mistake, Syd," said Rosie, coloring deeply as she spoke. "I don't always get a vowel."

"No, you don't always want one, but when you do, you seem to get it."

"So might anybody who was mean enough to peep and find out what the letter is before she takes it," remarked Lora in a half-jesting tone. Whereat the color on Rosie's cheek deepened still more. Then catching a scornful glance from Lulu's dark eyes, she rose hastily, pushing back her chair.

"If I am suspected of such doings," she said in tones trembling with anger and chagrin. "I'll not play anymore."

"Oh, now, Rosie, sit down and finish your game," said Evelyn persuasively. "I'm sure no one really suspects you of such dishonesty."

"Then let them say so," returned Rosie. But no one spoke, and turning haughtily away, she left them sitting there.

"Oh, girls, why didn't you speak?" exclaimed Evelyn, always inclined to be a peacemaker. "Let me run after her and tell her that of course you don't suspect her of any such thing."

"I can't," said Sydney. "For it wouldn't be true. I saw her peep."

"And so did—" began Lulu, but raising her eyes while the words were on her tongue and catching a glance of grave displeasure from her father, who noticing that something was amiss among the players, had drawn near and was now standing opposite her on the other side of the table, she broke off suddenly, leaving her sentence unfinished.

Her eyes fell and her cheeks flushed hotly under his glance, but he turned and moved away without speaking. The game went on but with less enjoyment than before on the part of the young players.

Lulu particularly, troubled by a consciousness that she was no longer in full favor with her dearly loved father, had almost lost her interest in it.

Rosie was still more uncomfortable, knowing that Sydney's and Lora's accusation was not at all undeserved, but she was far too proud of spirit to own it just.

She sauntered into an adjoining room, where the little ones were engaged in a game of romps, and was soon in their midst apparently the merriest of the merry, when in fact she was only making a determined effort to drown the reproaches of conscience. No one so carefully trained in the knowledge of right and wrong as she had been could be guilty of even the smallest act of dishonesty and deception without suffering in that way.

She, however, gave no sign of it till, on reaching their sleeping apartment, her mother turned to her with the most sadly reproachful look she had ever bestowed upon her.

Rosie's eyes sought the floor, while her cheeks burned with blushes. She had not thought "mamma" knew anything about her wrong doing, yet certainly she must, else why was her look so grieved and reproving.

Neither spoke for a moment, then, sighing deeply, Elsie said, "Can it be true that my dear, youngest daughter has been guilty of both fraud and deception?"

"Who told—why do you have such an idea, mamma?" stammered Rosie in confusion. "I—I never thought you'd believe anything so bad of me!" And she burst into a perfect passion of tears and sobs—a most unusual thing for her.

"Oh, Rosie, my dear child," her mother answered in tones tremulous with grief and affection. "I do not want to believe it. I can hardly bear to do so, and yet I must fear it is true till I hear the assurance from your own lips that it is not."

"Mamma, who has been carrying tales about me to you?" cried Rosie with great show of indignation. "I did not think anybody would be so mean. No, not even Lulu!"

"Rosie! Rosie!" exclaimed her mother in a tone that, for her, was very severe. "How can you be so wrong about Lulu? She is passionate, but I have never known her to be guilty of meanness. I have heard nothing from her to your discredit. But I did overhear a little talk between some of the others about your having cheated in a game, or perhaps more than one, and growing angry and forsaking their company when accused of it."

"Well, mamma, hadn't I a right to be indignant at such an accusation?"

"Not if it were just and true, my daughter." There was no response to the half-questioning rejoinder, and after waiting a moment, Elsie asked, "Was it true, Rosie?"

"Mamma, why do you—how can you ask me such insulting questions?" sobbed Rosie, hiding her face in her hands while a crimson tide mounted to her very hair.

"It pains me more than I can express to do so," sighed her mother. "But if conscious of innocence, my dear child, say so at once, and your mother will believe you." She paused and waited for an answer.

For a few moments Rosie seemed to have a hard struggle with herself, then she sobbed, "I can't mamma, because—because it is true. I did peep to see what the letters were, and—and before that when we were playing hide-and-seek and Lulu was hiding the slipper. But, oh, mamma, don't look so dreadfully grieved! I didn't really think how very wrong it was."

Tears were coursing down Elsie's cheeks, and her bosom heaved with emotion.

"Oh, mamma, dear mamma, don't! I can't bear to see you cry because of my wrong doing," sobbed Rosie, dropping on her knees by her mother's side and throwing her arms around her.

"It almost breaks my heart, my child, to learn that one of my darlings has stepped so far aside from the path of rectitude," returned her mother in tremulous tones. "Though you have spoken no untruthful word, you have been both untrue and dishonest in act."

"Mamma, mamma, how can you be so cruel as to tell me that?" Rosie exclaimed, hiding her face in her mother's lap and sobbing convulsively.

"'Faithful are the wounds of a friend,'" her mother said tenderly, softly smoothing the weeper's hair. "I must show you your sin in all its heinousness that you may see it to be hateful, repent of and forsake it, and go to Jesus for pardon and cleansing."

"I am sorry, mamma. I don't ever intend to do so again. I'll confess it to God, and I have confessed it to you."

"And do you think that is enough, my daughter?"

"Oh, mamma, don't say I must own it to the girls!" she entreated. "I couldn't bear to!"

"I perceive that your conscience is telling you you ought, and I hope it will not be necessary for me to add a must," Elsie said very gently and kindly.

Rosie was exceedingly reluctant. It seemed the hardest requirement her mother had ever made, but at length a promise of obedience was won from her. She went to bed to cry herself to sleep over the humiliation she must submit to on the morrow.

While she and her mother were talking thus together, Lulu had made ready for bed and received a visit from her father. She met him with a wistful, pleading look and the query, "Papa, are you displeased with me?"

He did not answer her immediately, but sitting down, drew her to his knee, smoothed the hair back from her forehead, and kissed her gravely. "Not very seriously, daughter," he said at last. "But what was the trouble between Rosie and the rest of you? Sydney seemed to be accusing her of some unfair dealing, and you, I thought, were beginning to utter a sentence of the same import."

"Yes, papa, I was, and I'm glad you stopped me before I'd said what I was going to," Lulu answered, coloring and dropping her eyes.

"And a moment before she left your circle I saw you give her a very scornful look. Do you think that was right or kind, especially remembering that she is your guest?"

"No, sir," acknowledged Lulu. "But, papa, I will try to do better if you just won't be vexed with me."

"I can ask nothing more than that promise, and I am not at all vexed with you now, darling," he said, repeating his caress.

"Oh, I'm glad!" she exclaimed, hugging him and returning his kiss. "Papa, do you think I would ever cheat at play, and so win the game unfairly? And if I should, wouldn't you think I was every bit as bad as if I flew into a passion?"

"Yes, quite as bad, and quite as deserving of punishment, but I do not think you would be guilty of anything of the kind. It has always been a great comfort to me to be able to believe my little daughter Lulu a perfectly honest, truthful child."

"Dear papa, thank you!" she said, her face lighting up with joy and love.

"It is a great pleasure to me to speak words of commendation to you," he responded. "As great a pain to have to reprove and punish you. So, dear child, if you love your father, try to be good."

"Don't you know that I love you, papa?" she asked, smiling into his eyes.

"Yes," he said, holding her close. "I haven't the least doubt of it. Now, goodnight. Get to bed and to sleep as soon as you can."

"There, now, I know papa wouldn't think Rosie a bit better child than I am if he knew all I do about her," Lulu said to herself with great satisfaction as he went from the room and the door closed after him.

❈ ❈ ❈ ❈ ❈

Rosie seemed strangely quiet and depressed the next morning, and she seemed to avoid meeting the glances of her mates.

"I guess she's ashamed of herself," remarked Sydney in an aside to Lora. "And she ought to be."

"Of course, she ought," said Lora. "Who would ever have believed that a child of Cousin Elsie's would cheat at play? I think Rosie has always had a very good opinion of herself. Perhaps it will do her good to find out that she's no better than other folks, after all. She's been hard on Lulu Raymond about her temper, you know. I must say I like Lu best, though she's no kin to me."

She involuntarily glanced toward Rosie, standing by a window on the farther side of the room as she spoke, and their eyes met.

Rosie's instantly sought the floor, while her cheeks flushed crimson.

It was shortly after breakfast and family worship, and they were in the parlor where the trouble began the night before. There were just the girls themselves and no one else, and Rosie perceived that there could be no better time than the present for her acknowledgment.

But how should she make it? "Oh," she thought, "it's the hardest thing I've ever had to do!"

Then, summoning all her courage, she spoke in low, faltering tones, her head drooping, her whole face and even her neck crimson with blushes.

"Girls, I—I own that Syd was right in what she said last night, Lora, too, and that besides, I did look when I was supposed to be hiding my eyes in the other games."

She ended with a burst of tears, turning her back upon her companions, as if too much mortified to meet their glances.

There was a moment of surprised silence, in which no one either moved or spoke. Then, Eva said in a kindly, sympathizing tone, "It is noble of you to own it, Rosie. So I think we should love you more than ever."

"Yes," said Lulu, hurrying to Rosie's side and putting her arms affectionately about her. "So we will, Rosie, dear, so don't cry. I'm sure you don't intend ever to do anything of the kind again, and we'll forget about it directly, won't we, girls?"

"We'll try," they answered. Sydney added, "So dry your eyes, cuz, and don't let us spoil our good times by fretting over what's done and can't be helped now."

"It will do for you to feel that way," sobbed Rosie. "All of you that haven't been doing wrong, but I ought to be ashamed and sorry whenever I think about it."

"Don't think about it, then," said Sydney in a jesting tone. "I wouldn't."

"And we won't," added Lulu, squeezing Rosie's hand affectionately.

"Lu, you're very good to be so very kind and understanding," murmured Rosie close to Lulu's ear. "For I haven't been kind and charitable to you when you were in disgrace, even when it was partly my fault that you had done wrong."

"Never mind. I hope we are not going to vex each other any more," returned Lulu. Just then Zoe came running in to say that some new tableaux had been thought of, in which they were all to have more or less part, and they were all wanted at once in Violet's boudoir.

CHAPTER THIRTEENTH

On SATURDAY MORNING the last of the guests had departed.

"Well, it's all over!" exclaimed Lulu with a sigh, as she turned away from the window whence she had been watching the carriage that bore them till it disappeared from sight. "Oh, but it does seem dreadfully lonesome now!"

Dreadfully? Quite that, daughter?" Captain Raymond asked, taking her hand and looking down into her lugubrious countenance with a smile of mingled amusement and affection.

"No, papa, I believe that's a little too strong," she answered with a not very successful effort to be bright and cheery. "But it does seem lonesome. Don't you feel a little so your own self?"

"Well, no, I can't say that I do. I have enjoyed entertaining our relatives and friends, but now I feel that it will be fully as enjoyable to have my wife and children quite to myself again for a time."

"I echo your sentiments, my dear," Violet said in a lively tone. "I have enjoyed the mirth and merriment of the past few days, but I would not be by any means willing to live in such a whirl of excitement all the time. So, no, I am full of content at being left alone with you and the children again."

"That's just the way I feel about it," Gracie said, nestling up against her father.

"That's right," he said, putting his arm round her. "And if any of us are lonesome we must draw the closer together, and each one try to be as kind and entertaining to the others as possible. Suppose I order the family carriage now and take you all for a drive? What do you say to that, Mamma Vi?"

"I am pleased with the proposition," Violet answered. "I shall go at once and don my wraps. But where is Max? Is he not to go with us?"

"Yes, on his pony—he is off to the stables to take personal oversight of the saddling and bridling. Now, daughters, go and get ready."

It was dinner time when they returned from their drive. Violet and the children were rosy and happy, saying they had enjoyed it greatly but were now hungry enough to be glad to reach home and the dinner table.

It did not seem a great while after leaving it when the short winter day closed in, the lamps were lighted, and, supper over, they gathered close together about the glowing grate in Violet's boudoir.

This was baby's usual time for a romp with papa, brother, and sisters. She and they were very merry tonight, enjoying the romp all the more because it had been omitted while the guests were in the house.

While Violet was away seeing baby put to bed, the three older children hung about their father chatting freely with him and each other.

When that had been going on for a few moments, the captain asked, "How about the lonesomeness now, Lulu?"

"Oh, I'm not a bit lonesome now, papa," she cried, giving him a vigorous hug and laying her cheek to his. "We didn't have a nicer time all the while the girls and boys were here."

"Ah, I wonder if Max and Gracie are of the same opinion, Lu."

"Yes, indeed, papa!" they both replied.

"Then you didn't greatly enjoy entertaining your young friends?" he said inquiringly.

"Oh, yes, sir! Indeed, indeed we did!" exclaimed all three.

"How would you prefer to spend the rest of the evening?" he asked, and again there was a simultaneous answer. "Hearing you read some nice book, papa."

"That is my choice also," said Violet, coming in at that moment.

"A unanimous vote," commented the captain with a pleased smile. "That is far more comfortable than a difference of opinion, or rather, in the present case, of desire."

He had always been a lover of choice literature and was anxious to make his children such, cultivating their minds as well as their hearts. He had already bought largely of standard works, history, poetry, biography, travels, and of the best juveniles — such as can be read with interest by adults as well as the young. Many an evening had passed delightfully for himself and Violet as well as to the children in making acquaintance with their contents.

The captain was always the reader at these times and would occasionally pause to give opportunity for a request for information or explanation, which he was fully capable of giving and always did give in the kindest and most painstaking manner.

"Well, children," he said, as he laid aside the book, "your holidays are over, and we must begin lessons again on Monday morning. I shall expect to find you all in the schoolroom at precisely nine o'clock."

"I'm not sorry, sir," said Max. "Though I've enjoyed my vacation very much."

"I'm not really sorry," said Lulu. "But I'm afraid I'll find it hard at first to sit still and study. Please, papa, won't you be a little easy with us for a day or two?"

"I hope you will find me not unreasonably strict or stern," he replied, smiling slightly. "But I can't allow too much self-indulgence or too ready a yielding to an indolent disinclination for work."

"But, please, papa, make the lessons short and easy for the first day or two," said Violet in a playful tone of entreaty. "That is the way mamma used to do with us after a holiday—getting us back into the traces gradually, you know."

"A good plan I think," responded the captain. "And it is very kind of Mamma Vi to plead for the children."

"Yes, so it is, but we don't need anybody to plead for us with our own dear, kind father," said Lulu, laying an arm across his shoulders, as she stood by his side, and gazing into his eyes full of filial love and trust.

"Indeed, no!" exclaimed Violet. "I know he loves his children dearly and would not be hard with them for the world."

"I trust not," he said, smoothing Lulu's hair caressingly and returning her look of love. "I think there is nothing I desire more strongly than their welfare and happiness here and hereafter."

"We are all sure of that, papa," said Max.

"Well, tomorrow is Sunday, when we have only our Bible and catechism lessons, and they are short and easy."

"Yes, papa never gives long, hard lessons in those things," assented Lulu.

"And you think he does in other things?" the captain said in a tone of inquiry.

"It does seem a little so sometimes, papa," she replied. "But maybe it's only because I'm lazy."

"Laziness is a very bad complaint—not at all to be encouraged," he said. "I think you are not indolent as regards physical exertion, but I fear you are sometimes a little so when mental effort is what is required of you."

"Papa," said Max, "you make Sunday a very pleasant day to us, and so did Grandma Elsie and Mamma Vi when we were at Ion. But before that—when I lived with that old—"

"Max—" interrupted his father in a reproving tone.

Max colored and hung his head.

"I would like you to refrain from speaking disrespectfully of even that man," his father went on. "I grant that he did not treat you with kindness or even justice. But, my dear boy, try to forgive and forget it all. I am very glad you find Sunday pleasant now. I would have you all esteem it as the pearl of days."

He spared no effort to make it both a happy and a sacred day to them—a day when worldly cares, labors, and amusements, even such as are lawful on other days were to be laid aside. The whole time was spent in a holy resting, in worshiping and praising God, and studying His word in order to learn His will that they might conform their faith and lives to it.

Three brighter faces than those that met his glance on entering the schoolroom at the appointed hour on Monday morning could hardly have been found anywhere.

"You do not look as though lessons were a terror to you today, my darlings," he said, smiling upon them with fatherly affection.

"Because we don't feel so, papa," said Max. "We've all been here studying for the last ten or fifteen minutes. You see we don't want you to find it a disagreeable business to teach us."

"No, indeed, papa," added Lulu. "We're just determined to be good and industrious, and you needn't make the lessons short and easy unless you think best."

"Both they and the time shall be a little shorter than usual, however," he said. "But I am glad my patience is not to be tried with a lazy set of pupils."

He perceived that, though they were earnestly endeavoring to do their best, it was difficult for them to sit still and give their minds to their tasks, so a full hour earlier than usual he said, "Gracie, you may go now to your play. Max, I want these letters mailed within an hour. You may ride your pony into the village and post them for me, if you will go and return promptly."

"Yes, sir, I will. I'd like nothing better," answered the lad, hastily laying his books away in his desk, taking the letters, and leaving the room.

"Papa, mayn't I stop studying, too, and do what I please?" asked Lulu.

"You may put away your books and come here," he said. "I have something to say to you."

"That's nice!" she exclaimed, obeying with alacrity for his tone was so kind that she felt sure he had no fault to find with her.

He drew her to his knee and put his arm about her waist.

"What is it, papa?" she queried, patting his cheek with affectionate familiarity. "I know you're not going to scold me, because I haven't been doing anything naughty, and besides, you don't look one bit stern."

"No," he said, caressing her hair and cheek with his hand. "I have no reproof to administer, and yet what I have to say will not be pleasant to you. But my little daughter must try to believe that her father knows best and loves her too well to require of her anything but what he deems for her best interests."

"I'll try, papa," she responded but with quite a troubled, anxious look stealing over her face. "I can't think what it can be! Oh, it can't be that you're tired of teaching me and are going to send me away to school?"

"Not quite so bad as that," he said. "I am not tired of teaching you or the others. I find it sweet work, because you are all my own dear children, but I am not qualified to instruct you in the accomplishments I wish you to have. Therefore, I must employ someone else to do so. Your musical education has been neglected of late, but now I have engaged a teacher for you, and you will take your first lesson from him this afternoon."

"From him? Then it's a man! Oh, papa, I don't want a man teacher! Won't you please let me be taught by a lady?"

"My darling, I want you to have the very best instruction, and from all I can hear, there seems to be no one else in the neighborhood so capable on imparting it as this gentleman."

"But I don't want to take lessons from him, papa—for he'll be sure to be cross and hateful and put me in a passion, and—and then you'll—you'll have to punish me. And you won't like that any better than I will," she added, putting her arm round his neck and gazing beseechingly into his eyes.

"My darling, I think you may dismiss that fear," he said, stroking her hair caressingly. "For it is my intention always to be present when you are taking your lesson and see that you are not ill-used, as well as that you do not misbehave."

"Then maybe I can stand it," she sighed. "I don't believe he would dare to strike me or do anything very bad to me if you are there to see. You won't let him; will you, papa?"

"No, I have already told him that if my little girl should be so naughty as to make it necessary to punish her in any way, I shall be the one to attend to it. I will not allow any one else to attempt it."

"And you don't like to do it either?"

"No, indeed I do not, yet if it should have to be done, I should be still unwilling to trust it to any one else."

"Is the gentleman an Italian, papa?" she asked.

"No, he is an Englishman."

"I wonder if that's any better?" sighed Lulu. "Professor Manton's an Englishman, and I can't bear him!"

"Hush, hush. I do not like to hear you talk in that way," said her father. "You may go now and amuse yourself as you please till dinner time."

"I don't care to. I've lost all my spirits," she sighed dolefully. "Oh, papa, do please change your mind."

"My dear child, it is too late. Even if I thought best to do so—which I do not—for I have made the arrangement and cannot honorably retreat from it."

"Oh, dear," she groaned. "Don't you think it may have been kinder if you had consulted me first?"

"No, not unless it were kinder to consider your present wishes rather than your future interests," he answered gravely, though there was a slight twinkle of amusement in his eyes. "What is the use of my little girl having a father if she is so wise that she knows better than he what is best for her?"

"But I'm not. Oh, I wouldn't be without a father for all the world!" she exclaimed, clinging about his neck again and pressing her lips to his cheek.

He drew her into his arms and kissed her fondly. "Then you are going to be good about this and not distress papa by stubbornness, pouting, or fretting?"

"Yes, sir. Why, it would be perfectly shameful for me to be naughty and rebellious after you have given me a party and everything! If I am, I hope you will punish me ever so hard."

"I hope I shall not have occasion to punish you. It would distress me greatly to do so. But what a doleful countenance! Put on your hat and coat, and we will take a little walk together."

Her face brightened at once, and she hastened to obey the order, for she esteemed a walk with papa, her hand in his, one of her greatest pleasures.

When they came in again, just in season for their dinner, her face wore its usual bright and happy expression.

They had scarcely left the table when the music teacher was announced. Mr. Morgan was his name.

Lulu decided upon the first glance that she was not going to like him at all, yet that he was less forbidding in appearance that Signor Foresti.

"And I shall not care so very much whether he is nice or not, as papa will always be by to see that he behaves himself," she remarked to Gracie in talking the matter over with her the first time they were alone together after the lesson had been given and Mr. Morgan had taken his departure.

"Was he cross today, Lu?" Gracie asked.

"No, of course not. Do you suppose he'd dare to be with papa there to see and hear everything?"

"No, I shouldn't think he would. Isn't it good of papa to do that?"

"Yes, indeed, and I mean to try as hard as ever I can to improve to please him."

"And to please our heavenly Father. Oh, Lu, isn't it good of him to notice when we try to learn our lessons and be obedient and good because we want to please Him?"

"Yes, but I think a great deal more about pleasing papa," acknowledged Lulu frankly.

They were in the library, sitting by the fire in the twilight. Their father and Violet had gone to pay some calls in the neighborhood, leaving the little girls at home.

"It's beginning to get dark," remarked Gracie. "I wish papa and mamma would come."

"There!" exclaimed Lulu. "I guess they have, for I hear wheels on the drive."

They listened for a little, then Gracie cried out joyfully, "Oh, yes, they have, for I hear their voices." The next minute their father came in alone, Violet going on up to her boudoir.

"Papa! Oh, we're glad you've come!" they both exclaimed, jumping up, running to meet him, and each taking a hand.

"Are you?" he said, seating himself and drawing them into his arms. "It is very pleasant to receive so warm a welcome. I hope my darlings have not been very lonely?"

"No, sir," they answered simultaneously. Lulu added, "I practiced a whole hour by the clock, just as you and Mr. Morgan told me to, and Gracie played with baby while I was doing that. Then we both came in here to sit and talk."

"That was right. I expect and hope to see you improving very fast under Mr. Morgan's instruction. It isn't so very bad after all to have to take lessons from a man, is it?"

"Not with you there, papa, but I think it would be without you."

"I have something to tell you," he said. "The little Joneses had their drive today—in a spring wagon which I hired for the purpose. I sent one of the servants over to sit with the mother so that all the children could go, and I think they enjoyed it greatly. They are much obliged to my two little girls for giving them the treat."

"Oh, I'm glad we did!" exclaimed Gracie. "It's better than getting a present or buying something for ourselves to know those poor children have had a good time."

"I think so, too," assented Lulu.

"Yes," said their father. "There is no better plan for making money contribute to our own happiness than using it for others, especially the benefit of the poor and needy."

"'Cept giving it to the heathen, papa?" Gracie said, half inquiringly.

"Surely, to be destitute of the knowledge of Jesus and His salvation is to be very poor and needy, my little daughter," he replied.

"Yes, so it is," she said thoughtfully. "Papa, I wish everybody in the whole world knew about Him and loved Him."

"So do I, my darlings, and we must not content ourselves with idle wishing, but we must earnestly strive to do all we can to spread the glad tidings and win souls to Christ."

Chapter
Fourteenth

THE REMAINING WINTER months sped swiftly by, nothing occurring to mar the domestic felicity of the family at Woodburn. Then came gentle spring with her soft breezes, buds, and blossoms, bringing new delights.

The captain planned and carried out various improvements on the grounds, taking not his wife only, but his children also, into his counsels. He consulted their tastes and wishes in a way that gave them a very enjoyable sense of joint proprietorship with him. He had a pleasant fashion of saying "our" instead of "my" house, grounds, or flower garden.

Max was given a garden spot to be all his own. Lulu and Gracie each had hers, and they were encouraged to work them according to their strength—the gardener being instructed to do for them whatever they were not able to do for themselves and to provide each with whatever plants and seed were called for.

It was but little Gracie could do with her own small hands, but she found great pleasure in directing the laying out of her own tiny domain—selecting the seeds and plants and deciding upon the order of their arrangement.

The captain was a firm believer in the efficacy of fresh air, and in suitable weather there were daily drives and walks about the grounds, through the woods, and along the country roads.

It was a dear delight to the children to hunt for wild flowers on their walks. And if they spied any on their drives, papa was always indulgently ready to stop the carriage and gather the floral treasures for his darlings, or even permit them to alight and pluck the tempting beauties for themselves.

Such a free, glad life was theirs, so filled with pleasant duties and pastimes, so surrounded with an atmosphere of tender parental care and love, that their young hearts seemed brimming over with happiness. Even Gracie's face grew round and rosy with health.

Violet, too, was very happy, merry and as lighthearted as a child. The captain sometimes said he felt as if he were renewing his youth. At which, Violet would laugh and say, "That is not so very strange, my dear, for you are some years younger than mamma, whom we all indignantly refuse to consider old, and you have neither gray hairs nor wrinkles."

Max and Lulu had not given up their fret and scroll sawing and carving, but they usually found at least a few minutes to devote to them every day. They had been for weeks engaged upon some pretty things for Gracie, to be presented upon her birthday, which was now near at hand.

It was a secret between themselves, known to no one except their father from whom they seldom desired to conceal anything. It was a dear delight to both that he was always ready to receive their confidences, listen with interest, and give hearty sympathy and help also, if it were needed.

Going into their workroom one morning, he found them there, both busily plying their tools.

"You seem to be very industrious," he remarked with a pleased smile. "Are you not nearly done?"

"Yes, papa," they answered. "We have only a little more to do, but we must make haste with that, for tomorrow is Gracie's birthday."

"I have not forgotten that," he said. "I shall have a gift for her, too."

"What, papa?" cried Lulu eagerly. "May we know your secret?"

"You may know tomorrow," he answered rather pleasantly. "This is very pretty, Lulu," taking up some of her work and examining it critically.

"Yes, papa, and this is the last piece I'm doing now. Then I'll fasten them together, and the cradle will be done — all but putting in the pink satin lining I have ready for it. It will just fit Kitty, Gracie's largest doll, and I've made such a sweet little pillow and spread for it — both of pink satin covered with lace. Oh, I'm sure Gracie will be delighted! Particularly because I've made everything myself."

"I haven't a doubt that she will," he said. Then, looking at his watch, "You have still fifteen minutes before school time."

"I think I can get done the carving in that time, papa," she said. "And this afternoon I can put in the lining. Maxie, you are nearer done than I, aren't you?"

"Perhaps just a trifle, Lulu," he answered. "Papa, what do you think of this clock case now that I am finishing up?"

The captain examined and admired, then bidding them be punctual in coming to their lessons, went out and left them.

They were careful to obey. Lulu entered the schoolroom with flushed cheeks and shining eyes.

"I'm finished, papa," she said to him in a low aside. "And so is Maxie."

"I congratulate you both," he answered with a look of interest and a kindly smile.

ネ ネ ネ ネ ネ

Her lessons over, Lulu hastened back to the work-room to gather up the small bits of carved wood upon which she had expended so much time and labor.

On the very threshold, she was met by a little Negro boy coming out with a hatchet in his hand.

"Dick! How dare you go in there? What have you been doing with that hatchet?" she asked in tones of mingled anger and alarm.

"Nuffin, Miss Lu," he answered, running off at full speed, while she hurried into the room and to the table where she had left her treasures laid together in a neat pile.

Her pile had disappeared, but on the floor beneath lay a heap of broken bits and splinters of wood which one horrified glance showed her were all that Dick's hatchet had left of her beautiful work.

With a cry of grief and dismay, she dropped into a chair, then laying her head on the table she began to sob in a heartbroken way.

Presently a hand was laid on her shoulder and her father's voice asked in tenderly sympathizing tones, "My darling, what is the matter? What can have happened to distress you so?"

"Look, papa, look! Dick did it with his hatchet," she sobbed, pointing to the telltale heaps of wood on the floor.

"Dick?" he exclaimed. "He is not allowed to come in here, and he should never be permitted to have a hatchet. I shall take measures to prevent a repetition of such mischievous doings."

"But he's destroyed them all, papa—every one, and I haven't time to make any more for Gracie's birthday now."

"No, dear child, and I am very sorry for you. What can I do to comfort you?" he asked, sitting down and taking her in his arms. "Will it console you a little to know that I am much gratified to find that you have borne this severe trial of patience without flying into a passion?"

"Yes, papa, it does comfort me some. But I hope Dick will keep out of my way for a while, because I'm afraid I might fly at him and box his ears."

"I shall see that he does not come near you," the captain said gravely. "And I must find some way to help you to get another present for Gracie. We will try to think of something to buy which she would be sure to like."

"But it won't be my work, papa!"

"No, of course not, but when we cannot do what we wish, we must try to be content with doing the best we can."

He hugged and caressed her for a few moments, then led her out into the grounds and tried to direct her mind from her loss by calling her attention to the growth and beauty of the plants and flowers.

It was the day for her music lesson—the hour for taking it was shortly after leaving the dinner table.

She had not learned to like Mr. Morgan and still esteemed it quite a trial to have to take lessons from him. His stock of patience and forbearance was hardly larger than hers, but the captain's presence had been a restraint upon them both. Hitherto there had been no decided outbreak of temper on the part of either.

But today, Mr. Morgan was testy and unreasonable from some cause known only to himself, while Lulu, in consequence of her great loss and disappointment, was not in a frame of mind to endure it even as well as she might at another time.

He scolded, called her stupid, asked how much time she had devoted to practicing her lesson. Upon being told, "an hour every day," he said he did not believe it.

"I don't tell lies, Mr. Morgan!" cried Lulu rather indignantly. "Please, ask papa if my word is not to be trusted."

"It is, sir, fully," said the captain, leaving the easy chair he had been occupying on the opposite side of the room and taking his stand near the piano, where he could look directly into the faces of both teacher and pupil.

"Doubtless you think so, sir, but I fancy you may be deceived, like many another doting parent," returned the Englishman in a sneering tone.

The captain received the taunt in dignified silence, not even changing color, but Lulu flushed hotly, flashed an angry glance at the speaker, then sent an entreating one up into her father's face.

"Yes, you may go," he said. "Go at once to the schoolroom." She made haste to obey.

"Sir!" exclaimed Morgan angrily. "I cannot have my pupils interfered with in this manner."

"The child is mine, sir," replied the captain. "And I decline to have her subjected to such a trial of temper as your captious fault-finding and unjust accusations have forced upon her today."

"I repeat that I shall allow no interference between myself and a pupil," returned Morgan, growing pale with rage. "If this thing is to go on, sir, you may look for another instructor for your daughter after the expiration of the present term."

"There is no need to wait for that," replied the captain in a calm, quiet tone. "Walk into the library, and I will draw a check for the full amount of your charge for the term and not ask you to give another lesson."

Lulu had gone to the schoolroom quivering with excitement and indignation, feeling as if the very thought of taking another lesson from Mr. Morgan was quite unendurable. She was hoping that her father was not disposed to blame her for her angry rejoinder to the man's rudely expressed doubt of her truthfulness, yet feared that he might. So, when he presently came in, it was with some apprehension that she glanced up into his face, asking tremulously, "Are you displeased with me, papa?"

"Come here," he said, seating himself.

She obeyed instantly, though still in doubt of what was awaiting her.

He drew her to his knee, put his arm round her, and, pressing his lips to her cheek, said, "No, daughter, I am not displeased with you. I think you have had sore trials of patience today, and you have borne them well."

"Oh, papa, do you? Oh, thank you for saying it! It makes me so glad, so happy!" She said this with a half sob, her arm round his neck, her cheek laid lovingly to his. "But, oh, I—I wish I never had to see that man any more."

"You need not. I have dismissed him and shall not engage a male music teacher for you—without consulting you," he added in a playful tone and smiled affectionately into her eyes.

"Oh, papa, how good of you!" she cried, hugging him close.

"Now," he said, "the next thing in order is to think what you can buy as your present to Gracie. How would you like to drive into the city with me this afternoon and select a gift for her?"

"Oh, very much, papa!"

"Then go and get ready as quickly as you can for we must start directly in order to return by tea time. Your mamma will go with us, and if Gracie chooses, we will take her as far as Ion and leave her there until we return."

"Oh, papa, how nice!" she cried, then hurried away to do his bidding.

Gracie was well pleased with her share of the drive, nor thought of any special reason for dropping her at Ion, further than that her father deemed it best.

Lulu came back in merriest spirits, accounting for them by saying that papa had been so very, very kind and had promised never to bid her take another lesson from Mr. Morgan.

It was Gracie's turn the next morning, when awakening, she found a small table by her bedside, quite loaded with pretty gifts from near and dear ones.

Lulu's was a lovely Paris doll with a trunk full of ready-made clothes. Max's a clock in a beautiful carved case. Papa, mamma, Grandma Elsie, and other friends had given her books and toys.

She was greatly pleased and very happy in her quiet way, especially when her father came in, kissed her fondly, and wished her many happy returns of the day.

But the most joyful surprise was when after breakfast and family worship, he led her and Lulu out to the veranda and showed them two pretty Shetland ponies, asking, "What do you think of those little fellows, children?"

"Oh! Oh! What darlings!" cried Lulu. Then half breathlessly, "Papa, are they for —? Whose are they?"

He smiled at her wistful, eager, half-hopeful, half-doubtful look.

"The larger one, called Fairy, is for a little girl who seems to have gained pretty good command over a fiery temper," he made answer. "The other, Elf, is for a birthday gift to Gracie. They are both from papa, who hopes his darlings will find much enjoyment in riding their small steeds."

Before he had nearly finished the long sentence they were in his arms, hugging, kissing, and thanking him in a rapture of delight.

He returned their caresses as warmly as they were given, helped them to mount their ponies, and gave Gracie a lesson in managing hers.

Lulu seemed quite at home in the saddle, and it pleased him to perceive it.

They went around the grounds several times. Then he had them dismount and go into the house.

"Your mamma has something to show you," he said and led them to their sitting room, where they found Violet and Alma waiting to fit each girl with a handsome riding habit.

Alma had been making them, measuring by some of their dresses, and they were so nearly done that she said she could have them both finished by dinner time. There was a dainty hat to match each habit, and when tied on they were pronounced very becoming.

"This is to be a holiday in Gracie's honor," their father said. "This afternoon several of her little friends of her own age are coming to help her celebrate her birthday."

Gracie's eyes sparkled with pleasure. "I'm glad, and I'm very much obliged to you, papa," she said. "Can Elf come to the party, too? she asked with a gleeful laugh.

"Yes, he may attend and have his fair share in entertaining the company by letting them take turns riding him about the grounds," replied her father, looking fondly down into the sweet, fair, young face upturned to his.

"I'm ever so glad for you, Gracie," remarked Lulu heartily. "Will you invite Fairy and me to your party, as well?"

"Why, yes, of course," said Gracie. "I couldn't enjoy it without my big sister that's always so kind to me, and if Fairy comes the girls can ride two at a time. Can't they, papa?"

"Yes, and when Lulu has her birthday party, she can make a return by inviting you and Elf."

"Oh, papa, am I to have one, too?" exclaimed Lulu, jumping for joy.

"Yes, if nothing happens to prevent it. And Max shall have one on his birthday, if he wishes."

"If nothing happens to prevent?" repeated Lulu, sobering down. "I suppose that means if I'm good and obedient and don't get into a passion?"

"A failure in that line would certainly be something to prevent it," answered her father. "But there might be something else—sickness, for instance."

Going close to his side, she said, "Papa, if I should get into a passion would I have to lose my pony?" she asked in an undertone.

"Yes, for a time. Ought you not to, since he is given as a reward for controlling your temper?"

"Yes, sir, that's just and right. Oh, I hope I shan't have to!"

"So do I. I should be very sorry to deprive you of her for even a day."

Gracie's guests arrived in due time. It was to be a lawn and garden party, and it came off a complete success—the ponies contributing largely to the enjoyment.

The captain stayed with the children constantly to assist in supplying amusements for them and to guard them against possible accident in mounting and riding the ponies, though the little ponies were almost as gentle and quiet as lambs.

CHAPTER FIFTEENTH

THE PONIES AT ONCE became the greatest pets with their young mistresses and soon would come to their call, eat from their hands, and submit to stroking and petting with as much docility as that of a dog or cat. It was a great pleasure to the captain to see the delight the children took in them.

It was some weeks before timid little Gracie would venture to mount hers or ride it without papa to hold the bridle and walk by her side to care for her safety. But after awhile she was content to let Max take his place, and at length grew bold enough to ride about the grounds at a moderate pace, guiding her small steed herself with only Lulu, mounted on Fairy, by her side.

Lulu was allowed to ride her pony within the grounds whenever she pleased, but she was strictly forbidden to go outside alone. Yet, as she could almost always have the company of her father, Violet, or Max, and not seldom of all three, there was little or no excuse for a desire to disobey.

Though Lulu had certainly greatly improved, there were still times when she was seized with the old willfulness and disinclination to submit to lawful authority. There were times when to have her own way and be altogether a law unto herself seemed a delightful thing, and for a time overcame the wish to please the father whom she did really love very dearly.

This happened one day—a month or more after the gift of the ponies. Morning lessons were over. Max went to the workroom, having a piece of carving he wished to finish, and Gracie, for once, preferred playing with her dolls to riding her pony. So Lulu set out alone with hers, not with any intention of going beyond the boundaries of the estate.

She rode round the drive, up and down the garden paths, and through the bit of woods several times. Then she turned longing eyes upon the road beyond, which, for some distance was shaded by overhanging trees, and did indeed look most inviting.

A side gate stood open, as a wagon, carrying some supplies from the house, had just passed through it. She reined in her pony close beside it.

"Why in the world shouldn't I go out there?" she said, half aloud. "It couldn't hurt anybody or anything for me to ride just a little way down that shady road. Papa's reason for forbidding me to walk alone in such places was that I might be in danger from tramps, but I'm sure Fairy could outrun any of them, and so I shouldn't be in any danger on her back."

Conscience whispered that whether she would be in danger or not, the act would be one of direct disobedience, but she refused to listen.

The reins were lying loosely on Fairy's neck, and just at that instant she started toward the gate of her own accord.

Lulu could have easily restrained her and turned her head another way, but she did not choose to make the effort.

"It's Fairy's doing, and I'm not to blame," she said to herself. "I'll only let her go a little way. I'll make her turn around in a minute."

She did not go very far, but the minute grew into five before Fairy's head was turned toward the gate again, and ten ere it was reentered and the two pursued their way back to the house.

Lulu found that somehow her ride had ceased to enjoyable, so dismounted and turned Fairy into the pasture where she and Elf were allowed to disport themselves when their services were not required. Then she sauntered about the garden for a little, then on into the house, vainly trying all the time to stifle the reproaches of conscience for the act of disobedience of which she had been guilty.

Presently she went into the library. Violet was there writing letters. Lulu took possession of the easy chair usually occupied by her father, took up a book that lay open on the table beside it, and began to read.

A few moments passed in silence. Then Violet, glancing up from her writing, said gently, "Lulu, dear, that is a book which your father would not approve of your reading. I am quite sure of it."

Lulu read on, paying no attention to the remark.

Violet waited a moment, then asked, still speaking in a gentle, kindly tone, "Did you hear me, Lulu?"

"Of course I did. I'm not deaf," came the quite ungracious, not to say, rude rejoinder.

"But you do not close the book."

"No, if papa doesn't want me to read books, he shouldn't leave them lying around."

"That is, you would have him treat you as one whom he cannot trust? Whom he considers destitute of a sense of honor? Since he has repeatedly told you that you must not read any book without first making sure of its being such as he would approve?"

An uneasy conscience made Lulu unusually irritable. "I do wish, Mamma Vi," she said quite peevishly, "you'd let me alone. I—"

"Lulu," interrupted a voice, speaking from the adjoining room in grave, slightly stern accents, "bring that book to me."

Both Violet and the little girl started at the sound, neither having had any suspicion of the captain's near vicinity. He had come in quietly just in time to overhear the short colloquy, while the portiere separating the two rooms concealed him from their view. It was quite accidental, he having no intention or thought of listening to anything not meant for his ear.

Violet, not wishing to be witness of a scene between her husband and his child, quickly and quietly withdrew by way of the hall, while Lulu rose and obeyed the order, appearing before her father with flushed face and downcast eyes. She silently placing the book in his outstretched hand.

He had come in somewhat weary, more in mind than body, and thrown himself into an easy chair.

He did not speak for a moment, and she stood, flushed and trembling before him, her eyes on the carpet at her feet.

At length he said, with a heavy sigh and in tones more grave and sad than stern, "I thought I had, in my Lulu, a daughter whom I could implicitly trust to be obedient and respectful to me and her mamma, whether in my presence or absence. I thought she cherished a sincere affection for her kind young mother and was quite sure that she loved, honored, and reverenced her father. But what I have accidentally overheard in the last few minutes has, I am deeply grieved to say, robbed me of that cheering belief."

Lulu hastily brushed away a tear. "Papa," she began in a trembling voice.

"No," he said. "I will hear nothing from you now. Go to your room and stay there till I come to you. I want you to think over your conduct since leaving the schoolroom this morning, and after due reflection upon it in solitude, give me your honest opinion of it."

A wave of his hand dismissed her, and she went silently from the room, up to her own, and sat down by a window overlooking the meadow where the ponies were browsing.

"I wonder," she thought with an added sense of shame and affright, as her eye fell upon them, "if papa knows where Fairy and I went? He said my conduct since I left the schoolroom, and that sounds as if he did. But I didn't think anybody saw us or would tell on me if they did. Oh, I wish I hadn't done so! I wish I hadn't spoken in that disrespectful way to Mamma Vi, and about papa! How could I do it and hurt his feelings so, when I do really love him dearly, dearly? He's such a good, kind father. Oh, I hate you for it, Lulu Raymond, and I should like to give you a good beating! I shan't make a word of objection if your father does, and in fact I believe I just hope he will. It's just what you deserve and you know it is."

She was deeply ashamed, and the more she dwelt upon her conduct, the more ashamed and penitent she grew. She rose from her chair and walked restlessly about the room.

"I wonder when papa will come, and what he will say and do to me," she sighed to herself. "I've been pretty good for quite a while till today and why couldn't I keep on? Why should I turn round all at once and be so dreadfully bad again? I haven't been in a passion to be sure, but I have disobeyed papa in two things, besides speaking disrespectfully to Mamma Vi about him. He certainly will have to punish me somehow, for I know he considers disobedience very, very bad indeed. I think half the punishment he gave me last time was for disobeying him. And it was kinder than to let me go on doing that dangerous thing."

At that moment, glancing from the window, she saw one of the Woodburn servants leading Fairy across the yard.

"Ajax," she called out the window, "what are you doing with my pony?"

The man looked up and answered, "De cap'n tole me for to tote she 'way off to Roselands. 'Spect Doctah Arthur gwine ride 'im when his hosses done wored out wid kyarin' de doctah 'bout de roads f'om mornin' to night."

"Dr. Arthur ride that little pony indeed!" exclaimed Lulu. "Why his legs would surely drag on the ground!"

She laughed over the ridiculous picture conjured up by the words of the servant and her own imagination. But then she began to cry, as she said to herself, "Papa is sending my pony away to punish me, and maybe he'll never let me have her again. I'd ten times rather he'd whip me."

The door opened, and the captain came in.

Lulu started up, hastily brushing away her tears, and stood before him with drooping head, hotly flushing cheek, and fast-beating heart.

He took her hand, led her to a chair, sat down, and drew her to his side.

"I have come to hear what you have to say as to your opinion of your own conduct today and any confession your conscience may impel you to make to your father."

"Papa," she burst out, hiding her face in her hands while the hot blood surged over it and her neck, "I'm ever and ever so sorry and ashamed of — of the — of what I said to Mamma Vi, and about you! Oh, papa, please, please forgive me! Please believe that I do really love and honor and reverence you!"

He waited a moment to see if she had finished, then asked gravely and with some severity of tone, "Is that all you have to say to me? Have you no confession of other wrong doing to make?"

"Yes, sir," she faltered, her head drooping still lower. "I — I disobeyed you before that by going outside the grounds."

"Yes," he said. "It so happens that I saw you, having had occasion just at that time to pay a visit to the observatory at the top of the house."

She looked up in surprise, but seeing the expression of grief and pain in his eyes, she dropped her head again and hid her face on his shoulder, sobbing out, "Oh, papa, don't look so hurt and sorry! I will try to be a better girl! Indeed, I will!"

"You have wounded your father's heart very sorely, little daughter," he said with emotion. "How can I be other than hurt and sorry on hearing that my dear child loves me so little that she is ready to speak disrespectfully of me and to disobey me repeatedly when she thinks I shall not know it?"

Her tears fell faster and faster at his words, and her sobs grew more violent.

"Oh, papa, I do love you!" she cried, twining her arms round his neck. "Oh, please believe me! I'd rather be killed than not to have you believe that I do!"

"I have no doubt that you have some affection for me," he said. "But—"

"Oh, papa, a great, great deal!" she interrupted. "I'm so angry with myself for being so disobedient and disrespectful to you, that I want you to punish me just as hard as you can. Won't you? And then forgive me, and love me again?"

"My dear child, I have not ceased to love you; very far from it. You are dearer to me than words can tell. But I cannot of course pass over lightly so flagrant an act of disobedience as you were guilty of today. I must punish you, and I have decided that your punishment shall be that Fairy shall be taken from you for a week."

"A week, papa? I was afraid you would never give her back to me, and I don't deserve that you ever should."

"It grieves me to deprive you of her for even that length of time," he said. "But if you are really as penitent as you seem, to lose her for a week will, I think, be sufficient punishment."

"Papa, I'm really discouraged with myself," she sighed. "I thought I'd learned to be pretty good, so that I would never be disobedient again, but now I have been."

"Do not allow yourself to be discouraged in a way that will lead you to give up trying to improve," he said. "Let your failures lead you to try all the harder and to pray more earnestly and constantly to God for help. Probably your failure was caused by your having grown too confident that you were really reformed and so relaxed your efforts and your watchfulness."

"Aren't you quite discouraged about trying to make me a good girl, papa?" she asked.

"No, I know too well that the battle with our fallen nature is a long and hard one, and I have had too many slips and falls myself to expect you to gain the victory at once. Also, I believe the promise, 'Train up a child in the way he should go, and when he is old he will not depart from it.' I must go on teaching and training you, praying to God for wisdom, and for a blessing upon your efforts, trying also to set you a good example, and God will surely at length fulfill His promise to me."

"Papa, is making me do without Fairy for a while the only punishment you are going to give me?"

"I hope that will prove sufficient," he said. "It pains me to have to inflict even that, for it has been a delight to me to see the pleasure you have taken in your pony. But I must train you to obedience, for that is according to God's command to me as a parent. You have told me that you are sorry for your bad behavior to your mamma as well as to me. I want you to make the same acknowledgment to her."

"Papa, I do hate to do that. Can't you tell her so for me?"

"I wish her to hear it from your own lips, and if you are really as sorry for your misconduct as you profess to be, you will do as I bid you without my having to resort to compulsion."

He rose as he spoke, then taking her hand, led her to Violet, who was sitting in her boudoir.

On seeing them enter, she instantly conjectured what was coming and sent an entreating glance on Lulu's behalf up into her husband's face. But he ignored it.

"Lulu has something to say to you, my dear," he said, and the little girl, coloring deeply and keeping her eyes upon the carpet, faltered out her apology.

"Mamma Vi, I'm sorry I spoke so disrespectfully to you. Please forgive me, and I'll try not to do so any more."

"Dear child," Violet responded, taking Lulu's free hand and kissing her affectionately. "I should by no means have required an apology from you. The offense was but a slight one, is entirely forgiven, and shall be forgotten as soon as possible."

"My love, you are very kind to make so light of the offense," remarked the captain. "But I consider it a serious one and shall be very greatly displeased if there is ever a repetition of it. Both your own lovely character and the position I have given you in relation to my children entitle you to respectful treatment from them, and they must yield to it."

"I have seldom had any reason to complain of their behavior to me," replied Violet. "They are dear children, and I can truly say that I love them every one."

"Thank you, my dear," he said, his eyes shining with pleasure.

Then catching a beseeching look from Lulu, he bent down and kissed her, saying, "All is right between us now, daughter."

But Lulu's conscience was not quite at ease. Violet's words had called up some memories that troubled it and her innate honesty and truthfulness prompted another confession.

"Papa," she said, bursting into tears, "Mamma Vi is kinder than I deserve. I have been very naughty to her a number of times, when you were away and didn't know anything about it—so ill-tempered and disrespectful that you would have punished me severely if you had been at home to see and hear it all."

"But that is all past and there is no occasion to bring it up again," Violet hastened to say.

"Yet I am glad she has made the confession," the captain said gravely. With a slight sigh, sitting down as he spoke and drawing Lulu into his arms, he continued, "It is a proof of honesty and truthfulness that gives me great hope that my dear, eldest daughter will yet make a noble woman—the pride and joy of her father's heart."

"Dear papa, how kind of you to say that," sobbed Lulu, hiding her face on his shoulder. "Oh, I will try to be everything you wish."

CHAPTER SIXTEENTH

꒰IT WANTED BARELY TWO weeks of Lulu's birthday when by her misconduct she lost sight of her pony for a time.

Of course, Max and Gracie inquired for what reason she had been sent away, and it was a mortification to Lulu to have to own that papa had ordered it as a punishment to her for disobedience.

"Well, Lu," said Max, "it does seem odd to me that you will disobey papa every once in a while. He never gives an unreasonable order and is always so kind and affectionate to us, yet sure to punish disobedience."

"Have you never disobeyed him, Max?" she asked a little angrily.

"Yes, several times in the course of my life, but not of late."

"I don't believe Lu will any more," said Gracie.

"I hope not. I don't mean to. It 'most broke my heart to see how hurt and sorry papa looked about it," Lulu said with a slight tremble in her voice. "It was worse than having Fairy sent away."

Max and Gracie offered the use of their ponies.

"Thank you," said Lulu. "It's ever so kind of you both, but I don't know whether papa would let me ride either of them now while I can't have my own."

They had left the dinner table shortly before, were now on the veranda, and Ajax was leading up Elf and Max's pony, Rex.

The captain stepped out from the open hall door, and Max asked, "Papa, may I lend Rex to Lu?"

"If you choose, but she is not to ride alone even about the grounds or to go out of sight from the house by herself."

"S'pose you ride on Elf, Lu, and have Maxie go along on Rex," suggested Gracie.

"And let you stay behind? No, indeed! You and Max go, and I'll amuse myself at home. I had a ride this morning and don't need to go again," Lulu answered.

"I propose that instead you two little girls shall have a drive in the family carriage with your mamma and me, Max riding alongside on Rex," their father said. They accepted his invitation with joyful alacrity, running up at once to their rooms to get ready, for he told them he had already ordered the carriage and that it would be at the door in a few minutes.

Lulu came down a little ahead of Violet and Gracie and found her father waiting for the carriage on the veranda alone.

Drawing near his side and speaking in a low tone, "Papa," she said, "I don't deserve to go along, and you are very kind to let me."

"I love to have you with me, dear child," he answered. "Though I have sent Fairy away for a time, it is not my desire to make the week an unhappy one to you."

Max's birthday would occur a few days earlier than Lulu's and that evening, when they were all together, his father told him he might celebrate it by having a party, inviting as many of his boy friends as he chose to spend the day, or part of it, at Woodburn.

Max was greatly pleased and began at once to plan amusements for his expected guests, asking advice and assistance from both his father and of Violet.

Lulu listened with interest to the talk, glad for Max, and hoping, too, that something would be said about the conditionally promised party for her birthday.

But it was not mentioned, and she concluded that probably papa did not intend to let her have one since she had behaved in so ill a manner. She was too sincerely penitent to feel at all rebellious or ill used, though she was sadly disappointed. Still, as it lacked nearly two weeks of the time, she did not entirely give up hope.

When she had gone up to her own rooms for the night and was getting ready for bed, her thoughts went back to the interview held there that morning with her father, and she seemed to see again the pained expression in his eyes that had so distressed her then.

"Oh, how could I be so naughty and disobedient to him—such a dear, good father!" she again sighed to herself, tears springing to her eyes. "I just hate you for it, Lulu Raymond, and I'd like to pound you well. I 'most wish your father would do it! I've a mind to ask him to. And here he comes," she said, as she heard his step nearing the door.

She looked up at him as he came in with tearful, wistful eyes. He opened his arms, and she ran into them, put hers about his neck and hid her face in his shoulder.

"What is it?" he asked, softly smoothing her hair. "Why are there tears in my dear little daughter's eyes. Is it because of Fairy's absence?"

"No, papa, but because I'm so sorry to have hurt you so today. Oh, have you got over it now?"

"Pretty nearly. The momentary doubt that my dear Lulu loved me more than just a little has vanished. I am quite sure she does love me — better, perhaps, than anything but her own self-will. But I shall never be quite satisfied till I can believe that she loves me even better than that."

"Papa," she pleaded, "please believe that I do 'most all the time."

"Yes, I do believe it and that you are really trying to overcome your faults. I want to talk a little with you about these besetting sins of yours and how to battle with them. Then we will ask God together to help you in the struggle, for Jesus says, 'If two of you shall agree on earth as touching anything that they shall ask, it shall be done for them of my Father which is in heaven!'"

"Papa," she said, clinging lovingly to him as, a little later, he bade her goodnight, "if your children don't grow up good, Christian people, I'm sure it won't be your fault."

"It is what I desire for them more than wealth, or fame, or anything this world can give," he answered, holding her close in a tender embrace.

She had grown very fond of Fairy and missed the pretty creature woefully, but she said never a word of complaint or entreaty for her restoration. Instead she strove earnestly to be faithful in the performance of every duty that so she might please her dear father and fully convince him of her devoted affection for him and Mamma Vi.

He noticed her efforts, gave frequent, loving commendation, and was kind as kind as could be during her long trial.

Yet the week seemed a long one. But at last it did come to an end, and on being dismissed from morning lessons, Lulu found her pony quietly feeding with Elf in the grassy plot in front of the schoolroom door.

She gave a joyous cry but turned and ran back to hug, kiss, and thank her father before bidding her sweet Fairy welcome.

"It pained me to take her from you, and now it gives me great pleasure to return her, my darling," he said. "Go and enjoy yourself with her, Gracie, and Elf, as much as you can, till dinnertime. I am sure I need not remind you that you must keep within the grounds, unless Max or I should join you."

"I hope not, papa, and I do thank you ever so much for trusting me again," she answered, as she hurried away.

The absorbing topic of conversation now was Max's approaching birthday and the party that was to celebrate it.

The little girls held many pleasant consultations with each other, and sometimes with papa and mamma, too, about presents for him, desiring to give something that should prove both useful and acceptable to him.

Max's satisfaction with what he received, when the day came, seemed to leave no room for doubt that they had succeeded. He was full of boyish delight, and more than once he expressed the belief that he was the most fortunate fellow in the world, for nobody could have a better father or kinder mother and sisters.

"And such a feast as papa has provided for us!" he went on. "How the fellows will enjoy it!"

"I think you must have been interviewing Christine and the cook, Max," laughed his father.

"Yes, sir, I have. You see I feel free to do pretty much as I please in my own father's house — at least as regards going up and down, and in and out, from garret to cellar, looking at whatever's going on and asking questions."

"That's right," returned the captain heartily. "Where should a boy feel at home if not in his father's house?"

"No where, I should say," answered Max. "And you've provided so many amusements for us that I don't see how it'll be possible for any one of us to have a dull moment."

"And am I not to have an invitation to share them with you, Max?" asked the captain.

"Oh, will you, papa? Will you really join in our games?" cried the boy, his eyes sparkling with great pleasure. "Why, that'll be perfectly splendid!"

"Possibly the 'other fellows' may be of a different opinion," laughed his father.

"If they are at first, I'm sure they'll change their minds when they find out what good company you are, sir," returned Max. "And, oh, papa, won't you tell us some of your sailor's yarns, as you call them?"

"Perhaps, if other amusements fail."

"Oh, thank you, sir! Mamma Vi, we'll take our noisy games far enough away from the house as not to disturb you."

"I shall not mind the noise," said Violet. "I have always been used to boys, and I take great pleasure in seeing them enjoy themselves."

Their talk was at the breakfast table, and an hour or two later, the guests began to arrive.

The sports were such as the little girls did not care to take part in, but they found much entertainment in looking on. Each felt a sisterly delight in seeing how intensely Max enjoyed it all.

The visitors were a polite, good-humored set, the captain's presence among them was a restraint as well as a pleasure, and nothing occurred to mar the harmony of fun.

When the time came for the good-byes, there were warm hand shakings and earnest assertions that never in their lives had they had a better time.

Max's party was now successfully over. Lulu's birthday was near at hand, yet nothing was said about its celebration. She waited from day to day, hoping that her father would mention the subject and say that she, too, should have a party. But kind as he was and thoughtful for her comfort and enjoyment in every other respect, he seemed to have forgotten that he had ever spoken of such an intention, never to reflect that she might reasonably expect the same indulgence that had been shown her brother and sister. So at length she sorrowfully concluded that he thought her late misconduct had rendered her unworthy of such a treat.

She was quite sure of it when the very last evening before her birthday had come and still she had received no intimation that any notice whatever was to be taken of it.

She was unusually silent all the evening, seemed to keep a little apart from the others, and now and then sighed softly to herself.

Several times her father's ears caught the sound, but he merely gave her a kindly inquiring glance and went on with his talk.

When he came to her room for a few goodnight words, as he almost always did, and found her shedding tears, he took her in his arms, asking tenderly, "What is the matter, daughter? Are you not feeling quite well?"

"I'm not sick, papa," she answered in tremulous tones, half averting her face.

"What then? Tell your father what troubles you. He will help and comfort you if he can."

"I'm ashamed to tell you, papa," she faltered, hiding her face in his shoulder.

"Is it that you fear papa has forgotten what an important day tomorrow will be to his little Lulu? If so, you may dry your tears. I have thought of it a great deal and prepared a pleasure for you. Eva is to come directly after breakfast to stay a whole week with you, and it shall be a week of holidays."

She lifted her head and looked up into his face, smiling through her tears.

"Oh, that is nice!" she cried joyfully. "Thank you, my dear papa."

"As nice as a party?" he asked with a smile.

"Almost," she said hesitatingly. "It's better than I deserve, because I was so so very, very naughty only a little while ago."

"Dear child, do you think your father could have the heart to keep on punishing you for wrong doing so sincerely repented of?" he asked in half reproachful tones.

"I—I thought I—I deserved it, papa."

"I do not think so," he said. "But did you want a party, Lulu?"

"Yes, papa, and I thought you meant to give me one if I'd been good."

"You shall have one some time before the summer is over," he promised. "And I hope tomorrow will be a very happy day for you in spite of your disappointment."

Then he kissed her goodnight and left her.

She was much comforted, and her troubles were soon forgotten in sleep.

When she awoke the sun was shining, and she started up with an exclamation of surprise.

Beside her bed stood a small table, and on it were a number of things she had never seen before—a pretty workbasket, a beautiful little clock, a lovely pair of vases, several handsomely bound books, and a box of kid gloves.

"Oh, how nice!" she cried. "They didn't forget me. No, not one of them! I'm so glad! It's so very pleasant to be remembered!"

She examined each gift, noting its beauties, and from whom it came—for they were all labeled—then sprang out of bed and began dressing in haste.

She had scarcely finished when her father entered noiselessly, stepped softly up behind her, and caught her in his arms before she was even aware of his presence.

"Good morning, my darling, and many happy returns of the day," he said, kissing her fondly.

"Good morning, my dearest papa," she returned, twining her arms about his neck. "Thank you for that lovely little clock. It is just what I wanted for my mantle."

"I am very glad to hear that it pleases you, daughter," he said.

Gracie had followed him in.

"Oh, Lu, I'm glad you've got a birthday!" she exclaimed. "But weren't you surprised?"

"At having a birthday, Gracie?" asked her father, laughing a little and hugging them both at once.

"No, papa. At the things on the table."

"Yes," said Lulu. "I didn't expect any presents at all."

"Here is another surprise for you," said the captain. Something glittering went over her head, and a small round object was laid in her hand.

She looked down at it and gave a cry of delight. It was a beautiful gold locket set with brilliants and attached to a gold chain, which her father had put around her neck.

She turned it over and found her initials on the other side.

"How very pretty, papa!" she cried.

He touched a spring and the locket flew open, disclosing a pictured face.

Lulu gazed at it in silence for a moment, then lifted her eyes inquiringly to her father's face.

"Mamma, our own mamma, isn't it?" she asked in tones half-tremulous with emotion.

"Yes," he said. "An excellent likeness, I think. She was very sweet and lovely in both looks and character. I hope all her children will resemble her in that last, as Gracie does in looks."

"Yes, papa, I do believe Gracie will look just like this when she's grown up," Lulu said, glancing from the miniature to her sister, then handing it to her. "And, oh, but I am glad to have it. You couldn't have given me anything else that would have pleased me so much, dear papa!" hugging him again as she spoke.

Gracie gazed fixedly at the picture for several minutes, then lifting tear-dimmed eyes to her father's face, said, "How dear and sweet she does look, papa! I can remember her only just a little, and this helps me to do it more. I'll always know now how sweet and pretty my first mamma was."

"Our own mamma," corrected Lulu emphatically.

"Yes, she was that," the captain said. "And I would not have her children forget her. Neither would your Mamma Vi. She so wishes you to remember this dear mother of yours, that she has spent many hours in painting, from a photograph, this likeness for you, Lulu, and another like it for Gracie. Also, she intends to paint one for Max."

"Where is mine, papa?" queried Gracie eagerly.

"Here," he said taking from his pocket another locket the facsimile of Lulu's except that the initials upon it were Gracie's own.

She received it with a transport of delight quite unusual for her, for hers was a much quieter temperament than that of her older sister.

"How good of Mamma Vi!" exclaimed Lulu. "Especially," she added, her cheeks growing hot with blushes, "considering the many times I've behaved badly to her."

"So I think, and I trust, my dear child, that you will never again treat her with unkindness or disrespect," said the captain gravely.

"Oh, I hope not! I'm sure I don't ever intend to!" cried Lulu.

"Let's go and thank her," proposed Gracie. "Mine's every bit as sweet and lovely as yours, Lu."

"Will you take us to her, papa?" asked Lulu.

"Willingly," he said, rising and taking their hands.

The breakfast bell rang just at that moment, and as they stepped into the hall, they met Violet coming from her room in answer to it.

Very sweetly she received the thanks of the little girls and congratulated Lulu, saying, "Truly, it was a great pleasure to paint for you the lovely face of your mother."

CHAPTER
SEVENTEENTH

AFTER BREAKFAST CAME family worship. It was the regular order of things at Woodburn. Then the captain smilingly bade his little girls go to their rooms and dress for company.

"Oh, yes!" cried Lulu, dancing away to do his bidding. "Eva is coming, Gracie. Papa told me so."

At that Gracie laughed and exchanged a knowing glance with her father and Violet.

But Lulu, hurrying on ahead, did not see it. She turned around at the door, saying, "Oh, papa, I forgot to ask what you want me to wear."

"Ah! Suppose we go with them, Mamma Vi, and help them in the selection of both dresses and ornaments," he said.

"Agreed!" said Violet, and they all went merrily upstairs together.

"Someone seems to have already made a selection for you, Lulu," remarked the captain as they entered her room, passing into it before going into Gracie's.

"Why, so they have!" she exclaimed, running up to the bed. "What a lovely new white dress—an elegant sash, too! Papa, are these presents from you?"

He nodded assent as she ran into his arms to hug and kiss him by way of thanks.

"Papa's gift and papa's taste," said Violet. "He made the purchase entirely alone, and I must acknowledge that I could not have done better myself," she added laughingly.

"They're just as beautiful as they can be!" said Lulu, examining them again. "Such lovely embroidery and the very handsomest sash I ever saw!"

"Really, I feel encouraged to try again one of these days," laughed her father.

"I hope Gracie has the same," said Lulu, looking up inquiringly into his face.

"Just the same, except the color of the sash," he replied. "I think she will find them on the bed in her room. Now I will leave you to put on your new finery, and when you are both dressed, come to me in the library and let me see how you look."

"Oh, just a minute and let me hug you once more, you dearest, kindest papa!" cried Lulu, running to him again.

"Twice, if you wish, daughter," he returned, laughingly submitting to her renewed embraces and hugging her so tight in return that she cried out, "Oh, not quite so hard, papa; you'll squeeze the breath out of me!"

"I should be sorry to do that," he said, kissing and releasing her.

"Oh, Gracie, what a dear, good father we have! What nice, nice surprises he's given me for my birthday!" exclaimed Lulu, as the door closed on him and Violet. "Did you know about them beforehand Gracie?"

"Yes, all but the lockets. Papa, mamma, and Maxie and I talked it all over together when you weren't by, you know. And it was such fun to think how surprised and glad you'd be. Now we'd better hurry and get dressed before Eva comes."

A little later, hand in hand and arrayed in the new finery, they presented themselves before their father and Violet in the library, asking, "Will we do, papa?"

"I think so," he said, regarding them with eyes full of fatherly pride and affection. "I certainly should not be ashamed to claim you anywhere as my own little daughters."

"You would not be that, my dear, if you saw them in rags," said Violet. "Your fatherly heart would only go out to them in stronger affection because of their unhappy condition."

"Yes, indeed, Mamma Vi," said Max, who had just come in from the grounds. "But papa would go without a coat himself before he would let his children be in rags."

"Oh, hark, I hear wheels! Eva has come!" cried Lulu, hurrying out through the hall to the front door, the others following.

To her surprise not only the Fairview carriage, but those of Ion and the Oaks were there on the drive, and her young friends Eva, Rosie, Lora, Sydney, Maud, and several others, all in holiday attire, came tripping in with merry greetings and good wishes.

And each one had a little birthday gift for her — flowers, fruit, confectionery, or some trifle — the work of her own hands.

"Oh, girls," cried Lulu, "I'm delighted to see you! It's a surprise party for me. I wanted a birthday party ever so much, but I didn't know I was going to have it."

"But Eva and I knew," said Rosie. "It was told us as a great secret, and we've been in ever such a hurry to see how surprised and glad you'd be."

The weather was delightful, the grounds were looking very lovely and inviting, everyone preferred them to the house, and the day was spent in out of door sports, in some of which the captain joined, Max taking part also.

At dinnertime a table was set in a beautiful grove not far from the dwelling and spread with abundance of dainty and delicious viands, as the children were unanimously of the opinion that it would be far more pleasant to eat there than within doors.

When their appetites had been fully satisfied, the captain gathered them about him in the shade of a beautiful magnolia and entertained them with stories of seafaring life and foreign lands.

Then their sports were renewed.

They went into the bit of woods belonging to the estate and played "Hide and Seek" and "Poor Puss Wants a Corner" among the trees.

The captain and Violet had left them for a time, having been summoned to the house to receive some callers, when a serious accident happened.

Rosie gave a sudden, piercing shriek and cried that a rattlesnake had bitten her. At the same instant several of the girls and Max also saw it gliding away through the grass. He seized a large stone, ran after and attacked it, while the frightened girls gathered round Rosie asking, "Where, where are you bitten?"

"On my ankle!" she cried. "Oh, oh, what shall I do? Oh, somebody run to the house and ask them to send for Cousin Arthur as quickly as they can. Oh, no, but I'll die before they can get him here! So it's no use."

But before her sentence was half finished several of them were flying toward the mansion.

Lulu was not one of them. She had dropped down on her knees beside Rosie, who was now seated on the grass, crying and wringing her hands. Without a word she rapidly tore off Rosie's slipper and stocking, tied a handkerchief tightly round her leg, just above the wound, then put her lips to it and sucked away the poison.

"Oh, Lu, Lu, don't! It'll kill you!" cried Gracie in great horror.

"Oh, Lu, how good of you! But how can you bear to do it?" sobbed Rosie.

But Lulu did not stop to answer either of them.

Meantime the cries and screams of the frightened girls had brought everybody running to see what was amiss. Among them was Dr. Conly himself.

He was a frequent visitor to Woodburn, being strongly attached to his Cousin Violet, a great admirer of the captain, and quite fond of all the children. He had stopped in passing but a moment before the alarm.

"A rattlesnake! A rattlesnake! It has bitten Rosie!" was the terrible announcement of the girls whom he and the captain met on the threshold. Both gentlemen hastened at the top of their speed in the direction of the woods, guided to the spot by the continued cries of the children there, and knowing that the least delay might prove fatal.

They found Lulu still sucking the wound.

"Brave girl! It is the best thing that could possibly have been done!" exclaimed the doctor. "I trust and believe that you have saved her life."

Max came panting up. "We've killed it!" he said. "Ajax came to my assistance with a pitchfork! Oh, Rosie, are you badly hurt?"

Rosie only sobbed in reply. She was thoroughly frightened. She didn't want to die and was very much afraid the bite might prove to be fatal.

"I think you may stop now, Lulu," the doctor said, and the little girl rose from her knees looking very white and faint.

Her father caught her in his arms and carried her away to a rustic seat a few yards distant, while the doctor took charge of Rosie.

"Papa, I feel very—very—sick," faltered Lulu, laying her head on his shoulder. "Do you think— it'll kill me?"

"No, my dear, brave darling," he answered in moved tones. "The poison does no harm taken into the stomach, although it is deadly when it gets into the blood. I think you are sick from the mere thought of having swallowed it. But how did you come to know so well just what to do?"

"I read it once, papa, and I thought, 'Now I'll remember that,' because Gracie or Max might get bitten, and though I'd hate dreadfully, dreadfully to do it, I'd be glad to save their lives."

"My own darling! My dear, brave, self-forgetful, little daughter!" he said, holding her close to his heart. "You have made your father a proud and happy man today! Proud and glad that his dear little girl has shown such presence of mind and willingness to sacrifice herself for another!"

She looked up with a flash of exceeding joy in her eyes, then dropping her head on his shoulder again, burst into a perfect storm of tears and sobs.

He knew it was simply the reaction from the excitement of what she had just gone through and merely continued to hold her in a close embrace, soothing her with words of love and the tenderest of caresses.

Then when she had grown comparatively calm, he half led, half carried her back to the house and made her lie down on a sofa.

Rosie had been carried to an upper room, put to bed, and was being cared for by the doctor, Violet, and her mother, who had just come to Woodburn, intending to spend the evening and take Rosie home. She had been met at the entrance with the news of the little girl's injury.

Gracie had followed her father and was close beside him when he laid Lulu down.

"Papa," she sobbed, "is—is Lu hurt, too? Oh, I was afraid she'd be killed doing that for Rosie!"

"No, dear, she is not hurt," he answered, drawing the little weeper into his arms.

"Then what makes her look so white?"

"She feels a little sick, but she will get over it very soon, I hope. Come in, my dears," seeing the other young guests gathered about the door. "This seems an unfortunate ending to your day's pleasure."

They came in very quietly, looking both sober and subdued, asking how Lulu was, and receiving the same replay the captain had given to Gracie.

"Where is Max?" asked the captain, but nobody there knew.

"I think it was very brave of him to run after that snake and kill it," remarked Maud Dinsmore.

Just then the boy appeared at the door. He was half-breathless with excitement.

"The men have found another and killed it, too," he announced.

"Ah, I am glad to hear it!" said his father. "It was doubtless the mate of the first one, and now we may hope we will be troubled with no more of them."

"What's the matter with you, Lulu? You weren't bitten, too, were you?" asked Max in sudden alarm, as he caught sight of the pale face on the sofa pillow.

"No," said his father, and several young voices began an eager recital of what Lulu had so unselfishly done for Rosie.

Max's eyes sparkled. "I'm proud of you, Lu," he said, going to the side of her couch.

"'Twasn't much—anybody could have done it," she returned, coloring and looking embarrassed.

"But 'tisn't everybody that would," Max said. "So dreadfully disagreeable, not to say dangerous. Wasn't it dangerous, papa?"

"No, unless she had a scratch or sore about her mouth, which I think she has not," he replied with a somewhat startled, anxious look at Lulu.

"No, papa, not a bit," she said, and his countenance expressed obvious relief.

"I must go and inquire about Rosie," he said, rising and turning to leave the room. "But I shall be back again in a few minutes," he added, catching an entreating look from Lulu.

When he returned Violet was with him. She went quickly to Lulu's couch, and bending down over her, kissed her several times, saying in tremulous tones, "You dear, dear child. How brave and self-forgetful you were! We all think you have saved Rosie's life. The doctor has strong hopes that she will get over it."

"I am glad to have been able to do it, Mamma Vi," returned Lulu, putting her arms affectionately round Violet's neck.

There was no more merry-making for that day. Tea was ready presently and shortly after leaving the table, all the young guests, except Rosie and Eva, took their departure. Max, Eva, Lulu, and Gracie spent a quiet evening together. Rather wearied with the excitement of the day, all were ready to go early to bed.

Gracie, being the feeblest, was the most weary of all. Her father carried her up the stairs and into her room. He did not leave her till her head rested upon her pillow, and the sweet blue eyes had closed in sweet slumber.

He was just turning to go, when the door leading into the children's sitting room softly opened and Lulu looked up at him with entreating eyes.

He answered the look with a smile and a nod of acquiescence, as he moved noiselessly across the floor in her direction.

"You know I could not do without my goodnight talk on my birthday, dear papa," she said as he joined her, and taking possession of an easy chair, he drew her to his knee.

"No, certainly not," he answered, caressing her. "I planned to make it a happy day for you, my darling, but I could not foresee the danger that met you and your mates in the woods."

"No, papa, and it was a very happy day till then. Oh, I am so sorry for poor Rosie!"

"So am I, yet feel most thankful that the bitten one was not either of my beloved children. I think, too, that Rosie will recover, and at some not very distant day will be none the worse for what has occurred.

"And the presence of mind, the promptness to act in an emergency, and the unselfish kindness shown by my dear eldest daughter are a very great gratification to me."

"Papa," she said, her eyes shining with joy, "it is sweeter than the sweetest music to hear such words from you."

He caressed her silently for a moment. Then he said, "You have made a good beginning of this New Year of yours. I hope, my darling, you will go on being cheerful, pleasant-tempered, and obedient, doing any and every noble, unselfish deed for which you may have opportunity. These anniversaries are milestones on the road we are traveling. At each one we should make a determined effort to press forward with redoubled energy toward the goal the Bible sets for us—to forsake evil ways and to seek to be the children of God, honoring and serving Him more and more faithfully as we draw nearer and nearer our journey's end. 'The path of the just is as the shining light that shineth more and more unto the perfect day!' Ah, my dear child, the longing desire of my heart is to see you treading that path."

CHAPTER
EIGHTEENTH

GRANDMA ELSIE SAT by the bedside gazing with much motherly solicitude upon the sleeping face of her youngest daughter. She had sat thus for hours, sending up silent petitions on the child's behalf, till now night's shadows had fled away. The sun had risen above the treetops, and a gentle breeze was stirring the lace curtains at the windows and wafting through the room delicious scents from the garden below.

Presently Rosie moved slightly, opened her eyes, and looked up into the sweet face bending over her.

"Mamma, I—I'm not going to die?" she queried in low, tremulous tones.

"I trust not. Cousin Arthur thinks the danger is past. My darling, thank God, as your mother does, for your spared life and devote it to His service."

"I—I mean to, mamma. It was Lulu—Lulu whom I have sometimes treated so unkindly—who saved my life." With the words, tears rolled down Rosie's cheeks. "Mamma, I want to see and thank her."

"I will ask her to come to you after awhile," Elsie said. "I think she has not eaten her breakfast yet. It is early, and I have not heard the bell."

There was a gentle tap at the door. Violet had come to ask how her young sister was. Lulu was with her on the same errand.

"Better. I trust the danger is past," Grandma Elsie said. "Come in and speak to her. Lulu, dear child, how shall I ever thank you? Cousin Arthur says we owe Rosie's life to you."

"I owe you a great deal more, dear Grandma Elsie," responded the little girl, returning with ardent affection the warm embrace Mrs. Travilla had given her along with her grateful words.

"Lu?" called Rosie feebly from the bed. "Oh, Lu, come here, won't you?"

Lulu complied at once, saying, "I'm ever so glad you are better, Rosie."

"If it hadn't been for you I'd have been dead before this," returned Rosie with a burst of tears. "And, oh, Lu, I didn't deserve it of you. I want to kiss you, if you'll let me."

"Of course I will," Lulu returned, bending down to give and receive a caress.

Rosie put her arms round Lulu's neck, sobbing, "I haven't always been kind to you, Lu. Please say that you forgive me."

"Indeed I do, but don't let us talk any more about it. I'm ever so glad to have had a chance to do you a kindness, though it wasn't so very much after all."

"Yes. Yes it was! I don't believe I could have done it for anybody, and it saved my life. I love you dearly now, Lu, and I always shall. I've been a real Pharisee in my feelings toward you, but now I know and acknowledge that you are far better and nobler than I."

"No, no," said Lulu. "You are not passionate or willful as I am. I wish I had as good a temper as yours, Rosie."

"You are both dear and lovable children," interposed Grandma Elsie. "Both have faults, and both virtues. We all love you both and hope that hereafter there will be no lack of affection between you. But Rosie must not talk any more now, I think."

"Then I'll run away, Grandma Elsie, till I'm told Rosie is able to see me again," said Lulu, and she hastened from the room.

In the hall she met Evelyn in a unusual state of unwonted excitement.

"Oh, Lu!" she exclaimed. "What now could you have supposed happened at Fairview last night? I have just had a note from Uncle Lester. He says a second little boy has come to them, and they call him Eric, for my dear father. Isn't it nice of them?"

"Oh, another baby?" cried Lulu. "That's nice! Eric's a pretty name, too. And your father was Uncle Lester's brother. I should think they would name the baby for him."

"I wonder," pursued Evelyn, "if Grandma Elsie and Aunt Vi have heard the news?"

"I don't believe they have," said Lulu. "But the breakfast bell rang a minute ago and here they come. So you can tell them."

"No," said Evelyn, "Grandpa Dinsmore and the doctor are coming up the stairs, and they will tell them. Let's wait a minute and see how they look when they hear it."

They stood aside as the gentlemen passed with a pleasant, "Good morning, little girls," then lingered to witness the interview between them and the two ladies.

Mr. Horace Dinsmore kissed his daughter and granddaughter, inquiring how Rosie was.

The doctor shook hands with both, saying, "We bring you pleasant tidings," and signed to his uncle to tell them.

"Elsie, my dear daughter," the old gentleman said with a smile, "you have a second grandson, I a second great-grandson."

"Ah, another treasure! Another cause for great gratitude to the Giver of all good!" she exclaimed. "And Elsie? Is she doing well?"

"As well as possible," answered the doctor. "And the child is as fine a fellow as ever you saw."

Both Eva and Rosie stayed the week out at Woodburn, and the captain made it a holiday time for all his children. They all enjoyed themselves very much in a quiet way.

Lulu and Gracie were urgently invited to make a return visit to both Ion and Fairview. Their father gave permission for the next week to be spent by them at the former place, partly promising, too, that some weeks later they should be allowed to pay a visit of equal length to the other, if they wished.

Gracie was doubtful about wanting to go, but Lulu seemed delighted with the prospect. But something happened to prevent her from going to Ion at the appointed time.

On the morning of that day, the captain came to the children's sitting room with a face even brighter and happier than its wont.

"Lulu," he said, when he had kissed his little girls good morning, "go up to Max's door and tell him I want him. He will find me here, but if he is not yet quite ready for breakfast, I will wait a little for him."

Lulu obeyed instantly, wondering, but asking no questions, and returned immediately, bringing Max with her.

The captain held out his hand to his son with a pleasant, "Good morning, my boy."

"Good morning, papa," returned Max, putting his hand into that of his father and looking up into his face inquiringly and with some little surprise.

"Lu said you wanted me."

"Yes," the captain said. "I want you all to come with me to the nursery." And taking a hand of each of the little girls, he led the way, Max following, and all three wondering what it meant.

Little Elsie lay sleeping in her crib, but another crib was there. To that one the captain went, and, turning down the cover with gentle hand, brought to view a tiny pink head, face, and doubled-up fist.

"Here, Max," he said with a joyous smile, "is a brother for you, for Lulu and Gracie, too," he added, glancing from one to the other.

"I've a warm welcome for him," laughed Max, bending down to look more closely at the tiny face. "You couldn't have given me a present I'd like better, papa. But dare a fellow touch the little chap?"

"Better not, just yet," said his father. "But what have his sisters to say about him?" turning to them.

"I'm ever so glad to see him," said Gracie.

"He's a darling, and I mean to love him dearly," said Lulu.

There was no cloud on her brow as at the news of Elsie's birth. There was no fear in her heart that her father would love her less for the advent of this new, little treasure.

"Papa," said Gracie, "are you just as much his father as ours?"

"Just as much, daughter, no more no less," answered the captain, laying his hand tenderly on her head and smiling down into her eyes.

"So now we have two brothers. That's nice!" she remarked with satisfaction.

"I have but one," said Max.

"We will go down to breakfast now," said the captain, carefully covering up the babe again. "I directed that the bell should not be rung for fear of disturbing your mamma, who is asleep." He led the way from the room, moving with care so as to make no noise.

"How strange it seems without mamma," remarked Gracie as they took their usual places at the table.

"Oh, papa," cried Lulu, "mayn't I sit in Mamma Vi's place and pour the coffee?"

"You may try," he said smiling kindly upon her. "That post of honor should be yours as my eldest daughter when there is no lady relative present. Grandma Elsie is in the house, but she also is lying down just now for a little rest and sleep."

Lulu felt proud of the permission and acquitted herself of the duties of her new position quite to her own and her father's satisfaction. He praised her warmly.

She colored with pleasure, but then with a wistful look into his eyes, she asked, "Are we to go to Ion today, papa, just the same as if Mamma Vi hadn't been taken sick?"

"Yes, if you want to," he said. "Her illness need make no difference."

"But won't you be lonely without us, papa?"

"No doubt I shall miss my dear little daughters," he replied with an affectionate look first at her, then at Gracie. "But it will give me much pleasure to think that you are enjoying yourselves."

"I'd rather stay at home if you need me, papa."

"I quite appreciate the offer, dear child," he said. "I shall do very well and perhaps enjoy you all the more when you get back; so go and enjoy yourself."

"I don't believe you need worry about papa being lonely without you and Gracie, Lu," remarked Max, a little teasingly. "You forget that he will still have more than half his children at home, at least when I am here."

"Why, so he will!" she exclaimed, as if struck by a new and not altogether pleasant thought. "But the others are only babies!"

"The little fellow won't amount to much for company, I suppose," laughed Max. "But Elsie can afford one a great deal of sport sometimes, can't she, papa?"

"Yes," answered the captain. Then to Lulu, "A week will soon pass to an old man like your father, my child."

"Papa, you're not old at all! I won't have you called old," she cried indignantly.

He laughed at that. "All the same, a week will be a short time to me," he said.

"Papa, what's our new brother's name?" asked Gracie.

"Edward, for his mother's father."

"Another little Ned," remarked Max.

"You are not an only son any longer, Maxie," said Lulu.

"Well, what need I care about that?" returned the lad. "Papa won't prize me any the less, and I've always coveted a brother."

"But you're so much older that he won't be any company for you," pursued Lulu, as if bent on making Max discontented and jealous.

"No," sighed Max, putting on a long face. "I presume he'll regard me as quite an old man when he's old enough to think anything about such matters. But I mean to be very good to the little chap, anyway, and see that no big fellow imposes on him," he added, brightening.

"I trust you will be a father to him, Max, in case anything happens to me," said the captain with grave earnestness.

"Yes, sir, I'll do the very best I can," returned Max, catching his father's tone.

How those two sentences came back to the boy an hour later, as if they had been prophetic.

The little girls, especially Lulu, had built great expectations upon this proposed visit to Ion. It was their old home, and a beautiful place.

Rosie was now disposed to be very kind, and Evelyn was to be her guest also for the week. She had lately received a pony from her uncle and aunt, and she would have it with her, riding it from Fairview. Lulu and Gracie were to have theirs with them also, so that each of the four little girls would be provided with a steed of her own, and they had planned to take a number of pleasant rides with Max as their escort.

He would not be at Ion all the time, but he proposed to have his pony carry him over every day that he might give the girls the benefit of his protecting care when needed. He felt himself almost a man in looking forward to taking so great a responsibility.

Immediately after family worship, the captain said cheerily to the children, "You may get yourselves ready now, my dears. I am going to ride over to Union but will be back within an hour if nothing happens to prevent and will take you to Ion myself."

"I have no preparations to make for Ion, papa," said Max. "Mayn't I ride Rex into the village along with you?"

"I shall be glad of your company, my boy," was the kindly reply, and they went out to the veranda together—father and son.

Ajax was just leading Rex and a larger horse, both ready saddled and bridled. The latter was a fiery steed, and not yet well broken—a recent purchase.

"You seem to have misunderstood your orders today, Ajax," remarked his master with some sternness. "I did not intend to ride this horse this morning, but bade you saddle Lightfoot. However, as I am in some haste, I will ride Thunderer into the village. But see that you have Lightfoot ready for me on my return, for this fellow would not be safe to go with the young ladies on their ponies." With the last word he sprang into the saddle, but the horse instantly began to rear and plunge in a frightful manner. In another moment the captain was lying motionless on the ground, while Thunderer dashed with lightning speed across the lawn, cleared the hedge at a bound, and disappeared from sight.

Max, who had not yet mounted his pony, ran to his father, and throwing himself on the grass beside him, lifted his head, rested it on his knee, and began to loosen his necktie.

"The doctor!" he gasped, addressing the group of frightened servants gathered around. "He's upstairs. Call him, but don't let Mamma Vi know. It would kill her."

But he had hardly spoken before the doctor was at his side. Lulu was there, too—both having seen the accident from the upper windows.

The captain's eyes were closed. He neither moved nor spoke, and he scarcely seemed to breathe. Both Max and Lulu thought him dead, and though they spoke not a word, nor made any outcry, their faces were full of agony.

"He lives," Arthur hastened to say. "But the fall has stunned him."

Under his direction, the captain was gently lifted from the ground, carried into one of the lower rooms of the mansion, and laid upon a couch, while Christine came hurrying in, bringing restoratives and whatever else seemed likely to be needed.

Arthur ordered everyone else out of the room but Max and Lulu, who had stationed themselves at the foot of the couch where they could watch their father's face. They stood still with such entreating looks that he had not the heart to enforce his order so far as they were concerned.

"You two may stay if you will be perfectly quiet and still," he said.

Max had his arms about his sister, and she was clinging to him, trembling with grief and affright but uttering no sound.

"We will, doctor," the boy promised in a hoarse whisper. "Only let us stay where we can see him."

The next minute the captain sighed deeply, opened his eyes, and asked quite in his natural voice, "What has happened?"

"You were thrown," replied Arthur. "Stunned to insensibility. I hope that is all. How do you feel? Any pain anywhere?"

"Yes, a good deal in my ankle—that old hurt, you know, Doc."

The doctor examined it. "It seems to have had a terrible wrench," he said. "You are in for fully six weeks of quietude. I don't think I'll allow you to so much as move about with a crutch before the end of that time."

"A pretty hard sentence that, doctor," replied the patient between a smile and a sigh.

"We may be thankful if that is all," Arthur said, adding something in a lower tone about the possibility of internal injury.

"You cannot tell yet?" was the response in an inquiring tone.

"Not certainly. I am strongly in hopes time will prove that there has been nothing more serious than the wrench of the ankle and the jar to the whole system—quite enough, to be sure."

"Quite! Ah, Max and Lulu," as his eye fell upon them. "What, crying, my dear children? You should rather rejoice that your father is alive and able to speak to you."

"But you are in pain, papa," sobbed Lulu. "Oh, I wish I could help you bear it!"

"Ah, my darling, I shall expect a good deal of help from you and the rest while serving out the doctor's hard sentence," he said with an attempt at pleasantry that was almost a failure, his features contracting with pain as he spoke.

"No more talking for the present," said Arthur.

"My wife—does she know? Keep this from her as long as you can," said the captain.

"Of course," returned the doctor. "It will not be possible to conceal from her that something has happened to you. I hope to be able to tell her shortly that it is nothing more serious than a sprained ankle."

"Max, you may take your sisters to Ion, if—" began the captain, turning his eyes on his son.

But Lulu interrupted with an earnest protest, "Oh, papa, please don't say we must go! I can't bear to! I want to stay at home and nurse you!"

"So you shall, dear child, but go now and take the air for awhile."

"Yes," said the doctor, who was busily engaged in dressing the wounded limb. "You three may as well ride over to Ion with the news."

"And come back as soon as you please," added their father. "Tell Gracie not to be distressed. Papa is not nearly so badly hurt as he might have been."

"Oh, please let me stay right here beside you, papa," pleaded Lulu.

"No, Lu," said Dr. Conly with mingled authority and playfulness. "I shall not allow you to be installed as nurse here unless you hold yourself in readiness to obey order. And I know the captain will agree with me that you must take exercise in the open air every day."

"Certainly she must," her father assented.

Then turning to Max, "My son, I shall have to entrust my errand to the village to you. You know what it was. Take your sisters to Ion first, then do your errand, and call for them as you come back."

"Yes, sir, I will," answered the lad promptly, moving toward the door as he spoke.

Lulu was about to accompany him but turned suddenly, sprang past the doctor, and dropping on her knees by the side of the couch, seized her father's hand. She lifted it to her lips and kissed it with passionate fervor.

"My little girl's love is a great comfort to me," he said in a low tone. "But go now, darling. You may come to me again when you return from Ion—unless the doctor forbids."

"Which I think the doctor will not," said Arthur. "Now run along like a good child."

Max found Gracie in the hall crying as if her heart would break.

"Oh, Maxie, tell me 'bout papa!" she sobbed. "Is he—is he 'most—'most killed?"

"No, Gracie, he knows everything and is able to talk. His ankle is badly hurt and pains him a good deal," answered Max, speaking as cheerfully as he could to relieve the fears of his little sister.

"Oh, can I go and see him?" she asked.

"No, not just now. The doctor is dressing his ankle, and papa says we must ride out for air and exercise, go over to Ion for just a little while, and when we come back, I think they'll let you see him."

This moment Lulu joined them. "Don't cry, Gracie," she entreated, taking her in her arms. "You and I are going to nurse papa and make him well again."

"You may as well include me in that. I'm the eldest," said Max. "We will all three do everything we can for him. Now go and get your things on—the ponies are at the door waiting—and we'll ride over to Ion at once. That's papa's orders, and I know he would say the first and best thing is to be obedient if we want to make him happy and help him to get well."

"Yes, we will," said Gracie. "But, oh," she sobbed, "it's so very dreadful that papa is hurt so!"

"But it might have been a great deal worse, Gracie," said her brother with a tremble in his voice. "I thought at first that papa was dead. He was so still and white, and he didn't know anything at all."

"Max," exclaimed Lulu, sobbing bitterly as she spoke, "I wish you'd take your gun along, and if we meet Thunderer, you could shoot him down dead."

"Why, no, Lu! I wouldn't dare do such a thing without papa's leave. The horse belongs to him and is worth a great deal of money, so I wouldn't have any right to kill him. Besides, papa has forbidden me to ever handle my gun when you girls are by, because accidents with firearms happen so often, even while they're in the hands of men."

"Well, I just hope he's broken his neck before this, jumping a hedge or something," cried Lulu fiercely. "Come, Gracie, we'll go upstairs now and put on our hats and habits.

Chapter
Nineteenth

A MESSENGER HAD been dispatched early that morning from Woodburn to Ion with the news of the arrival of Violet's son. Then Zoe and Rosie had ridden over to Fairview with the tidings and brought Evelyn back with them.

They were all three on the veranda now, waiting and watching for the coming of Captain Raymond or Max with Lulu and Gracie.

"What on earth can be keeping them?" exclaimed Rosie at length. "They must be greatly taken up with that new-comer — my third nephew. How nice and funny it seemed at first to be an aunt, but it's quite an old story now."

"And I can never be one," remarked Eva, between a sigh and a smile. "Though I confess the thought never struck me before now."

"Yes, you can, the same way that I am," said Zoe. "Marry a man with plenty of brothers and sisters, and you'll likely find it easy enough."

"Oh, here they come at last!" cried Rosie. "They're turning in at the gates. It's Max that's with them, not the captain. I never can remember to call him brother as he wants me to."

"Somehow they don't seem a very merry party," remarked Evelyn as the trio drew near. "They don't call to us or wave their hands or anything."

"No," said Zoe, examining them critically through an opera glass. "There is something dejected in the droop of their figures, and the girls have certainly been crying. Can it be that they are so distressed over the new arrival?"

"No, I am sure not," exclaimed Eva. "How could they be? A baby is the sweetest thing in the world, I think!"

"So do I," said Zoe. "And Max and Gracie were delighted when little Elsie was born."

"And Lu, I am sure, loves her dearly now," said Rosie. "No, it can't be that. Oh," with sudden affright, "what if Vi is very ill?" She ran hastily down the steps just as the ponies were reined in beside them.

"What's the matter?" she asked breathlessly. "Why are you so late? And what have you been crying about? Oh, don't tell me that—that anything is very wrong with Vi!"

"No, the doctor says she is doing well," replied Max, alighting and beginning to assist the now bitterly sobbing Gracie from the saddle.

Lulu slipped easily from hers to the ground. "It's papa," she said tremulously and with streaming eyes. "Thunderer threw him, and he's badly hurt. We're not going to stay. We want to nurse him ourselves, but he said we must come and tell you all about it. Then we could come back."

They had all three come up onto the veranda by this time. Mr. and Mrs. Dinsmore had joined the little group, and questions, condolences, and exclamations of both sorrow and dismay were poured out from the listeners in rapid succession.

"How did it happen? Where is he injured? What does the doctor say?"

"Oh, the dear, good captain!" cried Zoe. "It does seem too bad it should have happened to him!"

"I'm very fond of him, and as sorry as I can be for him and Vi, too. It'll most kill her not to be able to go to him and nurse him," said Rosie.

But Evelyn only clasped Lulu in her arms and wept with her.

"I really do hope—I think the doctor does, too," said Max, when the excitement had calmed down a little, "that papa has received no permanent injury, though he'll have to suffer a good deal for weeks with that wrenched ankle. I must go to the village now," he added. "I am to call for my sisters as I come back."

With that he bowed a polite adieu, ran down the steps, mounted his pony, and rode away.

"Max is growing very manly," remarked Zoe, gazing admiringly after him. "He's quite the little gentleman, but he always was that ever since I have known him."

Grandma Rose took the weeping Gracie into her kind arms. "You are quite worn out with your grief, dearie," she said. "You must lie down and rest till Max comes for you again." And with that she led her into the house.

Evelyn had drawn Lulu to a seat, and with her arm round her waist and her hand clasping Lulu's, was trying to comfort her.

"Don't cry, dear Lu," she said. "Your father is left to you, and he is brave and patient. He will bear his pain well, while it will be such sweet work to wait on him and nurse him."

"Yes, indeed it will," said Lulu, wiping her eyes. "Oh, if I could bear the pain for him!"

"He wouldn't let you if you could," said Eva.

"No, not he," said Zoe. "He's quite too fond of his children not to prefer suffering himself, rather than to let them suffer."

"That is quite true, I know," assented Lulu. Then with a sigh, "We were all so happy this morning, before—before papa's accident, and so glad over the new baby. I hardly wanted to come away—though I looked forward so to this visit and expected such a pleasant time and so much fun. I tried to get papa to say he needed me at home to keep him from being lonely, with Mamma Vi sick, but he wouldn't. He didn't want either Gracie or me to be disappointed over the loss of the visit."

"But can't you come anyhow?" asked Rosie, hospitably. "There are plenty of people there to nurse and wait on your papa."

"Oh, Rosie, I couldn't bear to be away from him when he is suffering! And I'm 'most sure he'd rather have me to wait on him than anybody else—except Mamma Vi, of course. I thank you, all the same, though, for your kindness in asking me."

"You needn't," Rosie returned. "It's almost pure selfishness, for I expected to enjoy your company very much."

At that Lulu's face lighted up with pleasure for the moment. It was so nice, she thought, that at last Rosie had become really fond of her.

Max wasted no time doing his errand, and he was back again at Ion sooner than anyone expected to see him. But Lulu and Gracie were ready and eager to go home.

On their arrival at Woodburn the doctor came out to help them dismount and with so cheerful a face that their hopes rose.

"How is papa? May we go to him?" all three asked eagerly.

"Doing very well. There's not much amiss with him, I think, except the sprained ankle. And the brave, patient man, such as he, will not make much of that. Yes, you may go to him. If you behave well, as I have no doubt you will, your presence will be a comfort rather than an injury," replied the doctor. Then he added laughingly, "Odd as it may seem, he is certainly very fond of you all."

Hardly waiting to hear the end of the sentence, they hastened to avail themselves of the permission.

The captain was in great pain, but he lay with his eyes on the door, his ears attentive for the sound of childish footsteps. As his three children appeared at the threshold, his face lit up with a welcoming smile.

"Ah, my darlings, I am glad to see you," he said. "Come to me, all of you," extending his hand. "I want a kiss and a loving word from each."

They waited for no second invitation but ran to him, putting their arms about him and half-smothering him with caresses mingled with smiles and tears. They each poured out assurances of their ardent love and sympathy in his sufferings.

"Ah!" he said, noting the traces of tears on their cheeks and about their eyes. "It grieves me to see how your young hearts have been wrung on my account! Gracie, dear, you look worn out. Max, help her upstairs. She must lie down and rest.

"Lulu, daughter, you may go along and change your riding habit for a house dress. When you have seen Gracie comfortably established in her bed, come back and be papa's little nurse.

"Max, when Gracie needs you no longer, come and report to me about the errand I trusted to you."

"Yes, sir, I will," returned Max, taking Gracie's hand and leading her away, while Lulu lingered a moment to give their father another hug and kiss. She said joyfully, "Thank you ever so much, dear papa! I am so glad I may be your little nurse! I shall just love to wait on you and do everything I can to help you to forget your pain. Oh, papa, if only I could bear it for you!"

"My dear, loving little daughter," he said with emotion, holding her in a close embrace, "it would be far worse to me to see you suffer than to bear the pain myself. Don't be distressed for me, my child. It is no more than I can very well bear, especially remembering those sweet Bible words: 'We know that all things work together for good to them that love God,' and that my kind heavenly Father will not suffer me to have one pang that is not needed to make me fit to dwell with Him at last."

"Papa," she said, gazing wonderingly into his eyes, "it does seem to me that you are as good as you can be now, so I don't see why you should ever have any pain or trouble at all."

"'The Lord seeth not as man seeth; for man looketh on the outward appearance, but the Lord looketh on the heart,'" he quoted.

"My little daughter can't see her father's heart, but God does. And though He sees love there for Him and an earnest desire to live to His honor and glory, He sees also remains of the old evil nature born in us all. That has to be taken entirely away before we can be fit for heaven—so in His great love and kindness He sends trouble and trial to root it out.

"'Whom the Lord loveth He correcteth; even as a father the son in whom he delighteth.'"

"Or the daughter," murmured Lulu thoughtfully. "Yes, I see how it is that you punish me to cure me of my faults, even though you love me very much."

"Because I love you very much," he corrected. "It would often be much easier and more agreeable to me to let them pass unnoticed. But go now, my child. Gracie will be wanting you."

She had scarcely gone when Max returned, and sitting down by his father's side, he proceeded to give a satisfactory report of what he had been doing in the village.

There were some improvements in progress on the estate to which the captain strongly desired to give personal oversight, but his injuries now made this impossible, unless by bringing them to a halt till he should be able to get about again.

Fortunately, however, he had all along talked freely with Max of his plans and purposes, giving the lad a thorough understanding of them. Max was a bright boy quite capable of comprehending his father's explanations. Also, it was delightful to him to be taken into that father's confidence and treated by him as one whose opinion was worth having and who was to some extent a joint proprietor with himself.

"Max," said the captain with a look of fatherly pride and confidence that made the boy's heart throb with pleasure, "you will have to be my man of business now, reporting the progress of the workmen to me, taking my orders to them, and seeing that they are obeyed."

"Will you trust me, papa?" cried the boy delightedly. "I'm sure it's very good of you!"

"I am very glad to have a son whom I can trust," was the smiling and kind rejoinder. "I have entire confidence in you, and as you are more fully acquainted with my plans and wishes than any one else, you are the very one I prefer before all others to see them carried out."

He then went on to give some directions in regard to the work for that day.

Before he had finished, both the doctor and Lulu had returned to the room.

"Attending to affairs in spite of everything, captain?" said the doctor. "I should have supposed you were suffering enough with that injured ankle to forget all about the improvements you are making on the place."

"I prefer to try to forget pain in interesting myself about something else," returned the captain, suppressing a groan and forcing himself to speak lightly.

Arthur was changing the dressing on the wounded limb, and Lulu was standing beside her father, her hand in his and her eyes, full of both love and sympathy, fixed upon his face.

"Dear papa, are you in very much pain?" she asked. "Oh, I am so sorry for you! I wanted Max to take his gun and shoot Thunderer, but he wouldn't without your leave."

"Quite right," was the quick rejoinder. "By the way, I had utterly forgotten the horse. Do you know what has become of him?"

"He jumped over the fence and ran away, papa," said Lulu.

"But was pursued and brought back," added Arthur. "He is in his stall in the stable now, somewhat quieted down by his race of several miles and the journey back again."

"Papa," cried Lulu vehemently, "I wish you would have him killed, because he deserves it, and I'm afraid he'll kill you someday, if you don't. Doctor, don't you think it would be best?"

"Possibly, your father may be a better judge of that than either you or I, my little girl," was the reply. "I am inclined to suspect the groom may have been a worst culprit than the horse. Perhaps before being brought from the stable, Thunderer had been subjected to cruel and irritating treatment, which put him in a passion and led him to throw his rider without waiting to make sure that it was he who was to blame."

Lulu's heightened color and her downcast eyes seemed to indicate that she suspected the doctor of intending his remarks to have some personal application for her.

"Do horses get into passions?" she asked.

"They have feelings and tempers pretty much like human creatures," returned the doctor. "And are certainly more excusable than humans when indulging a fit of rage."

"Then I ought to have a good deal of charity for Thunderer," remarked Lulu with a sigh. "But, papa, I do hope you'll never mount him again. Won't you promise not to?"

"I promise not to for six weeks to come," answered the captain laughingly, as he squeezed her hand and looked fondly into her eyes. "Don't you think she'll make a careful nurse, doctor?"

"A capital one when she has gained experience."

Lulu's eyes sparkled.

"I mean to get that as fast as I can," she said.

Both gentlemen laughingly said, "How?"

"By nursing you, papa," she answered. "I shall watch everything the doctor and Christine do for you, so that very soon I'll be able to do it for you all by myself."

"Is she not a dear child?" her father said, passing his arm around her as she stood by his couch and gazing into her face with eyes shining with love. "She gave up the week of holiday at Ion that she had been looking forward to for so long in order that she might wait upon and comfort her father in his pain."

"Ah, it is an old saying that love begets love," the doctor remarked, smiling on her also. "And I think an affectionate parent is quite apt to have affectionate children."

"I don't deserve any praise for it," Lulu said, though blushing with pleasure even as she spoke. "Because I prefer to be here with papa."

"But a selfish child, who thought only of pleasing herself, would not prefer it," the doctor said, regarding her approvingly.

"I want to begin my work at once," said Lulu. "What can I do for you now, papa?"

"You may bring me a glass of ice water and a fan," he answered. She obeyed with a cheerful alacrity that proved the sincerity of her professed desire to do something for him.

CHAPTER TWENTIETH

"YOU CAME FROM Violet's room just now?" the captain said inquiringly to the doctor.

"Yes, she's sleeping and has been for some hours. She knows nothing yet of your accident."

"That is well. Do not let her be uneasy about me."

"Not if I can help it," returned Arthur with a slight smile. "She will, of course, miss you soon and demand a reason for your desertion of her. Then what can be done better than to own the truth?"

"Nothing, certainly, but make your report of my condition as favorable as you can."

"I will do that, and I can say truly that there is no reason to apprehend anything worse for either of you than an enforced separation for a few weeks — even while in the same house and almost near enough to carry on a conversation. You can exchange messages every hour of the day if you deem it desirable."

"And I can carry them for you, papa," said Lulu, returning with the ice water and fan.

"So you shall, daughter," he said, taking the glass from her hand. Then, as he returned it, "Bring me a writing desk, paper, and pencil, and I'll prepare one for you to take."

"And I may sit and fan you while you write it, mayn't I?"

"Yes, I shall be glad to have you do so."

Grandma Elsie was watching over her daughter's slumber, carefully guarding her from disturbance, and especially from any intruder who would bring the evil tidings of her husband's injury.

At length Violet woke and looked up into her mother's face with a bright, sweet smile. "I feel very comfortable," she said. "I must have slept a good while, have I not? How kind of you, dearest mamma, to watch over me so tenderly. I fear you must be fatigued, and it strikes me you look a trifle weary and troubled. Is anything wrong?" Then with a quick glance round the room, "Where is my husband?"

"Downstairs."

"I wish he would come up. Please send him word that I am awake and want to see him. He will come up at once, I know."

Elsie bent down and kissed the pale cheek before she answered.

"If you can spare me for a few minutes, I'll go and tell him myself," she said with a playful look and a smile.

"But why not send a servant, mamma dear? I don't want you tiring yourself going up and down on my errands."

"But I have a fancy for doing it this once. I've been sitting still a long while, and a little exercise will be good for me."

With that, she left the room.

She found the captain writing his note, the doctor still with him.

"Vi is awake and asking for her husband," she said. "Arthur will you come up and give her as good a report as you can with truth?"

"Certainly, dear cousin, and it need not be so bad a one as to cause her special uneasiness."

"And here is a report from the patient himself," remarked the captain, smilingly handing a slip of paper to his mother-in-law. "Don't let her be despondent over the enforced separation, mother. Remind her that it is at least a little better than if I were on a voyage that would keep us apart for six months or a year."

"That should be a comforting reflection," said Elsie. "But you are suffering, captain!" as a sudden spasm of pain caused an involuntary contraction of his brow.

"Well, yes," he replied. "But not more than can be easily endured. Make as light of it as you can to my dear wife."

They broke the sad news to Violet as gently as possible, treating the matter as of as little conse-quence as they conscientiously could, then gave her the captain's note.

It was written in a cheerful, even merry strain, which did much to remove her apprehensions. He spoke of the morning's accident as something in the nature of a repetition of the mishap that had been the means of bringing them into intimate associa-tion for weeks, till they had learned to know and love each other—a consummation for which he, at least, would have cause to be grateful all his days.

"So there was a blessing in that, love," he con-cluded. "Let us hope there will be in this also."

Violet could not, of course, fail to be distressed on her husband's account because of the pain and weariness he must inevitably suffer, and for herself that she must be so long deprived of his dear companionship. But she would not allow herself to fret—no murmur or complaint escaped her lips. She vied with him in the cheerfulness and merriment of her messages and notes, when she was well enough to obtain permission to write them.

As to the captain, while thus deprived of the society of his wife and tied down to a couch of pain, he found the greatest solace in the companionship, devoted affection, and endearments of his children.

Max came and went, doing his errands, conveying his orders to workmen and servants, and writing letters at his dictation. Gracie hung about him with pretty, loving embraces and was always glad to do any little service in her power. Little Elsie was brought to him for a short daily visit, but Lulu was his devoted nurse, seldom absent from his side during the day, except to take her meals and the daily exercise in the open air that he would not allow her to omit.

It was a dear delight to her to wait upon him and to feel that she was necessary to his comfort.

When the worst of it was over, and when he was comparatively free from pain, he had the children resume their studies. He heard recitations as he lay on his couch. Useful occupation seemed to him the best panacea for pain and the tedium of a long confinement to the house. Having his couch wheeled out to the shady veranda was for weeks the only practicable change.

His wife's relatives were kind and attentive to both her and him, making frequent friendly calls and offers of service, but his chief dependence for entertainment and constant, loving attention was upon his children.

He loved to have them gather about him at all times, but especially in the evenings when the day's duties and pleasures were over. He would have them tell him what they had seen in their walks and drives, thus teaching them to observe and describe. Also he encouraged them to talk freely of their thoughts and feelings, so winning their confidence, correcting their mistakes, and giving instruction in a way that was pleasant to both teacher and taught.

He thought much of their future in both this world and the next; how best he could prepare them to meet successfully life's trials, toils, and struggles; and how to find and to do the work intended for them. Often his heart went up in prayer to God for grace and wisdom to guide them aright.

Remembering the inspired declaration that "we must through much tribulation enter into the kingdom of God," he did not ask for exemption from trials and troubles, though his heart yearned over them at the thought of what they might be called to endure. But his request for them was that when called to pass through deep waters or fiery trials, they might ever find the eternal God their refuge underneath His Everlasting Arms. He prayed that through all their lives they might prove good soldiers of Jesus Christ, able and ready to endure hardness for Him, and that they might be kept by the power of God through faith unto salvation.

"My darlings," he would sometimes say, "I would not have you of the number of those who seek first their own ease and gratification. 'Man's chief end is to glorify God and enjoy Him forever.' Make it the aim of your lives to know, love, and serve Him—to do His work and His will, to do all in your power to bring others to Him, and He will take care of the rest."

"Papa, you love us so very much, don't you want us to have easy, pleasant times?" Gracie asked on one of those occasions.

"I do love you all dearly, and I am afraid that would be what I should choose for you if the choice were left to me," he answered. "But it is not mine, and I rejoice that it is not. God, our heavenly Father, in whose hand are all these things, loves you far better than I do and is infinite in wisdom. He will choose for you and never make a mistake."

"It makes me glad to think of that, papa," she sighed, creeping closer into his embrace, for she was leaning against his couch with his arm round her. "I am not very strong, you know, and when I hear about having to run a race and fight a battle, it seems as if I could never do it, but Jesus will help me to do both, won't He, papa?"

"He will, dear child. He says, 'In Me is thine help.' 'Happy art thou, oh, Israel: who is like unto thee, oh, people saved by the Lord. The shield of thy help, and who is the sword of thy excellency? Our soul waiteth for the Lord: He is our help and our shield.'"

"Does everybody have to run a race and fight a battle to get to heaven, papa?" queried Lulu.

"Yes, my child, there is no escaping it. We belong to a fallen race, and we are born into the world with a sinful nature that must be gotten rid of before we can enter heaven. We would not be happy in that holy place with that evil nature, even could we gain admittance there uncleansed from it. We have it to struggle against and put away with the help of God and by the application of the blood of Christ, which cleanseth from all sin. And we have the snares of the world to avoid and a warfare to wage with many spiritual foes, malignantly intent upon our ruin."

"That's just dreadful, papa!" said Lulu. "I don't see how anybody ever gets saved."

"By trusting in the Lord Jesus Christ, who is mightier than all our foes, able to save to the uttermost, and who died to redeem us."

"What does that word redeem mean, papa?"

"To buy back, to deliver from bondage, or out of the hands of justice. In our case, it is bondage to sin and Satan. It is God's justice that demands the death eternal of every sinner who is not ransomed by the blood of Christ."

"Are all the people who don't love and serve God servants to sin and Satan, papa?"

"Yes. 'Know ye not, that to whom ye yield yourselves servants to obey, his servant ye are to whom ye obey: whether of sin unto death, or of obedience unto righteousness?'

"Oh, my dear children, I cannot bear to think of any one of you being a servant to sin and Satan instead of a servant of God and Christ!"

A few moments of solemn stillness succeeded the last words. Then the captain said, "It is time for evening worship. Call in the servants, Max."

He had not once omitted the morning or evening sacrifice of prayer and praise. Though unable to kneel, he could read the Word and pray from his couch.

Firmly he had resolved, "As for me and my house, we will serve the Lord."

He had for some time seen reason to hope that Max and Gracie, young though they were, had entered that service, but not so with Lulu. Though truthful, conscientious, affectionate, and usually obedient to him, really striving to overcome her easily besetting sin and rule her own spirit, she showed no love to Christ and professed none.

He was anxious about her, and he often lifted up his heart on her behalf, for he knew that, being old enough to fully comprehend the plan of salvation, she was not safe while neglecting or refusing to come to Christ.

He noticed that she was unusually thoughtful and attentive during the short service this evening. She lingered a little behind the others, as she was wont. So, he drew her to him and held her in a close and loving embrace, asking tenderly, "My darling, when are you going to leave the service of sin and Satan for that of the dear Savior?"

"Papa," she said, hiding her face on his shoulder, "I—I can't bear to think of being Satan's servant, and—and I do mean to be a Christian some time. I—I'm not good enough yet. I've got such a bad temper, you know. And I like my own way so well that—that it does seem as if I can't keep from disobeying you once in a while.

"So I couldn't be a good kind of a Christian, and—and that's the only kind I'd want to be."

He sighed deeply. "My child," he said, "what is all that you have been saying, but your own acknowledgment that you still love and choose the service of sin?"

"I was just telling you the truth about how I feel, papa. How can I help it, if I'm made so?"

"By coming to Jesus, who saves His people from their sins. He is able to save to the uttermost, to save all from sin who will come to Him. He never saves any in their sins, and He is the only Savior—the only one who can deliver you from bondage to sin and Satan. He can take away the evil in your nature and implant the love of holiness.

"You can never conquer your love of sin without His help. You will never really grow better while you stay away from Him."

"But I'm only a little girl, papa. I think I could do it better when I'm older."

"No, it is Satan who tells you that. He knows that the longer you delay, the harder your heart will grow, and the more difficult it will be to bring it to Jesus.

"Many and many a soul has been lost by listening to Satan telling it to wait for a more convenient season and so putting off repentance till it was forever too late.

"But God's time is always now. 'Behold now is the accepted time; behold now is the day of salvation!' Come now—this hour, this moment—my dear child, and He will fulfill to you His gracious promise, 'Him that cometh unto me, I will in no wise cast out.'"

"Papa, are you ordering me?"

"No, my child, I am entreating you. Jesus entreats you, 'Son, daughter, give Me thine heart.' He says, 'Behold I stand at the door and knock; if any man hear My voice, and open the door, I will come in to him, and will sup with him and he with Me.'

"Open the door of your heart to Him now, my child, lest He should turn away and never knock there again."

"Does He ever do that, papa, before people die?" she asked in an awed tone.

"Yes. He says, 'My Spirit shall not always strive.' Of some He says, 'Ephraim is joined to his idols; let him alone,' and that sentence may go forth years before death comes. Of Esau it is said, 'He found no place of repentance, though he sought it with tears.'

> *"'There is a time, we know not when,*
> *A point we know not where,*
> *That marks the destiny of men,*
> *To glory or despair.*
> *There is a line, by us unseen,*
> *That crosses every path,*
> *The hidden boundary between*
> *God's mercy and His wrath.'"*

He paused, and shuddering and hiding her face, she murmured, "Papa, I do intend to try before very long, when I'm just a little older."

"But you may not live to be any older. Who can say that you will live to see the light of another morning? Or that the invitation may not be withdrawn? My child, the only time you are sure of is now—just now; come now."

"But how, papa?" she asked, as again he paused.

"Just as you would if you could see the Lord Jesus here in this room. It would not be difficult for you to go and kneel at His feet and ask Him to take you for His own, to wash away all your sins, and teach you to love and serve Him."

"No, papa, but—I'm afraid I—I don't want to."

"Oh," he exclaimed, "how can you help loving One who is so lovely in character? So kind, so good, so loving, so unselfish that He died the cruel death of the cross that we might be saved?

"One who has been so patient and forbearing with you all these years that you have lived in rebellion against Him and is still entreating you to come to Him and be saved!"

He paused for a reply, but none came.

"You think that you belong to me? That you are my very own?" he said inquiringly.

"Oh, yes, papa! Indeed I do!"

"You love me very much?"

"Indeed, indeed I do!"

"And you value my love?"

"Oh, papa, I don't know how I could live without it," she cried, nestling closer to him and kissing him with ardent affection.

"You look to me for protecting care? You feel safe in my arms?"

"Oh, yes, of course, papa! You would never let me be harmed."

"Not if I could help it, dear child. I would protect you with my life. But I cannot always do so. Some day, daughter, your father will have to die and leave you."

"Oh, don't, papa, don't talk of that!" she exclaimed, catching her breath with a half sob.

"I don't speak of it to distress you, my darling," he said, softly smoothing her hair. " But I want you to reflect how desirable, how necessary it is for you to secure a nearer, dearer, more powerful Friend. One who sticketh closer than a brother, whose love is deeper and stronger than a mother's, and who will never leave nor forsake you, never die. The Lord Jesus, who is all these and more, now offers you His friendship and His love. But how long He will continue the offer, none can tell. Will you not come to Him now, this moment?"

"Papa, I can't. I can't make my heart want to do it," she said despairingly.

"Make the effort, and He will help you, as He did the man with the withered hand. That man might have said, "I cannot stretch it forth. I have not been able to move it for years." But instead, he tried to obey, and Jesus gave him strength. And so will He help you to obey His call. 'Come unto me,' if you will but try to do so."

"But perhaps He doesn't mean for me to try just now, papa," she said, struggling with herself.

"No, that cannot be so. His time is always now, today—never tomorrow, or next week, or next year.

"Today, if you will hear His voice, harden not your heart as in the day of provocation.

"'Behold, now is the accepted time; behold now is the day of salvation.'

"And you will be but giving Him of His own. You are His because He made you—His because He has kept you alive all these years—His because He has bought you with His own precious blood. He has lent you to me for a time, but you belong to Him. Do not refuse Him His own, my child.

"I hope and believe that all the rest of us are walking in the straight and narrow way. Will you not come with us? Oh, how can I bear to see my daughter traveling the broad road that leads to eternal death?"

"Papa, pray for me. Ask Jesus to help me to do it just now," she sobbed, sinking to her knees beside his couch.

He laid his hand tenderly on her bowed head, and in low, earnest tomes confessed for her that she was a sinner, lost and undone without the atoning blood of Christ, that she had in herself no power and no desire to turn from sin unto holiness, that she had often rejected God's offered mercy and forgiveness and refused to accept the Savior's gracious invitation, 'Come unto Me.' Then he pleaded for her that her sins might be forgiven and blotted out for Jesus' sake so that He would take away all the evil of her nature, wash her thoroughly from her iniquity, cleanse her from her sin, and enable her to give herself wholly and unreservedly unto His service.

As his voice ceased, she followed him in a few broken sentences. "Dear Lord Jesus, I am a great sinner, just as papa has said. And, oh, I am afraid I don't want to be any better. Please make me want to, and to love to belong to Thee even more than I do to be papa's very own. I will—I do give myself to Thee. Oh, take me and make me all good—no bad at all left in me. For thine own names' sake. Amen."

For some moments there seemed a solemn stillness in the room. She was still kneeling there with her father's hand resting tenderly on her head. Then in low tremulous tones, she asked, "Papa, do you think He heard me and will take me for His?"

"I know it, my child, if you asked with your heart, as I believe you did, for He is the hearer and answerer of prayer!"

Then again he poured out an earnest supplication on her behalf, asking that she might be kept ever near the Savior's side, growing in grace and conformity to His will all the days of her life on earth, and at last be taken to dwell forever with Him in heaven.

Again a solemn hush ensued, only broken at length by Lulu's voice in a low, sweet tone. "Papa, I think He has heard our prayers. I do begin to love Him in my heart and want to be His."

"'Bless the Lord, oh my soul; and all that is within me, bless His holy name!'" exclaimed her father, his tones tremulous with emotion. Then as she rose from her kneeling posture, he drew her to his heart and held her there in a long, tender embrace ere he bade her goodnight and sent her away to her rest.

CHAPTER
TWENTY-FIRST

QUITE EARLY THE NEXT morning, fully half an hour before breakfast time, Lulu and Gracie came hand in hand and with loving greetings to the side of their father's couch.

The young faces were very bright, and looking searchingly into Lulu's, he thought it wore a sweeter expression than he had ever seen on it before.

"Papa, I am very happy this morning," she said softly, putting her arm round his neck and laying her cheek to his.

"I am very glad, my darling," he responded. "Your happiness lies very near your father's heart."

"It's because Jesus loves me, papa," she went on in low, earnest tones. "Oh, I find His love is even sweeter than yours—though that has always been so sweet to me! Oh, now I'm glad to belong to Him, and I want to serve Him all my days! It seems strange that I haven't always wanted to."

"It is passing strange," he sighed, "that it is not the joy of every human heart to belong to Him and do Him service."

"Papa, I want to be good and do everything He tells me. Do you think I shall ever be naughty again—disobedient to you—willful—passionate?"

"My dear child, to think you would not would be like expecting you to win the prize as soon as you have started to run the race—to gain the victory as soon as the battle is begun. Not so easily can our spiritual foes, or the evil of our natures, be overcome. The fight will go on till we reach the verge of Jordan."

"Death, papa?"

"Yes, 'tis only then we can sing the victor's song. And yet, trusting in the Lord Jesus, who is called 'the captain of our salvation,' we may be sure of final victory—certain that we shall be 'more than conquerors through him that loved us.'"

Max joined them presently and asked his father what orders he was to carry to the workmen and men-servants.

When that matter had been attended to, the captain, giving the lad a look of proud fatherly affection, said, "Max, my boy, you are growing fast. You will be a man one of these days, should it please God to spare your life. What do you think of making of yourself? I mean," seeing a slightly puzzled look on the lad's face, "what would you choose as your principal employment for life?"

"I don't know, papa," Max answered with some hesitation. "What would you like best to have me do, papa?"

"Whatever you have the most talent and inclination for, if we can find out what that is," returned his father. "That will be the thing you can do with the greatest enjoyment and most successfully."

"That is very kind of you, papa," said Max. "But I would rather have you decide for me. You are much wiser than I, and I don't think I have any particular fancy for any one thing yet."

"Well, my son, there is no need to decide in haste," his father said. "It will be better to take plenty of time to consider the question, so that we will be more likely to come to a wise decision.

"But, my boy, whatever your choice may be, I want you to seek to glorify God in doing your work and to be the servant of God, not the servant of men.

"'Ye are bought with a price, be not ye the servants of men!'

"Let not the question with you be 'How shall I obtain wealth and fame? How shall I gain the approbation of my fellow men?' but 'What shall I do that I may please God? How shall I best honor and glorify Him? How shall I do the most for the upbuilding of His cause and kingdom?'

"'For ye are bought with a price; therefore glorify God in your body and in your spirit which are God's.'

"Gracie, can you tell me what that price was?"

"Yes, papa, one of my Bible verses says, 'Ye know that ye were not redeemed with corruptible things, as silver and gold, from your vain conversation received by tradition from your fathers, but with the precious blood of Christ, as of a lamb without blemish and without spot.'"

Here the conversation was interrupted by the bringing in of the captain's breakfast.

Max sprang up and rolled a small table to the side of the couch, while Lulu quickly brought and spread upon it a snow-white damask cloth that she took from a closet. Upon that the servant set the silver waiter she had brought in. Then Lulu poured out a cup of coffee for her father, while Max broke and seasoned his egg and Gracie handed him a plate and the buttered toast.

It was evidently a delight to each of them to wait upon him and to him to receive their loving service.

They hovered lovingly about him till his meal was finished and then went to the dining room for their own.

While they were thus engaged the captain had a delightful surprise.

He lay there quietly musing — thinking, in fact, of the wife and babies upstairs and longing to go them. He longed particularly for a sight of her sweet face. As he did so, a slender, girlish, white-robed figure glided in at the open door and to the side of his couch. Almost ere he was aware of its vicinity, two arms were about his neck and two lips were pressed to his in a long kiss of ardent affection.

"Vi, my precious little wife, my darling!" he cried, clasping her close in an ecstasy of delight. "Can it be you, love? I did not know they would let you come to me yet. Ah, I hope you are not exerting yourself too much, glad as I am to see your dear face and have you in my arms again."

"I couldn't stay away another minute," she said, repeating her caresses. "Arthur gave his consent, and now they shan't keep us apart any more.

"Oh, my darling, tell me, are you suffering? It was so hard to know you were in pain and not be able to come to you and at least try to give you some relief."

"I think it has been pretty hard on us both," he said, stroking her air and gazing fondly into her eyes. "No, love, I don't suffer now when I'm careful to obey orders and not move the injured limb." He added merrily, "Here, take this chair close by my side. Ah, I begin to think Max knew what he was about when he wheeled it up! I rather wondered at the time but asked no questions."

"Yes," she said, leaning back in the chair and gazing on him with devouring eyes. "I let our Maxie into the secret—dear boy that he is—but charged him not to tell his father. I wanted to give you a sweet surprise."

"You succeeded. Ah, dearest, what a feast it is just to lie and look at you."

"I echo your sentiments," she returned merrily, then getting more serious. "My dear husband, I want you to promise me that you will never mount that horse again."

"You are making common cause with Lulu against the poor fellow, I perceive," he said with a humorous smile.

"Poor fellow, indeed! He must be very vicious to throw so good a master, and that without the slightest provocation."

"Ah, my love, there you are mistaken, for I have learned that the poor animal had been subjected to very bad treatment just before being brought from the stable. I have therefore dismissed Ajax and engaged another man in his place. But set your heart at rest. For your dear sake and my children's, I have consented to sell the horse. Negotiations are being carried on now with a gentleman who desires to own him, and they will probably be completed even today."

"Oh, I am glad to hear it," she cried. "Not for twice his money's worth would I have him given another opportunity to do you an injury."

"I'm afraid I must acknowledge," laughed the captain, "that I feel a strong desire to teach him that

I am his master. But for your sake, my love, I consent to forego that pleasure."

"Ah, who should ensure your success in that effort?" she asked with a mischievous look. "You are, I know, a man accustomed to obedience from those under your authority, but possibly you might fail in exacting it from Thunderer."

"Very true," he returned good-humoredly. "But perhaps the doubt makes me all the more eager to prove my ability. Ah, here come the children!" he said as childish footsteps came pattering down the hall.

"Mamma! Mamma Vi!" exclaimed the little girls, catching sight of her as they crossed the threshold. "How nice to see you down again!" And they ran to her to give and receive loving caresses, for even Lulu had grown fond of her beautiful and lovable young mother. Persevering, unwavering kindness had done its legitimate work.

"Thank you, dears," Violet said. "You can't be more pleased to see me here than I am to be here. It has been very hard for me to stay away from your papa while knowing that he was suffering. But it has been a very great comfort to feel sure that he had loving attention from his children."

"They have been the best and dearest nurses," he said, smiling tenderly upon them.

"Here's the mail, papa," cried Max, coming in with the bag and handing it to his father.

The captain opened it with a key that he took from his pocket, handed Violet her letters, and began opening his.

"Ah!" he exclaimed presently. "Mr. Mason accepts my terms and Thunderer is sold."

"Oh, good! Good!" cried Lulu, dancing up and down in delight. "Now, papa, I think he'll never have a chance to throw you again."

"No, I presume not," said the captain. "I suppose you are well pleased that he is disposed of."

"I certainly am," said Violet.

"I, too," said Gracie. "Oh, papa, I should have been afraid for you every time you got on his back."

Max had not spoken, and his father, looking at him with a humorous smile, asked, "And you, my boy? What have you to say about it?"

"I suppose I ought to be satisfied, papa," returned the lad with some little hesitation. "But—"

"Well, out with it, my son," laughed the captain. "You did not exactly want him sold, eh?"

"I—I believe I rather liked the idea of seeing you conquer him, papa," answered Max, a trifle shame-facedly. "I wouldn't have you hurt again for anything, I'm sure," he went on earnestly. "But I don't believe he could throw you again, for you would be on your guard another time as you were not before. You are a fine horseman, and I'm certain, almost, could conquer any horse that ever was made."

At that his father laughed outright, but there was certainly no displeasure in his mirth.

"Perhaps it is just as well for my reputation for skill and prowess that they should not be tested too far," he said.

"Max," said Violet, "I like that speech of yours. And I believe if I were a boy with such a father as yours, I should feel just as you do about it."

"What do you say to a holiday, children, in honor of your mamma's coming downstairs?" asked the captain.

There was a unanimous vote from all three in favor of the motion.

"Then so it shall be," he said. "Ring for the servants, Max. It is time for family worship. After that, we will send for the two babies to join us and see what a merry time we can have."

Little Elsie had been an almost daily visitor to her father but the newcomer only an occasional one. It was now some days since his last visit.

"Does he grow, Vi?" asked the captain while they were waiting for the coming of the nurses.

"Yes, indeed, and develops new beauties every day," she answered merrily. "At least so his mother thinks. Ah, here they come, the darlings!"

"Papa, papa!" shouted little Elsie, eagerly reaching out her arms to her father. "Take Elsie, papa."

"Yes, bring her here," he said.

He was still unable to stand or walk, as the injured limb had not yet gained strength to bear his weight. But he could now assume a sitting posture, so for the first time in several weeks, the baby girl was treated to a seat upon his knee.

She seemed to appreciate the privilege. "Elsie sit on papa's lap," she cooed triumphantly. Then, putting one arm round his neck, she patted his cheek with the other hand and showered kisses upon him, while he hugged and kissed her.

But she soon was quite ready to get down and go to her play.

Lulu had possession of the tiny baby. She was holding him very carefully and gazing affectionately into the wee face, Max and Gracie standing beside her, doing likewise.

"The little chap has grown, sure enough," remarked Max.

"Whom does he resemble, Max?" asked Violet.

"Nobody but himself, I think, Mamma Vi."

"Oh, Max, how disappointing!" she laughed. "Now, I have been thinking I could see quite a striking likeness to both your papa and yourself."

"Very complimentary to us both, Max," laughed the captain in his turn. "Bring him here, Lulu, and let us see if I can find that resemblance."

"Well?" Violet said inquiringly, as he took the babe in his arms and regarded him with quite an earnest scrutiny.

"I must say I think it is largely in your imagination, my dear," replied her husband. "Though I can't say that he looks more like anyone else than like Max or his father."

"Well, time will show," she said laughingly, as she gazed at her babe with all a mother's admiring love. "We'll see what you and Max have to say in another month."

After that no day passed without a visit between the captain and his wife, and as soon as both were able for the short journey, they went to Ion for a week, taking all the children with them. The Lelands were there at the same time, and a very delightful holiday it proved to all—old and young, guests and entertainers.

Then for another week the same company gathered at Fairview.

It was now late into the summer season, and it seemed that everyone from every household was longing for sea breezes. Someone expressed the desire one evening as they all sat on the veranda, and the queries started around whether it would not be advisable to go to some seaside resort and which was most preferred.

The first question was soon decided agreeably in the affirmative.

Then Zoe exclaimed, "Let us go to Nantucket! We had such a delightful time there, and we can travel nearly all the way by sea, so that the journey will not be hard for our recovering invalids."

The motion was carried by acclamation.

"Oh, I'm glad!" cried Lulu, clapping her hands. "I'd rather go there than to any other place I can think of. I liked it so much before, and it'll be twice as nice for me with you along, Eva. 'Twill be such fun to show you all the interesting places. And, oh, papa, may we take the ponies with us?"

"Yes," he said. "I shall arrange for that, quite for their sakes, of course," he added jestingly. "No doubt they will enjoy the sea breezes as much as the rest of us."

"Oh, you are such a dear, good, kind papa," laughed Lulu, giving him a vigorous hug. "You'd never allow ponies or horses to be abused, but I guess I know which you care most for — the ponies or the children."

"Yes, indeed, we do," Gracie said, seizing his hand and lifting it to her lips. "You love us ever so much more than you do the ponies. But, oh, I am so glad we are going, and that we may take them along. It'll be so nice to ride them there."

Little preparation was needed, and in a few days the voyage was begun. That and the sojourn upon the island that followed were almost one long delight to the children and enjoyed but little less by the older members of the party.

CHAPTER
TWENTY-SECOND

EVERY HOUR OF THE sojourn at Nantucket had been enjoyed by the Raymonds, yet when they came in sight of Woodburn with its nice lawn, trees, shrubbery, and woods glorious in their autumn robes of crimson, scarlet, russet, and gold, every face was wreathed in smiles.

"Fleeting glories, but very beautiful while they last," remarked the captain.

"Yes, indeed," said Violet. "I know no more charming place than home after all!"

"Such a sweet home as ours is, Mamma Vi," supplemented Max.

"Yes, it is just the sweetest of homes," cried Lulu with enthusiasm. "And yet it is nice to go away to the sea sometimes."

"Yes," replied her father. "Change is pleasant and beneficial to almost everyone. And, no doubt, we shall enjoy our own home all the more for having been absent from it for a time."

The carriage drew up at the door, and they all alighted to receive a joyous welcome from Christine and the servants gathered about.

A delicious supper was waiting and was presently served up. Ample justice was done it by the hungry travelers, especially the children. Then, as there was still a good half hour of daylight, they roamed over house and grounds, delighted to renew their acquaintance with all their old familiar haunts, and were greatly pleased to find everything in perfect order.

The weather was charming, both on that day and for several subsequent days, and the captain and Violet thought it well to take advantage of it for paying and receiving visits among the family connection before settling down to the regular routine of home duties and occupations. The days were pretty well filled with walks, rides, drives, and social gatherings.

After that, Violet busied herself with the direct oversight of dressmakers and seamstresses, and the captain resumed his duties as owner of the estate, employer of household servants and out-of-door workmen, and tutor to his children — the latter being required to at once begin again their long-neglected studies.

Confinement to the house for several hours on the stretch and steady application to their books were at first irksome, but papa was lenient and his pupils were sincerely desirous to merit his approval. There were neither reprimands nor complaints. Study hours were made short, and the afternoon walks and rides on the ponies found all the more enjoyable for the industry that had preceded them.

But the second week of November brought with it a long, cold rainstorm that put an end, for the time, to all outdoor diversions.

Both Max and Lulu had always been very fond of exercise in the open air, and they now found it extremely wearisome to be shut up in the house day after day. Lulu's trial of the confinement and same-ness was rather more continuous than her broth-er's, as he could occasionally venture out in the weather, which their father considered quite too inclement to be braved by a little girl.

She had been remarkably good, docile, and very obedient for months—ever since that time when she had had to do without Fairy for a week. She began to look upon herself as quite a reformed char-acter. But her father, though greatly pleased and encouraged by the improvement in her behavior, felt quite certain that there would be times when the old tempers and habits would resume their sway for a season.

One morning when the sun had scarcely shown his face for a week, Lulu woke feeling dull and irri-table. She became all the more out of humor upon discovering that she had overslept herself and would have scarcely time to dress properly before the breakfast bell would ring.

She sprang up instantly and began dressing in feverish haste.

Punctuality was one of the minor virtues that the captain was particular in enforcing, but to appear at the table looking otherwise than neat would be a still more serious breech of discipline than to be a trifle behind time.

"Oh, dear, why did I sleep so late?" she said, giv-ing herself an impatient shake. "I shan't have time to do everything I ought to and get to the dining room to sit down with the rest, and papa will be displeased. I do so hate to have him displeased with me. There, I hear his voice in the next room! Gracie will have him all to herself, and I shall miss every bit of the nice talk before breakfast."

The old adage, "The more haste, the less speed," found exemplification in the experience on this occasion. In vain she tried to dress with dispatch — the comb tangled in her hair, a button came off her boot, she couldn't pin her collar straight, and in the midst of her efforts to do so, the bell rang.

"There it goes! And I haven't said my prayers yet. I'll have to omit them this time. But perhaps papa will ask me about it. He sometimes does."

She knelt for a hurried sentence or two, putting no heart into them, rose up hastily, and ran down to the dining room.

The blessing had been asked, and her father was helping the plates. He gave her a grave look as she took her place at the table.

"Good morning, daughter," he said. "You are quite behind time. What is the excuse?"

"I overslept, papa, and then everything seemed to go wrong with my dressing."

"You must try to be more punctual," he said. "I was sorry to miss my morning kiss from my eldest daughter, and the little chat we usually have before breakfast," he added in a kindly tone.

"Oh, mayn't I give you the kiss after breakfast?"

"No, I will take it now and also another after breakfast," he answered with a smile. She sprang to his side, eager to give and receive the accustomed morning caress.

"Is that the punishment for being unpunctual, papa?" asked Max facetiously.

"For the first offense," replied his father. "I don't expect a repetition of it from my usually prompt, eldest daughter."

"She is that," acknowledged Max. "I'll be more likely to be unpunctual another time than she. And then, papa, I'll expect the very same punishment you have given her."

"Ah, don't be too sure of it. Circumstances alter cases, and much will depend upon the excuse you bring, my son."

Lulu felt grateful at the time for her father's leniency, but her fretfulness and irritability soon returned. All seemed to go wrong with her. Her recitations were poor, and when told her lessons must be learned over, she sulked and pouted.

Her father thought it best not to seem to notice her ill humor, but he did not relax in his requirements. She must give her mind to her tasks and recite them creditably, he said, before she could be dismissed to her play. She had scarcely succeeded in that when the dinner bell rang.

Her face did not wear its usual pleasant expression during the meal, and she had nothing to say, though all around her were chatting in their accustomed cheery fashion. Once or twice her father gave her a troubled look, but he administered no reproof.

On leaving the table, he repaired to the library to attend to some correspondence. He was giving all his thoughts to that when a jesting remark in Max's voice, speaking from the adjoining room, caught his ear.

"What a very amiable countenance, Miss Raymond! How very agreeable you've made yourself all day!"

"Max," returned Lulu's voice in angry tones, "if you don't quit teasing me, I'll—"

"Max! Lulu!" interrupted the captain, sternly. "Come here to me—both of you."

Max obeyed instantly, appearing before his father looking very red and ashamed, but Lulu did not move from her spot.

"Lulu, did you hear me bid you come to me?" asked her father with added sternness in his tones.

"Yes, sir," she answered. She then immediately added in an undertone, "But I'll not come a step till I get ready."

As low as the tone was, he heard her. A deeply pained expression swept across his features. He turned suddenly pale but rose without a word and moved with a calm, quiet step in the direction of his rebellious child.

Lulu started to her feet as he appeared in sight. "I will, papa. I'm coming."

"Tardy obedience following upon an insolent refusal to obey," he said, taking her hand and leading her to the side of the chair from which he had just risen.

He resumed his seat and dropped her hand. She stood there with burning cheeks and eyes fixed on the carpet. Her refusal to obey had been upon the impulse of the moment and not intended for her father's ear, but she had spoken the insolent words louder than she was aware of doing.

The captain addressed himself first to Max. "I am sorry, my son, to find that you have not sufficient regard for either your sister's feelings or my wishes to lead you to refrain from teasing her, though you know it is an easy matter to rouse her quick temper and so get her into trouble."

"It was very thoughtless and wrong of me, papa," said Max frankly. "I beg your pardon, and Lulu's, too, and I will try not to do so again."

"That is right, my boy, and I am not angry with you now. But as this is not the first time I have had to reprove you for the same fault, I think I must inflict a slight punishment to impress the lesson upon your mind. You will go to your room and stay there till the tea bell rings."

"Yes, sir. It is a much lighter punishment than I deserve," Max said, moving instantly to obey.

He had gone, and Lulu was left alone with her justly displeased father. There was silence for a moment. She still stood by the side of his chair, and though her eyes were downcast, she felt that his were fixed upon her. Her countenance was sullen. He could perceive in it no sign of penitence.

"I am quite certain," he said at length, speaking in a grave, sad tone, "that it will not be long before my little daughter will be almost overwhelmed with remorse on account of this day's behavior toward the father whom, I know beyond a doubt, she loves with all her heart."

Before he had finished his sentence, a change had come over her. "Oh, papa," she cried, suddenly moving closer to his side and throwing her arm round his neck, "I'm sorry now. Oh, so, so sorry and ashamed! Please, please forgive me for saying such naughty, naughty, rebellious words to you. And please punish me for it just as hard as you can!" Dropping her head on his shoulder, she ended with a storm of tears and sobs.

"I am afraid I must punish you for your own sake," he said, sighing deeply. "It would hardly do to pass lightly over so flagrant a breach of discipline and so insolent a refusal to submit to lawful authority."

"I didn't mean to speak so you'd hear me, papa."

"Ah! I am not at all sure that that admission sets your conduct in a more favorable light."

"Papa, I am sorry. Oh, I didn't think I'd ever be so bad again! But everything has gone wrong with me today!"

"Surely then, you did not begin the day aright? Did you ask with your heart that you might be kept from sin?"

"I did say a prayer, papa, but I was so late I had to hurry."

"And so offered only lip service?"

She was silent.

"Ah, my child," he said, "no wonder you were left to fall into grievous sin! Approaching the King of kings with haste and irreverence that would be insulting to even an earthly monarch."

"Oh, I never thought how very wicked it was!" she sobbed. "You'll have to punish me for that, too. Please do it now, papa, so I'll have it over."

He did not answer her for several minutes. Then he said, "I think I shall try a new plan with you. As you were pleased to refuse obedience to an order from me, I shall not give you another for some days. For the four remaining days of this week you may try self-government, regulating your conduct to suit yourself, except that you must not go out of the house while the weather is inclement or out of sight of it at any time.

"I shall give you no command, direction, instruction, or advice concerning your daily activities, nor must you feel at liberty to come to me for any or to treat me with any greater familiarity than you would toward a gentleman in whose house you were only a visitor. Duties and privileges are not to be separated, and while released from the duties of a child, you can have no right to claim a child's privileges."

"But I don't want to be released, papa," she burst out in her vehement way. "I want you to order me, and I mean to obey the very moment you speak—always, always!"

"So you think now," he said. "But I am not at all sure that your good resolution would last for any length of time. You may be quite as willful and rebellious tomorrow as you have been today. You need and must have the lesson I hope you will gain by being left to be, for a time, a law to yourself.

"Understand that I do not propose to subject you to any harsh treatment. On the contrary, I shall be as polite and as considerate of your comfort as if you were my guest."

"I don't want to be company!" she exclaimed. "I don't want you to be polite to me! I want you to punish me, and then let me be your very own child—just as I always have been! Oh, papa, please, please do!"

"It is very far from being a pleasure to me to punish you," he returned, again sighing deeply as he spoke. "And I have quite decided to try this other plan. I do not expect to enjoy it, either, any more than you will. It will be a sad thing for me to have to do without the loving attentions and caresses of my dear, little daughter, Lulu, even for four days."

She looked up into his face in blank dismay.

"Oh, papa, you can't mean that I am not to kiss you or have you kiss me for four whole days? I could never, never stand it!"

"I do not say that. I should not refuse a kiss to a little girl visitor, should she ask for it, and I might even offer her one. But I certainly should not expect to treat her, or be treated by her, with the same affectionate familiarity which you and I have been accustomed to use toward each other."

"Oh, I shan't know how to behave to you at all!" she cried despairingly.

"When in doubt, you will only have to consider how you would expect a little girl visitor — Eva, for instance — to act toward me. Now you may go, for I have not time to talk any more to you at present."

"Am I to go to my own room and stay there?"

"You will go where you please and do what you please. You are your own mistress for four days."

Her own mistress! How often had she looked longingly forward to the time when her right to be that should be acknowledged. But now — oh, it wasn't felicity at all! It was misery to think that for four whole days she was to be only like a stranger-guest to her papa, instead of his own dearly loved and coddled child.

Slowly and feeling much like one who had been suddenly turned out of paradise, she went from his presence and on up the stairs to her own rooms.

Gracie was in the nursery, at play with the baby sister. She heard their voices and merry laughter as she passed the door, but she had no heart for joining them and sharing their merriment. She did not pause till she had reached the tiny room in the tower — the most private spot to which she could have access at that time.

She sat down by the window, and leaning her arms on the sill, gazed out into the grounds — looking desolate enough just now under leaden clouds swept by wind and sleet.

"It looks exactly as I feel out there!" she sighed to herself. "Oh, dear! Four whole days! Such a long, long while to be treated as only a visitor!"

Then she fell to considering in what respect her father's treatment of her would differ during the four days from what it ordinarily was, and in what way she must alter her conduct toward him.

Eva would certainly never think of running to him to put her arms round his neck and gaze lovingly into his eyes or take a seat uninvited upon his knee. Nor would he invite her to that seat or draw her into his arms to hold her close to his heart and kiss her over and over again, as if he thought her one of the dearest and sweetest things on the earth.

Oh, no, those were among the privileges and delights that had to be dispensed with along with the duties of daughterhood. And, oh, what delights they seemed now that they must be resigned for a time! Ah, if papa would but relent and commute her sentence to the severest punishment he could possibly inflict, what a relief it would be!

Then recalling the insolent, rebellious words she had addressed to him, she buried her face in her hands, almost overwhelmed with both shame and remorse at her actions.

What would she not give never to have spoken them! Oh, what base ingratitude to the kindest and dearest of fathers! How those dreadful words must have pained his loving heart! How had she found it in hers to hurt him so? For, oh, indeed, she did love him dearly, dearly. Though she could hardly expect him to believe it any more!

What if he should decide that she didn't love him, and so that he didn't want to keep her for his own. What if he should tell her she must go away and be her own mistress always, or somebody else's child?"

Her heart almost stood still at the dreadful idea, but in a moment she remembered with relief that he had once said he would have no right to let her go away from his care and authority—even if he wanted to be rid of her—because God had given her to him to be protected and provided for and trained up for His service. So, there was no danger of that, for papa was a good Christian man who always tried to do exactly as the Bible said.

It was growing dark. The supper bell would soon ring, and—should she go down to the table?

She dreaded meeting the family and felt ashamed to even look her father in the face. And since she was her own mistress, she could do as she pleased about it, but she would much rather do as she supposed papa would wish. Besides she began to feel hungry.

The bell rang and she obeyed the summons.

As she stepped out into the hall she and Max met face to face.

His eyes opened wide in surprise.

"Why do you look at me so," she asked angrily, feeling her cheeks grow hot.

"Because I thought you would surely have to stay in your room for at least a week after talking as you did to papa this afternoon. I should never dare to speak so to him, and I wouldn't for the world hurt his feelings so. If you had seen the pained look that came over his face."

"Oh, Max, don't!" she cried with a burst of tears. "I could kill myself for it! I don't know what possessed me! I didn't really mean to say the words, but I thought out loud before I knew it."

There was no time for anything more, for they had reached the door of the dining room. As they passed in, Lulu hastily wiped away her tears, finding themselves in the presence of their parents who had just sat down to the table.

Max and Lulu took their plates in silence, the latter carefully keeping her eyes down, that she might not meet those of her father. He asked the blessing, then helped the plates, giving her, when her turn came, what he knew she liked without question or remark. She ate in silence, the others chatting pleasantly among themselves as usual.

Presently a servant, passing a plate of waffles, handed them to Lulu.

The captain thought it not best for children to eat hot bread at night, but he sometimes made exceptions.

"Papa, may I have one?" she asked.

"I have nothing to say about it," was his reply.

Violet gave her husband a look of surprise.

Lulu's lip quivered. "I'll not take it," she said in a low tone to the servant. Then, a very little louder, and with a perceptible tremble in her voice, "Mamma Vi, please excuse me," and hardly waiting for an answer, she rose and left the room.

Again Violet looked at her husband. "I fear the child is not well," she said inquiringly.

"Possibly not," he sighed. "Though I have heard no complaint of illness."

A light broke upon Violet, and she began talking of something else.

But the captain's fatherly heart was stirred at the thought that perhaps his child was not quite well or that there might be found in threatened illness some excuse for the misconduct of the day. Upon leaving the table, he went in search of Lulu.

She was in the little tower room again, and hearing him call to her from the adjoining room, she hastened to obey the summons.

"I am here, papa," she said, appearing before him with drooping head and downcast eyes.

"Are you not well?" he asked, and his tone was very kind.

"Yes, sir," she answered tremulously and without raising her eyes.

"I want you always to tell me when you feel at all ill," he said. "We are all expecting to spend the evening together in the usual way, and we will be glad to have you with us," he added then turned and left the room.

"He didn't call me daughter, or his child, or anything but Lulu," she sighed to herself. "Any other time he would have taken my hand and led me with him. Oh, it isn't at all nice to be treated like a visitor!"

She had always greatly enjoyed the evenings when they were just a family by themselves, yet she shrank from accepting her father's invitation, feeling that she could not be one of them as heretofore.

But she found it lonely staying by herself, and at length sought the room where the others were.

Gracie, seated on her father's knee, hailed her appearance with a glad, "Oh, Lu, so you've come at last! I was thinking I'd have to go and find you. You've missed the fun with the babies—they've just been carried away. Here's a chair Max has set for you close beside papa, or perhaps you can sit on his other knee."

"I'll sit here," Lulu said, taking possession of an easy chair on the opposite side of the fire.

"Why, Lu!" exclaimed Gracie in astonishment, "What can be the matter with you? Always before you've wanted to get just as close to papa as ever you could."

There was a moment of silence, then Lulu answered in a low, half tremulous tone, "I have not been a good girl today, Gracie, and I don't deserve to sit close to papa."

Then Max made a diversion by asking his father a question in regard to his lessons for the next day.

"Gracie, would you get papa his slippers?" the captain asked presently.

"Oh, yes! If I may, papa," she answered brightly but with an inquiring look at Lulu, who had always hitherto claimed that little service as belonging to her.

"Papa doesn't want me to do it, Gracie," she said in a low, hurt tone.

He took no notice. Gracie brought the slippers and was rewarded with a smile and a kiss.

Then Violet came in with a bit of fancywork in her hand. Max brought out the book they had been enjoying together for several evenings past, and he handed it to his father.

While the captain was turning over the leaves in search of the place where he had left off the night before, Lulu drew quietly near the table and took up a paper cutter and a magazine that had come by that afternoon's mail.

"Don't trouble yourself to cut those leaves, Lulu," her father said. "Max will do it for me."

She dropped the magazine and knife as though they had burned her, turned away with quivering lip and eyes full of tears, and presently stole away to her own room. She went to bed and cried herself to sleep.

She knew it was not worth while to stay up for the usual goodnight visit from papa. He would never think of paying one to a little girl guest.

In the morning when he came to the children's sitting room, Gracie had him to herself.

Lulu met him first at the table, when he greeted her with a pleasant, "Good morning, Lulu," but offered no caress, and she did not ask for one, though she had never felt more hungry for it.

She went to the schoolroom at the appointed hour and applied herself industriously to her task, but he did not call her to recite. The others were heard and dismissed, but she sat unnoticed at her desk. At length she rose and drew near him.

"May I say my lessons now, papa?"

"I do not teach visitors," he said in a tone of polite astonishment. "I instruct only my own children."

"But I am your own—your very, very own! I know I am for you have told me so many and many times!" she cried, bursting into sobs and tears.

"Yes, you are," he said gently. "And I purpose to claim my right in you again one of these days—for not all the gold of California would I resign it entirely. But you must remember that for the present you are considered only a visitor and your own mistress."

"But I don't want to be my own mistress! I want to be taught and directed and controlled by you. Oh, papa, if you would only punish me and forgive me, I don't think I'd ever want to be rebellious again!"

"You shall be restored to all a daughter's duties and privileges when I deem that the proper time has come, but that is not yet," he said. "I love you just as dearly as ever, but I think you need the lesson I am giving you and that you could get it no easier way. It grieves me more than I can tell you to see my dear little daughter unhappy, but now and always I must seek her permanent good, rather than her present pleasure."

"You're kind to tell me that you love me   yet, papa," she said, wiping away her tears. "I don't deserve that you should. And I 'most thought you had stopped. Papa, I hate myself for hurting you so yesterday."

"I don't doubt it, my child, and when the right time comes I will listen to all you wish to say to me about it, but now I must attend to my correspondence."

"Then I'll go away, but, oh, mayn't I have one kiss first? You said you'd give Eva one if she asked for it."

Then he drew her to him, kissed her twice with warmth and affection, and she went away feeling less unhappy than she had since her rebellious reply to the last order he had given her.

She found Gracie in their rooms dressing a doll.

"Oh, Lu," she cried, glancing up at her sister as she came in, "you've been crying! What ever is the matter? Is papa angry with you?"

"He says I must be my own mistress all the rest of this week, because — because I was disobedient and rebellious yesterday."

Gracie looked puzzled. "Don't you like it, Lu? I thought you always wished you could be."

"I used to, but, oh, it isn't a bit nice, Gracie! I'm ever so much happier when papa tells me what to do."

"Yes, I like that best."

"And he won't let me do a single thing for him," Lulu went on. "It's simply dreadful, for I just love to wait on him and do all his little errands about the house."

She did not attempt it again, however, until restored to a daughter's place.

CHAPTER
TWENTY-THIRD

LULU JOINED THE rest of the family that evening and listened to the reading, but she was careful not to take any liberties inconsistent with her position as only a guest. She asked for a goodnight kiss and received it, but that was all. There was no close, loving embrace given with it, as in former days, and no words of tender fatherly affection were spoken.

The next day and the next passed very slowly to her with no lessons to learn, no loving little services to render to her father, no delightfully confidential chats with him. While by reason of mental disquietude, all employments had lost their usual interest for her, and her heart was very heavy because she felt she was not in full favor with either her earthly or her heavenly Father.

For months past she had been very happy in the consciousness that Jesus loved her, and that He was her Savior and she His disciple. She was his servant, belonging to Him even more entirely than to the father whose "very own" she loved to call herself.

But in rebelling against the authority of that earthly parent she had broken God's command,

"Honor thy father and thy mother," and the light of His countenance was withdrawn from her.

The captain sat reading alone in the library on Friday evening, the rest of the family having retired to their rooms for the night. A slight sound caused him to look up from his book to find, much to his surprise, Lulu standing by his side and wearing a very troubled countenance.

"What is it?" he asked. "You bade me goodnight some time ago, and I thought you had gone to bed. Are you not well, my child?"

"Yes, papa, but — papa, if Eva was troubled in her mind and came to you for help, wouldn't you listen to her and tell her what to do?" she asked, low and hesitatingly. Her head was drooping, and her eyes sought the carpet.

"Certainly, I should be very glad to do anything in my power to relieve her, and if instead of Eva, it were one of my own children, I surely should not be less ready to help and comfort. Tell me freely what it is that troubles you."

As he spoke he laid aside his book and took one of the small hands in his, holding it in a tender and loving clasp.

Lulu's tears began to fall. "Papa," she sobbed, "when I behaved so rebelliously toward you I sinned against God, and I am afraid He is angry with me. Oh, papa, what should I do?"

"Go at once and ask His forgiveness, daughter. Ask in the name of Jesus, and for His sake.

"'If any man sin, we have an advocate with the Father, Jesus Christ, the righteous.'"

"'If we confess our sins, He is faithful and just to forgive us our sins, and to cleanse us from all unrighteousness.'"

"Papa, I thought I was a Christian. I thought I loved Jesus and had given my heart to Him. But now I am afraid it was all a mistake. Oh, do you think a real, true Christian could behave so wickedly as I did the other day?"

"If a man running a race should step aside for a moment from the path, or stumble and fall, and then get up and go on, I should not think he had proved himself to have been mistaken in believing that he had really set out to run it in the right path. Should a soldier fall back for a moment before the enemy, I should not think that he did not love his country and his flag and would never fight bravely for them.

"But, my child, there is no need to settle the question whether you really came at the time you thought you did. The way is open still and you may come now. Come anew, or for the first time. Jesus still invites you, still says sweetly to you, 'Come unto me and I will give you rest.' 'Him that cometh to Me I will in no wise cast out.'"

"Papa, pray for me," she entreated. "Please ask Jesus to forgive me and love me—to help me to come to Him now, and always keep close to Him."

Then, with her hand still in his, he knelt with her by his side and earnestly besought the Lord for her, "his dear, erring, but penitent child."

They rose from their knees, and lifting her tearful eyes to his face with a look of ardent filial love, she said, "Thank you, dear papa," in faltering tones. "I said the words after you in my heart, and I do believe Jesus heard and has forgiven me and loves me now."

"Yes, dear child, we have His own word for it. 'Him that cometh to me I will in no wise cast out.'"

He still held her hand in his, and now, laying the other tenderly on her head, he said solemnly, "'The Lord bless thee and keep thee, the Lord make His face shine upon thee, and be gracious unto thee. The Lord lift up His countenance upon thee, and give thee peace.'"

Then, with a goodnight kiss, he sent her away to her rest.

"What a dear, dear father he is," she said to herself as she went softly up the stairs again. "How I do love him! And, oh, how I did want to put my arms round his neck and hug him tight! It would have been disobedience, though, and so I couldn't. But tomorrow night I may, for then this dreadful time of being my own mistress and only a visitor will be over, and he'll take me for his very own child again. Then, oh, how happy I shall be!"

The next evening, as the goodnights were being said, she gave him a most wistful, longing look.

"Yes, my daughter," he said in a grave, serious, yet kindly tone, "I am coming to your room for a little goodnight talk."

"Oh, I am so glad, papa!" she cried, her face lighting up with joy. She then went skipping and dancing to her room, hurried through her preparations for the night, and when she heard his approaching footsteps, ran to open the door and bid him welcome.

"It seems such a long while I've been without this, the pleasantest of all my times," she said, as he sat down and drew her into his arms with the old fond gesture and tender caress.

"Well, daughter," he said, "shall I give you another week of freedom from my control and being your own mistress? Or have you had enough of it?"

"Oh, quite, quite enough, papa! A great deal more than enough!" she exclaimed, nestling closer in his arms. "I do think I'll never want to be my own mistress again while I have such a dear, wise, kind father to rule and direct me—to love and care for me. Papa, I actually feel hungry for an order from you, that I may have the pleasure of obeying it. And, oh, it will be so delightful to wait on you and do all sorts of little things for you again, if only you will let me!"

"Gladly, dear child," he said, holding her close to his heart. "You can scarcely rejoice more than your father does in your restoration to a daughter's place. I have found it a sad thing to have to do without the loving services of my dear daughter, Lulu, and this sweet exchange of endearments with her."

"Oh, it is ever so sweet to me!" she said. "But," as if struck by a sudden and not pleasant thought, "aren't you going to punish me now for my disobedience? Don't you have to, because of your Bible orders?"

"I think not. I think you are penitent enough this time to make it right for me to accord you free forgiveness, and I am very, very glad to do so," he said, repeating his caresses.

The End